I scrambled to my feet, pushing my hair out of my eyes, and then North was behind me, pulling me toward him. I didn't have time to move; he wrapped his black cloak around us, up and over our heads, and blocked out the image of crumbling stone.

"What—?" I choked on my own words, my heart dropping again into my stomach. We were sliding sharply downward, the air buzzing and singing. The world went dark around us, but there was no more fear in my heart.

Ah, I thought, feeling the first brush of tingling warmth as we fell into the unknown. *Magic.*

OTHER EGMONT USA
BOOKS YOU MAY ENJOY

BRIGHTLY WOVEN

ALEXANDRA BRACKEN

EGMONT

USA

NEW YORK

EGMONT

We bring stories to life

First published by Egmont USA, 2010
This paperback edition published by Egmont USA, 2011
443 Park Avenue South, Suite 806
New York, NY 10016

Copyright © Alexandra Bracken, 2010
Map illustration by Heather Saunders
All rights reserved

1 3 5 7 9 8 6 4 2

www.egmontusa.com
www.alexandrabracken.com

THE LIBRARY OF CONGRESS HAS CATALOGED
THE HARDCOVER EDITION AS FOLLOWS:
Bracken, Alexandra.
Brightly woven / Alexandra Bracken.
p.   cm.
Summary: Sixteen-year-old Sydelle Mirabil, an unusually
talented weaver, must master her mysterious power and join a
young wizard in stopping an imminent war in her land.
ISBN 978-1-60684-038-2 (hardcover)
ISBN 978-1-60684-061-0 (reinforced library binding ed.)
ISBN 978-1-60684-195-2 (eBook)
[1. Weaving—Fiction. 2. Wizards—Fiction. 3. Fantasy.] I. Title.
PZ7.B6988Br 2010
[Fic]—dc22   2009025115

Paperback ISBN 978-1-60684-210-2

Printed in the United States of America

CPSIA tracking label information:
Printed in May 2011 at Berryville Graphics, Berryville, Virginia

FOR MY PARENTS,
DAN AND CYNDI,
WHO HAVE THEIR OWN
GREAT LOVE STORY

�֍   �֍   ✷

Astraean Nation:
PALMARTA

Salvalite Nations:
AUSTER
SALDORRA
RUTTGARD

RUTTGARD

NORTHRANGE

Arcadia

Mariton

Sapienshire

Westwood Road

DELLARK

Cliffton

Wickerby Road

Andover

FAIRWELL   Road

Wiltfordshire

SASINOU MOUNTAINS

Road

Farfield

Westfield

Prima

Cloverton

PALMARTA

SALDORRA

CHAPTER ONE

The day the rains finally came was like any other, with blistering air coating the canyon in a heavy stillness. By late afternoon, the only thing more suffocating than the air was the dust kicked up by our feet. We were as quiet as the dead, moving from rock to crevice, always watching the paths for a sign of movement. Not even a desert hare emerged from the shade. In a way, we were grateful to be left alone, but it was a haunting reminder of what waited for us in the valley below: a village of deserted streets, of wood and mud houses, and of the slow, creaking swing of the well's empty pail.

I crouched beneath the cover of the jutting rocks, my legs aching with exhaustion and my chest as tight as dry leather. The dust was hot between my fingers, and my knees stung with all the jagged little rocks that dug into them. I was awful at this game—I was awful when I was a kid and still awful now, years later, when Henry had decided that the best way to watch his little brothers was to play go-seek-find.

Even with all of the hiding places the Sasinou Mountains had to offer, none ever seemed good enough to mask the red hair that grew out of my head in every which way. I wasn't exactly an image of grace and lightness of foot, either, which made hiding more difficult.

Earlier that day, Mother had given us a disgusted face when Henry came to our house, begging me to join them in the mountains. For weeks, she had worn the strip of black cloth like armor, knotting it fiercely around her upper arm every morning in the dark since the news had reached Father by post.

"Out playing games—now, of all times? It'll do nothing more than show the young ones how to be disrespectful," she had said, working a slab of dough on the countertop. I gripped the silver pendant around my neck and held my tongue.

Mother and the others her age had grown up with the king. They remembered his early ascension to the throne, his many years of pushing Auster's forces from our shores, and had admired him for his fair rule. Three years prior, when the king had married the young, beautiful Eglantine, the entire country celebrated the wedding. To everyone my age, he was only a face on a portrait. To our parents, he had been a hero.

"The king's been buried for a month," Henry said gently.

"A month and already forgotten," she said. "Never

thinking of what will become of us, now that the dear old man is gone. The queen is far too young to rule."

Henry and I shared a look. All of the adults had uttered the same line at one point or another. My father had called a village meeting the night he had received the terrible news. Parents had filed into the great hall, where they remained all night, away from the prying ears of children. The queen was a sore subject with my parents. "Too young," my mother said. "Too inexperienced," my father added. "Her world is her wardrobe."

All of this was true. Eglantine was only a few years older than I. She had married a man old enough to be her father and had earned only scorn from the people when she failed to produce an heir to the throne.

The next morning, our parents all emerged from the meeting with the same pale strained look. A pact had been made. We young people knew that that single letter announcing the king's death had done more to shake the roots of our village than our ten-year drought.

At the time, Henry and I were sure that the adults were only worried about Queen Eglantine neglecting the western villages. The king had taken a special interest in our region and had offered the use of the Wizard Guard's finest wizards to try to coax the rain out of the clouds. When that had proved futile, he set up a peaceful trade of water between Saldorra, an otherwise hostile country, and us, the town of Cliffton, in the country of Palmarta. Our yellow dirt, when mixed with water, could be fired into the hardest ceramics the world had ever seen. Our sand was the only currency we had.

My mother turned to Henry. "I know that *you* at least have better things to do with your time."

"We're done salvaging the corn," Henry said. "There isn't much to go around, but Father said it should last at least a month. I've finished my chores, and Father and I won't leave to make the mud deliveries until tomorrow morning."

My mother stopped kneading, her hands releasing the battered dough. She glanced up through the small window that overlooked our bit of land.

"Sydelle, did you start the rug for Mrs. Anders?"

I nodded, my eyes drifting back to the loom leaning against the wall. All Mrs. Anders wanted was a yellow rug to help hide the dust tracked into her rickety little home. I would be done in a day, maybe two.

"All right, but take the basket and bring back some dry root. I need to grind a new batch for your father after you ruined the last of it with your clumsy hands."

Henry said, "We'll find enough to last for the next few months, I promise."

And then, amazingly, she let us go.

* * *

Three hours later, I was crouched down behind the rocks until my knees were shaking with pain. Just as I was about to launch myself forward, Henry appeared beside me, grinning like a kid. I let out a small, surprised squeak. He held a finger to his lips.

I thought, not for the first time that day, that something was a bit off. We hadn't had this heavy a cloud cover in years, and Henry's tan skin and brown hair were looking especially dulled in the unusual dimmed light. He faded easily back into the mountains, while my pale skin, burned pink by the sun, made my efforts to hide all the more difficult.

He crawled past me, sticking his head out to gauge whether his brothers were still around.

"I think I lost them a ways back," he said. "Ready?"

"Why do I have to go first?" I complained. "You always make me go first—ever since we were ten."

"And six years later," he whispered back, "I still like you enough to give you the glory of the capture, Sydelle Mirabil. Don't forget we have our honor to uphold."

"You mean *your* honor," I said. "Against your six-year-old brothers. If one of those scamps hits me with a rock, you're taking my chores for a week."

Henry glanced out one more time and nodded. I sprang forward, heading for the scrap of fabric tied to the trunk of the hollow tree. Henry was right behind me, his long legs carrying him quickly across the small path. Above us, we heard the cries of the twins and the thudding of the rocks they launched in our direction. Demons.

Something did hit me. Something wet, which might have

been sweat had it not been so cool. It rolled down the back of my neck, nearly jolting me from my skin. At first, I didn't recognize it for what it was. It had been years, truly *years*.

I whirled around to face Henry, to see if he had felt it, too. He was staring up into the sky, his eyes wide. The twins launched one last rock from the cliffs overhead. It fell inches from my feet, but I didn't move. There was a moment of absolute silence before the thunder cracked and the sky opened.

We were drenched in a moment. The rain fell from the sky in heavy, fat drops. I let out a choked sound, half delight, half surprise. Henry and I stared at each other, holding our breaths for fear it would be over just as quickly as it had begun. We had been six, maybe seven at the last rain, but the twins hadn't been born yet. They looked up at the sky, and it was clear by the looks on their faces that they were mystified.

"Come on!" Henry said, turning to run. "Allan! John! Back to the village."

"My basket!" I said.

"Get it later," Henry insisted.

"I'll meet you down there," I said. "Just go—you have to watch your brothers."

The twins charged down the steep trail and passed right by us. We could hear shouts from the valley below, the village waking from its long, dry slumber.

Henry gave me a long look. Was he honestly worried I would get lost? I watched the rain smear the dust on his cheeks into long, snaking lines and smiled. That was just the kind of friend he was, ready to fall over himself with concern.

"Go!" I said, giving him a playful push. We turned away from each other at the same moment, he back toward the village, barely visible through the sheet of rain. I was heading up, to the highest point of the canyon.

It had been raining for less than a minute, and already the dust had melted into patches of sticky mud. The raindrops were fat and unrelenting—a feast after a ten-year famine.

I stumbled over the loose rocks, but I never stopped, not even for a moment. I wanted to be in the village, to hear the songs and prayers of thanks. To see the look on my mother's face, and the weight lifted from my father's shoulders. Each raindrop was sending up a little splatter of dust, and I had never seen the dirt so dark as it was in that moment. The cracked, withered soil seemed to melt together beneath my feet.

When the men from Saldorra came to trade their water for our dirt, I thought, wouldn't they be surprised at what they found?

The scent of rain and dust was dizzyingly wonderful, and I wished for a bottle to capture it. A new carpet practically wove itself in my mind, and I could see how to bring the blues together with the silvers and browns. I could almost imagine what the village would look like spotted with green. We wouldn't be forced to work so hard, every single day.

The possibilities were freeing beyond my wildest dreams.

I found my basket right where I had left it, where the sun could dry the roots that Henry and his brothers had helped me pull from the ground. They were a soggy mess, but I didn't think my mother would mind.

I wrapped my arms around the basket, holding it closely to my chest, breathing deeply. I would stay up here a little while longer, where only the rain could touch me.

Suddenly I could hear voices rising from below even with the fierce pattering of rain against the rocks. Only they were not raised in joy, they were shouts coming in a different tongue.

I pushed the wet hair off my cheeks and was to the ledge in three short steps, bracing my basket against my hip.

There were horses and men in the field just beyond the mountain, hundreds of them. Their scarlet uniforms were a blur from my vantage point, a long, twisting line of men and beasts.

My eyes drifted along the river of red, twisting down the pass. Behind the first group of horses were wagons, their wheels now trapped in the yellow mud. It looked as if the soldiers behind them were pushing vainly as the horses struggled to pull them free.

They weren't bringing in the usual trade of water.

I took a step back, colliding with something solid, my startled cry muffled by a hand. I was pulled away from the ledge, spinning toward the overhang of rock.

"Don't scream," someone said in my ear. "I'm going to let you go, but don't scream, all right?"

I nodded, holding my basket tightly.

The man let me go without a moment's hesitation. I whirled around, the basket coming up to smack the side of his face. He staggered back, but before I could bolt past him, he had me by the arm again, and this time his grip wasn't as forgiving.

"What are you doing here?" he asked. I kept my eyes diverted, looking for a way to escape, to overpower him. He wouldn't let me; he hauled me around and pinned me there. The happiness in my heart was entirely gone, replaced by fear.

The stranger wasn't dressed in a Saldorran uniform as I would have expected a scout to be, but in simple clothes. He looked to be about my age, maybe a few years older. I watched the rain drip down the length of his long nose and collect in his dark, uncombed hair. There was a small cut on his face where the sharp edge of my basket had caught his skin, but it was nothing compared to the bruise on his other cheek.

I let myself admit that he had a roguish charm about him. Some hint of softness in his eyes, at least. No, he wasn't a soldier, but he was still a stranger, a vagabond, maybe. Even if I hadn't seen his face, his worn boots and torn cloak would have told his story. The pressure of his hand on my arm became nearly unbearable, yet it wasn't until I let out a gasp of pain that he released me.

"Are you from the village?" His words came out in an urgent rush. "From Cliffton?"

I nodded. "Why are the soldiers here? Do you have any idea why—?"

"Can you take me to the elder?"

"My father?" At that, I did take a step back.

"Is he in the village now?" I wasn't sure how to respond, and he must have been able to tell. He took my arm again, this time far more gently. "You can trust me—I'm here to help you. Is your father in the village, or has he left for the capital?"

The sound of horses and men below drifted in and out of my ears. I searched for a reason to distrust him, but instead I saw the desperation in his face, the real concern.

He had a kind face, even with the dirt, even with his wounds.

"Yes," I said finally. "He is. I can take you to him."

He took my other arm, pulling me toward him so quickly the basket slipped from my hands. It was the last sound that reached my ears, for in the next moment even the rain disappeared. The man brought his black cloak up around us, pulling me close to him. The world spun away under our feet. I felt my stomach lurch and an explosion of pain behind my eyes, and just as quickly, darkness fell over us.

*　　*　　*

I woke, not in the yellow mud of the mountains, but in the dark chill of my room, under a pile of blankets. Somehow, the afternoon had fallen into night without my knowing it. If the slow growl of thunder and the steady pattering of rain hadn't been there to greet me as I opened my eyes, the entire day might have been a dream.

How had I gotten down from the pass? I had slipped and knocked my head against the rocks before, but never so badly as to lose all recollection of it. And the stranger, what about him?

"Sydelle, are you awake?" Mother whispered. I turned my head and allowed the dizziness to wash over me. The usual rasp in her voice was gone.

"What's happened?" I asked, waiting for my eyes to adjust to the darkness. She held a candle up to her face, its flickering light catching the strands of her pale hair. I saw that my loom had been disassembled and moved from the main room of the house into my cramped room.

"That man I met in the mountains—is he here?"

There was sadness in her eyes where I had expected to find anger. I didn't know whether to be relieved or frightened by it.

"I'm sorry about the roots," I said quickly. "When the rain clears, I'll find more."

She brought the candle closer to my face, and for the first time, the warmth it provided was a relief. My hair and dress were still damp, and the rain had cooled the air enough for me to shiver beneath the blankets.

"I'll go tell your father you're awake," she said. "He's with our guest."

My mother left without another word, leaving me alone, my questions still unanswered. I sat up slowly, wishing she had left the candle with me. All I could make out in the darkness was my loom and the shape of my father's leather bag next to it on the floor. It looked full. What had the man asked—if my father had left for the capital yet?

". . . would you . . . Sydelle . . . it's . . ."

The words came in soft fragments. I strained my ears past the slow drumming of rain to the conversation on the other side of the wall. Layers of mud and plaster muffled the voices, but the stranger's rich voice was clear, almost as if he was in my room.

". . . from the capital?" asked my father.

"No, but I have spent a great amount of time there," the stranger replied after a long pause.

"Just how old are you, Mr. . . . ?"

"North," the man said, neatly sidestepping my father's question. "Wayland North, if you'd prefer."

"What are you doing around our parts?" Mr. Porter, Henry's father, asked. I hadn't realized he was there. "It's unusual to find a wizard so far west, given that we're so close to Saldorra and they don't take kindly to your . . . kind."

A *wizard,* I thought numbly. The word rolled around inside of me. That man had been a wizard, one of Astraea's disciples . . . and I had been so disrespectful. Had he brought the rain?

"After the king was murdered, some of the details didn't

align for me," said the wizard. "I needed proof, so I traveled west."

I pressed my ear up against the wall.

"We were told the poison came from Auster. Are you saying that it came from Saldorra?" my father asked. His voice was too calm—I almost couldn't hear it above the pounding in my ears. *Poison?* Henry and I had guessed an illness, an accident perhaps . . . but murder . . . ?

Wayland North let out a sharp laugh. "I have it on good authority that the wizards haven't the slightest idea where the poison came from. They only know it was put in his nightly glass of wine."

"So we've declared war against Auster for nothing?" Mr. Porter asked, and I didn't need to be by the wall to hear him. "On a whim—a guess? Did the Wizard Guard send you out here to search for information?"

"The Guard is still pursuing Auster as the primary culprit," the wizard said. "You have to understand that if we go to war with them, it won't be because they killed our king. With the king dead, Auster's king is claiming his right to the throne."

"By what right?" Mr. Porter said. "It's absurd."

"No," my father said. "It's not. The king of Auster is our king's second cousin, the last of his living relatives, and you know as well as I do that our laws say that a woman cannot inherit the throne, regardless of circumstances."

"You said a law had been introduced to change that," Mr.

Porter said, "on the chance that the queen didn't deliver a male heir."

"There was to be a vote on it next month," Father said. "We can vote it in, but there's a real possibility that Auster won't recognize the law as valid."

"They've been waiting for an excuse to invade our country under legitimate circumstances," North said. "Saldorra's soldiers will join their forces. I would say they're maybe half a day from overtaking your village."

"Sydelle!" a voice hissed. I started, tearing myself away from the wall. It had come from outside, slipping through the small hole in my wall that was meant to be a window, without glass or fabric.

"Delle!" It was Henry. If he had been any louder, the entire village would have heard him. I looked out to see him hunkered down in the mud, drenched straight through his clothes.

"What?" I asked, annoyed.

"Are you all right? I waited for you in the market," he said. "And out of nowhere you appeared with the wizard—I thought you were dead, you were so pale. Did you faint?"

"Not now!" I whispered. "I'll tell you everything tomorrow. Just go!"

I didn't wait to see if he would listen. Two steps later and my ear was back against the wall, catching the wizard's voice.

". . . and they won't stop," North said. "I used the rain to slow them as much as I could—I didn't realize it would be such a help to you."

"You have no idea what you've done for us in bringing the rain. I can't even begin to fathom how you succeeded where other wizards have failed," my father said. He sounded tired. "Anything we can give in return, *anything*, we'll give you."

"If you're still willing to give up what we discussed before, then there's nothing more I could ask for." North cleared his throat. "But we shouldn't stay much longer. Auster and the officials in Provincia have agreed on a two-month deadline to try to resolve this without magic and sword, but I'm afraid it may take me just as long to get there, and I don't trust the mail service to deliver the report safely."

"I insist you stay the night, then. You look worn—even your cloaks need looking after."

I sat up a little straighter on the floor, tucking my legs beneath me. I knew what was coming.

"They all do, I'm afraid," North said. "I saw a bit more action in Saldorra than I had expected. But wizard tailors are pricey, and I haven't been across one in a few months. I have an entire country to cross, and less than two months to do it. It'll have to wait until I get to Provincia."

"Nonsense, my daughter will do the same for free."

"It requires a bit of skill—" North protested.

"She's the best in the village, I assure you," he said. "Sydelle!"

I stood quickly, brushing the dust from my dress and

hands. He called my name again, impatient as always.

Only the wizard looked up at me when I entered our sitting room. Jugs of water and plates of our precious bread were scattered on the table's surface.

"Sydelle, you'll mend Mr. North's cloaks and show him to your room," Father said. "You can stay with your mother and me for the night."

I nodded and said nothing, though it killed me not to ask the questions that were running through my mind. If I embarrassed my father now by opening my mouth, I wouldn't hear the end of it for months—probably years, knowing his legendary temper.

North stood and stretched. I waited until he came toward me, close enough to smell the mix of sweat and rain clinging to his clothing and skin, and to see the dark circles under his eyes.

"You don't have to mend them," North said as we entered my small room. "Honestly, they've been far worse."

I watched him out of the corner of my eye, studying him as I would a book or drawing. How could I not? He was the only wizard I'd ever met—in all likelihood, the only wizard I ever would meet. It seemed so strange to have him look so ordinary. After all the stories I'd read about their adventures and magic, I never expected them to look like any man or woman. There was only one difference, slight enough that I almost missed it, and that was the warmth that surrounded him, a warmth that was so much softer than the heat of our sun.

"Are you afraid I'll ruin them?" I asked, assessing my small supply of thread and needles. He lifted the cloaks one by one, and I was startled to see how many there actually were—black, red, green, blue, yellow. Why did he need so many?

"I'm sure you're very good," he said. "But these cloaks are special. Do you know anything about how magic works?"

I shook my head. "Not in the least."

"Well . . . ," North began. "These cloaks are what I use for magic. If they're not mended carefully, I won't be able to use them."

I held out my hand, still unable to look him fully in the eye.

"I'll be careful," I said.

North sighed. "One to begin with, all right?"

He tried untying them from around his neck, but the strings had become badly knotted, and his gloved hands were shaking so badly that I had to do it myself. The moment my hands touched him, he stilled.

"Are you all right?" I asked.

"Fine. A bit tired."

"Are you sure?" I said, watching him more carefully now.

He nodded, holding perfectly still as I worked on the stubborn knots.

"Thank you for bringing me back to the village," I said. "I don't know that I've ever fainted before. I guess I was more overwhelmed than I thought."

"And here I thought you swooned at the sight of me." He gave me a crooked smile.

"Do you do this a lot?" he asked, when I had finally pulled the cloaks free and placed them in his arms. I didn't answer, but accepted the yellow cloak as he handed it to me. They were made from a thin wool: rough but sturdy. I set to work immediately, sinking down next to him on my small pile of bedding. He glanced around the room, at my half-finished blankets and rugs and the small scenes of Cliffton I had created with yellow, brown, and red thread. His eyes fell on the silver circle on my wall, a larger version of my necklace. I would have to pray beneath the one in my parents' room that night.

"It's not much," I said. "I'm sorry I don't have a bed for you."

"No, no," North said quickly. "It's not that. I'm just surprised that you're a weaver."

"Why is that?" I asked, pulling together a jagged tear in the stained yellow cloak.

"I just meant that you're very young to be so good. At weaving, I mean."

"I'll have you know that I just turned sixteen," I said, knotting the thread and cutting the excess. "Aren't *you* a little young to be a wizard?"

"I'll have you know that I just turned eighteen," he said, mimicking my tone almost perfectly. "That's four years out of apprenticeship and two years your elder."

So much for wizards and their legendary kindness and courtesy. He was no different than any of the boys I had grown up with.

"Very funny," I said. "A wizard *and* a joker."

North shrugged, still looking around. "I see red . . . yellow . . . brown . . . ah, a little green, and of course our own Palmarta purple—no gray?"

"Why would I have gray?" I asked, giving him a sidelong glance. "We haven't seen a rain cloud in years."

He glanced up, toward the old blanket I had strung over my bed. What had once been an expertly woven image of Provincia's castle and its surrounding lake was now faded and stained.

"Ah, but there's the castle!" he said, craning his neck for a better look. "That's a decent likeness. Have you been to the capital?"

"Of course not," I said. "That was given to me by a woman who was traveling across the country selling her work. She gave me the blanket and told me to meet her in Andover when I was old enough."

"And when will you be old enough?"

"When I'm born in a different village in another lifetime," I said.

"But you want to go," North said. He bit the side of his thumb, his expression troubled. It was not long before his eyes found the old map of Palmarta tacked up in the soft plaster of my wall. Each circle of string marked a city where Henry had traveled, making deliveries of our yellow dust. With Auster looming to the east and Saldorra to the west and south, our country looked ready to be swallowed whole.

"What I want will always be different from what everyone else wants for me," I said, knotting the thread.

"You're talented enough, if you really do want it," North said. "You could support yourself if you settled in a city."

I shook my head, surprised at the prick of anger inside me. He could flit in and out of towns and cities at will. I should never have brought the old woman up in the first place, but every time I looked at the blanket, I could feel her soft, wrinkled palms as she had brushed the dirt from my cheeks.

"Would you leave," he asked, "if you could?"

"It's not my choice," I said. "It must be nice to go wherever you want. Have you decided how you're getting to Provincia?"

He shrugged. "I'm taking the most direct route possible, cutting straight through the center of the country. There are a few cities like Dellark and Fairwell along the way, but I'll be spending most of my time outdoors. You could start over, buy yourself a new, bigger loom—"

"Never," I said. "That's my loom, and it's the only one I want to use."

The loom had been with me since I was a little girl, watching my grandmother weave her own blankets and stories into it. It was an extension of me, as familiar as the face of my father. It had always been an escape—from drought and from every painful emotion.

I handed him the yellow cloak, watching as he turned it over in his hands, inspecting my work.

"Your father wasn't lying," he said. "But now comes the real test."

He threw the yellow cloak into the air, and it disappeared from sight. Impossibly, a strong breeze blew past us. It shook the hanging blankets and sent my mass of red curls up around my face. A moment later, the yellow cloak reappeared in front of the wizard, floating gently back into his hands.

The wizard turned his face toward me, his dark eyes studying me with a mixture of shock and fascination. His pale face was drained of what little color it had possessed before, and he twisted the yellow fabric so roughly between his fists that I thought it might tear. He didn't move—he looked to be barely breathing.

"You . . . ," he began, his voice low with disbelief. "You're really . . ."

I waited for him to continue, but the words never came and his eyes never left mine.

"Sleep well," I said, standing. "Let me know if you need something. There's a basin in the corner if you'd like to wash up before praying."

"I don't," he said.

"Don't what?" I said incredulously. "Don't pray?"

He lowered his eyes.

"Sydelle?" he said, just as I was about to step through the doorway. He was still holding the yellow cloak in his hands. "I know you were listening to what I told your father. If you can find the courage to leave, then you need to go soon . . . before things are set in motion."

"Then the war . . ." I almost couldn't get the words out. "Then it'll really happen?"

"It's happening now," he said. "Your village must prepare for the worst. Saldorra is Auster's western ally. It's only a matter of time before they reach you."

"Astraea will protect us," I said. "We trade with Saldorra. They'd never—"

"It would be better if you could protect yourself," he said, and blew out the candle.

Hours later, as I turned restlessly on a blanket on my parents' floor, his words returned, until I was sure that they would be burned there forever, that they would follow me into sleep every night. *It would be better if you could protect yourself.*

I listened to the rain and wondered.

CHAPTER TWO

I was still awake when the temple's bells began to ring out in an unfamiliar pattern, and my mother began to cry loudly, brokenly, from somewhere deep inside her chest.

"Now?" she moaned. *"Now?"*

"Up, Sydelle!" my father said, dragging me from the tangled bedding. "Put on your dress and your boots."

"What's happening?" I choked out. The wizard was waiting in the main room, far more alert than he had been the night before. He was holding my disassembled loom.

My mother took me, wild-eyed and frantic, into my room and began to pack dresses and yarn into a small leather bag.

"What's happening?" I cried. "Tell me what's going on!"

My mother placed the bag over my shoulder, and I was sure I felt her warm tears drip onto my neck.

"Be a brave girl," she said. "I know you have it in you."

My father reappeared in the doorway, his face flushed. "Hurry—move quickly!"

"Tell me what's going on!" I said. *"Tell me!"*

"Those soldiers you saw before in the canyon are here now," North said from the other room. "You're coming with me."

"I offered Mr. North a reward for breaking the drought," my father explained, "and he's chosen you. Do you understand?"

I was the one crying now, and I couldn't tell my anger from my fear.

"Sydelle, tell me you understand," Father begged, and Mother only cried harder. "You'll help him get to the capital, you'll do whatever he asks, you won't look back."

"Do I have no choice in this?" I cried, as the wizard appeared behind my father. The smile on his face was small, but it was still there.

He thought he was helping me, did he? He thought that he was doing me some sort of favor. A prisoner of my village or a prisoner of a wizard. What was the difference when you could not decide your own path?

The sound of bells died out, only to be replaced by the sound of a hundred villagers emerging into the early-morning sky.

"They're here." North was suddenly right beside me, taking my arm. I turned toward him wildly, hearing the sound of rolling thunder, of hooves.

"What's happening?" I asked. "What—?"

"Sooner than expected," my father said. He patted my shoulder twice, as he would a complete stranger. "Go before they find you here."

"No!" I said. "I don't want to leave, not now!"

North held my things as my father pulled me outside. He had a bag of his own, one I hadn't noticed before. A fine mist of rain and fog cooled the flushed skin of my cheeks. I watched my mother, still expecting her to speak. She only looked away.

Henry had come to find me. He was standing a short distance away from our door, his lip pulled back in anger, maybe disgust. I had never seen him wear such a hostile face—ready for battle. I tried to picture the boys I had grown up with in the dark militia uniforms, but the best my mind could conjure up was the image of Henry's brothers playing in the mud, hitting their sticks against each other as if they were swords.

The dirt and rocks trembled beneath our feet as the sound of galloping horses and hollering men reached our ears.

"Go now!" My father pushed me toward the wizard. *"Go!"*

"Saldorra!" a woman screamed, and it was all the encouragement North needed. He surged forward, shoving Henry to the side and taking me by the arm.

"Delle!" I heard Henry shout, and then nothing more. A shroud of darkness wrapped around the wizard and me, and we were falling.

✳   ✳   ✳

The earth found us again, its jagged rocks and familiar dust breaking our fall. By the time my vision cleared, North was crouched in front of me with my loom and bag at his side, examining the scene in the valley below. The screams from Cliffton floated up to us.

We were in the mountains, but how or why we were there seemed inconsequential. I watched as dozens of horses and men in hideous crimson uniforms overran the village below. They flooded the streets like a river of fire, moving among the scattered homes, encircling the crowd of people we had left only a moment before.

"Did you know?" I cried. "You knew they were coming, you knew they'd—!"

I couldn't finish.

I was too far away to recognize anyone. The soldiers disappeared into shops and homes, dragging the few lingering villagers outside. Chaos fell like a wall of sand, devouring everything at once. Troughs, buckets, pots, and vases were all kicked to the ground, the precious water inside wasted on dust.

"Why are they doing this?" I whispered.

"Your village has been dependent on Saldorra for bringing you water." North cast a sidelong glance at me. "The soldiers need to camp here and wait for instructions from Auster about invading our country. They were planning on exchanging the water for the villagers' silence about them being there, which is why they can't let the villagers have their own supply. It's exactly what they did to Cloverton and Westfield. I warned your father last night this would happen."

"You warned him?" My fists lashed out blindly. I couldn't tell my anger from my fear. "You were the one who led them here! They're chasing you! You took that information—!"

"Information that said they would overtake Cliffton and wait out the two-month deadline before invading the rest of Palmarta," North snapped, catching my hands. "Listen to me! Saldorra is taking over the western villages and blocking all communication between them and the capital so the Wizard Guard and the queen won't know their soldiers are invading from the west. Auster isn't responsible for killing the king, and if I can convince the wizards of that, they'll call our own war plans off! That's why your father told us to go, because we can tell them! I have the proof they'll need to believe us—letters, maps, everything. I need you to come with me, though, in case something happens and I can't get there myself. I *need* you."

I shook my head, struggling to pull away. The wind was picking up around us, howling through every crack and crevice of the mountain pass.

"You're a wizard," I cried. "Can't you do anything?"

"There's nothing you or I could do against that many men," North said. "Any sign of rebellion and they'll burn the village to ashes. Westfield already suffered that fate, and I won't risk more innocent lives."

"You mean *your* life!" I cried. "You won't risk *your* life!"

I cast my eyes to the familiar landscape below. The villagers remained huddled together as the soldiers continued to rip through the streets, taking livestock, blankets, anything of value. There would be nothing left in a place that already had so little.

What were wizards if they couldn't protect the powerless? I had heard the story of their inception thousands of times, in temple and at home. In the great competition deciding which goddess would have authority over men, Astraea had granted the chosen people of our country, Palmarta, the magic to defeat the evils of the world, while her sister, Salvala, had merely given swords to her people, the citizens of Auster, Saldorra, Ruttgard, Libanbourg, and Bellun. When only the wizards were capable of defeating the wicked dragons and sinister men, they became Palmarta's champions. Their purpose was to protect us, even against the worst of odds.

"You said before that you had no choice," North said. "But here's one right in front of you. You can go back down to your people and suffer quietly with them, but if do, you really will be trapped there, with no relief. It'll be at least a month and a half before I get to the capital, and longer before the Wizard Guard can come to help you."

"Trapped with them or trapped with you—" I began.

"Not forever," he said. Something hard and unbearable had wedged itself in my throat. "If you help me get to the capital, I swear on everything good in this world that after we deliver the information, I'll take you anywhere you want to go. It *will* be your choice."

It was happening too quickly, with no time for good-byes, for lingering last looks. Was it possible that only yesterday it had rained for the first time in years, that people had been singing and dancing instead of crying and screaming? Now the rain was gone again, leaving behind only a fine gray haze, and the only thing left for me was to go with the wizard.

It was a cruel twist of fate, I thought, finally to have the chance to see the world beyond Cliffton but only in the worst, the most terrifying of times.

"Why did you pick me?"

North picked up my bag and loom, helping me to my feet.

"Why me?" I repeated over the deafening wind. "You could have had anyone!"

"Yes," he said, taking one last look at the village below. "But I only need you."

✻   ✻   ✻

The sun hadn't fully arched into the sky when we found the first soldier. I don't know why I hadn't expected to find them lurking up in the mountain passes, waiting to see if they could catch an escaped villager or a traveler trying foolishly to enter the valley.

North saw him a moment before I caught the flash of the arrow tip, strung on the scout's bow. There was a chance the scout hadn't seen us at all, but North yanked me back against him. For a moment, I thought he meant to use me as a shield, but the force of it sent us stumbling behind the nearest rock formation in a tangled heap. I pressed my hand against my mouth.

I glanced around one side of the rocks, searching for some path I recognized. Out of the corner of my eye, I saw North rise to his knees, his green cloak in one hand.

"Don't you dare!" I hissed. "If you use magic against that scout, you'll call the rest of them to us."

"It's the only choice we have," he said. "We can run for it in all the confusion."

"What's so confusing about a wizard using magic?" I asked. "They're likely looking for you, and if you do this, you might as well paint the targets on our backs."

"If you're going to knock down my suggestion, you'd better have one to replace it." The irritation was plain on his face.

I glanced around the side of the rock again. The path we were on was one Henry and I had used many times before, but instead of going left, toward the caverns, North had taken us right. We needed to get back to the caverns unnoticed.

"Can you distract him?" I whispered. "Just for a moment? He needs to turn his back on us."

"Oh, so now you require my services?" he asked humorlessly, and brought up the same yellow cloak I had mended the night before.

"Not too much," I warned.

The gust of wind that emerged kicked up the loose rocks and dirt, and the scout staggered backward. He didn't turn, but it was all the distraction we needed. I grabbed a fistful of North's cloaks and dragged him after me. Our boots slid against the mud as we ran, and I didn't dare look back as we cut through every rock formation and crack in the earth I could find. I thought I heard the call of a horn behind us, and North's arm tensed as he tried to slow me down. It was the only way we could slip out unnoticed, though we would waste hours crawling through the caverns.

The wizard had some difficulty sliding down through the cavern's entrance, and in any other situation I might have laughed at the way his feet struggled to find purchase against the slick rocks.

Henry and I had used the caverns as a way to escape the heat. We had spent days down in the darkness, feeling our way when our eyes failed us. Once, I had hoped to find a hidden pool of water, like the one in my storybooks—but now all I needed was a safe route to the northern road.

There was a thud behind me, followed by a string of curses so violent it made my ears burn.

"Careful," I whispered, glad for the darkness that hid my smile. North crept up beside me, one gloved hand clutching his forehead, the other still holding our bags and my loom.

"Rotting good path you've found us," he whispered furiously. After that, there was nothing but the echo of dripping water to mark time.

I wished someone had thought to pack me a pair of gloves to keep the rocks from cutting my hands. The skirt of my dress was soaked through with the rainwater that had collected in the cavern overnight, but I kept us moving downward, deeper into the water.

"We'll be swimming soon," North said. "You should have just let me use magic—!"

"Here," I cut him off. My hands had found the gap in the dark stone I had been searching for. I pressed my body between its narrow walls. The exact moment I caught the first hint of sunlight, I felt for North's arm to make sure he was still behind me.

The path had widened, giving me a clear view. I scanned the rocks above, searching for a glint of metal or scarlet. When I was sure it was safe, I pulled us both free from the darkness.

Once he saw where we were, North tried to take control of the situation, turning to run in the very same direction from which we had come.

"North!" I said, as loudly as I dared. "*This* way!"

He kept his eyes on the path before him.

"We just came that way," I said. "Honestly, do you have no sense of direction whatsoever?"

North bristled. "How was I supposed to know? The mountains are all the same! For all you know, my way could work, too."

"The Westwood road runs west to east, not north to south, wise one," I whispered, checking to make sure no one was within earshot. "It's the main road to the eastern coast. If we want to get out of these mountains, we need to find it."

"And how in the seven hells would you know that?" North asked, blocking my path with his arm. "You said you've never left Cliffton."

"Because one day I wanted to take that road out of Cliffton." I shoved his arm out of my way. "Unlike you, I actually bothered to learn how to read maps and what roads lead to where."

North was quiet for a moment. "So . . . if one wanted to, let's say, go to Dellark . . . how would one do that?"

"Just be quiet and follow me, all right?" I shook my head and began to pray as I started down the path.

*　　*　　*

By the time we broke through the Sasinou Mountains' endless maze of sharp brown stone two days later, my feet had gone numb and my back was hunched under the weight of my bag. North had found a way to throw the loom over his shoulder, for which I was grateful. I wasn't sure I could carry anything else.

I leaned forward, trying to balance the weight of my bag with the lightness in my head. It was a mistake. My vision spotted with black and colors. Henry had told me once it took him and his father two days to reach Dellark, but I had hoped to get there faster.

The path down into the valley was steeper than I had originally thought, and I was forced to take small, steady steps in order not to fall the rest of the way down. The frame of my loom rattled and railed within its tight restraints; it was the only sound I could hear above my harsh breathing.

The sun was sinking behind us, the lingering heat on our backs no more than a painful reminder of what I was leaving behind. I had no eyes for the red flowers growing amid the tall grass or the river winding lazily across the land.

"Are you sure I can't carry your bag for you awhile?" North asked, tucking his hands into his pockets. "Your loom doesn't weigh much at all."

I whirled around so quickly I nearly lost my balance. North saw, of course, and his hands flashed out to steady me. His fingers weren't on my arms for more than a moment before I pushed him away as hard as I could.

"Don't *touch me*," I said. "You want to help me? Go back and force the soldiers out of Cliffton!"

He tried to pull the bag from my shoulders, but I held on to it.

"Syd," he said calmly. "Be reasonable. I know it's heavy. Please, let me take it for a while."

"Are you hard of hearing?" I asked, the words coming out in a furious storm. "Leave me alone!"

North held up his hands in surrender, and we spent the next few hours in silence, with only the sound of the bugs in the tall grass and the dim lights of a distant city to guide us.

The moon was under a cover of clouds, which didn't make navigating through the fields any easier.

With my eyes on the city ahead, I didn't see the hole at my feet. I did, however, feel it as my body careened forward and the ground rushed up to meet me. My chin came down hard against the ground as my fall knocked the air from my lungs. I wasn't sure how long I was on the ground, but I couldn't pull myself back up, and I wasn't sure I wanted to.

North's heavy boots came shuffling toward me.

"Don't," I protested weakly.

His hands lifted me to my knees and released me just as quickly. He removed the bag from my shoulders and placed it over his own. I felt better immediately, but it didn't stop the hot tears that spilled onto my cheeks all the way to Dellark.

*   *   *

Somewhere amid all his ramblings, North had mentioned that Dellark was a major port on the river. I saw several wooden ships, but mainly I saw bridges, dozens of them, maybe even hundreds. The bridges over the river were wood, rising and falling with the passing ships. Those that rose over the streams branching from the river were smaller, built from the same old gray stone as the buildings. It was an intricate network—a maze, truly.

Above us, the purple banners of Palmarta were flapping in the evening's breeze. North and I crossed two of the larger bridges before I stopped outside a grim-looking tavern. The sign hanging above it had rotted to the point that the wording on it was indecipherable . . . but I had to stop. If I moved one more step, I was sure I would collapse.

"I have a little money if you want to sleep inside tonight . . . ," he began.

"Here," I said.

"Fine." North pushed the door open, his dark hair hiding his face. He looked filthy, but I probably looked worse. It only made me despise him more.

North dropped our bags down at the only free table and headed straight for the large blond man behind the bar. I dropped down into my chair and rested my head against the table. There wasn't a part of me that didn't throb with exhaustion. Barely able to keep my eyes open, I hardly noticed the uproar of laughter and song. On the wall opposite me were two portraits, one of the king when he was still young and beautiful, and the other of the fair-haired, blue-eyed Queen Eglantine.

My eyes drifted shut against my will, but I couldn't slip into sleep. The smell of a pipe from across the room instantly recalled dinners at Henry's house, his father puffing rings of smoke to amuse the twins. Was it possible . . . ?

I brought my head up to see where the smoke was coming from, looking past North at the bar, around the animal heads and dead fish mounted on the walls to a far, dark corner. The man smoking the pipe wore a pale overcoat and a hat that covered his eyes. It wasn't Henry's father—of course not—it was just my stupid mind playing tricks. As if sensing my gaze, the man leaned forward in his seat and gave me a slight nod. For a moment, it looked as though he would stand.

A plate slammed down in front of me. I glanced at the shreds of meat and pile of vegetables and pushed the plate away.

"This is all he had left for the night," North said, settling across the table. "Sorry it's not much."

He had his own plate, strangely less full than mine, and two pints, both for him, I realized. He downed one in a single swig and reached for the next.

"You know," he continued, "I get that you're angry. I know you don't want to be here with me, but you not eating isn't punishing me. You can starve yourself all you want, but it won't do anything other than slow us down."

"Why did you bring me, then, if you knew I was only going to hold you back?" I asked.

North glanced up at the ceiling.

"Tell me," I said, leaning back in my chair.

"I don't know. Perhaps I thought that burning hatred in your eyes would give way to some faster walking?" North stood up to refill his pints. "I just wanted a lovely assistant?"

"Don't you mean slave?" I called after him.

He glanced over his shoulder. "Assistant, though, if you'd prefer . . ."

He was right not to finish that thought.

I waited until his back was to me before I looked down at my plate again, my heart fighting with my stomach. I would eat it, I thought, but only because I needed to be strong enough to keep going tomorrow. We still had an entire country to cross.

Looking up to make sure he wasn't watching, I brought a spoonful of vegetables to my mouth and didn't stop eating until the plate had been cleared. And even then, I was still hungry.

✴   ✴   ✴

North had had only four pints, or at least four pints that I had seen, when he lurched forward in his seat.

"Syyyyd," he whined. I turned my head away sharply, disgust settling in my stomach like a rock. The man in the pale overcoat was still there, hours later. I shifted uncomfortably in my seat, trying to dodge his gaze.

An hour later, the tavern still throbbed with life and off-key ballads, but my head just throbbed in pain. And North? He was singing at the top of his lungs in the midst of them all. His usually deep and melodic voice was hoarse by the time he collapsed back into his seat. Another man sent an appreciative pint his way, which I promptly poured out at his feet.

It was like watching a man transform into some kind of beast, I thought. North's unshaven face, usually lit with a carefree ease and an uneven grin, had taken on a pinched expression. The dark eyes that I once had thought kind, even intelligent, were glassy and framed with red. The sharp angles of his high cheekbones flushed pink with fits of laughter, which rang out loudly and unevenly over the deafening clamor.

"Syd, Syd, Syd," he said, shaking his head.

"What?" I asked flatly. "Can we go up to our rooms yet?"

"Rooms!" He laughed. "What makes you think I got more than one? I'm not a money bag, you know."

I sucked in a sharp breath. "That is *completely* inappropriate! It's— It's not proper, but apparently *you* wouldn't know that. You wouldn't know a moral if it slapped you in the face."

North leaned back in his chair, whispering conspiratorially to the man sitting behind him. "Not proper, she says. After everything we've been through!"

The other man shook his head, as if he had been privy to our entire story. "You've caught yourself a cold fish, my friend," he said, and the other men and women at his table laughed.

North rocked forward in his chair again, narrowly missing my foot. He leaned—fell, really—across the table, reaching for my hands. I snatched them away immediately. The heat was rising in my face, no matter how many steadying breaths I took. I could hear my father's voice in the back of my mind, whispering an old proverb. *Of all things in life, forgiveness is the most difficult. If we can forgive, we can let go of the insidious anger that moves our souls to grief.*

It was the most difficult—too difficult.

"Give me the key," I said. "I'll go upstairs by myself." All I really wanted to do was weave myself into a mood that resembled calm. North dug around in his pockets for the key.

He waved the thing through the air with great fanfare and ceremony before placing it in my hand. I closed my fist around it, wondering if I could lock him out.

"If you want, Syd, you can share my . . . my . . ." North's voice trailed off.

I kicked my chair out of the way, pushing through the crowd toward the stairs.

"Syd!" he called, and everyone else quieted down. "Syd, I was going to let you have the bed!"

The woman to the left of me laughed so hard she was practically sobbing into her pint. I knocked into the next man, nearly taking him down to the floor. I couldn't hold it in any longer.

"I hope you choke on your tongue, you miserable human being!"

"Wizard," I heard him correct me weakly. "I . . . am . . . a wizard!"

"Some wizard you are!" I whirled back around. "How about using some of your magic to sober your sorry, drunken self up? And stop calling me Syd!"

I stormed up the staircase, ready to slam our door shut

against the tavern's laughter and North's infuriating smile. My hand was tight on the railing, my eyes firmly on the trail of muddy footprints leading to the upstairs hall. The suffocating heat and movement of the tavern was behind me, but its smell was inescapable.

The single window in the hallway was propped open by a thin book. I went toward it and forced the stubborn wood frame open the rest of the way. When it finally gave, a rush of cool air was my reward.

I stuck my head out into the night, and for one peaceful moment, I just breathed. We hadn't stopped moving since leaving Cliffton, save for the few hours each night I could convince the wizard I needed to sleep. He was always talking, always moving, never stopping.

At this time of night, the bridges of Dellark were haunting but not frightening. Every now and then a couple would cross a bridge, laughing, so wrapped up in each other's company they didn't notice the full moon's reflection in the dark water. Its face hovered there among the stars until a breeze came along and smeared them all away.

I leaned back, retreating into the warmth. The stars weren't nearly as bright as they were in Cliffton, though I could make out each constellation. Astraea the magic giver, Salvala the sword bearer . . .

I barely noticed the tap on my shoulder, but it was impossible to ignore the full, flushed face of the man who had appeared behind me.

"Has anyone ever told you your hair is the color of Astraea's?"

He was almost as short as I was, with hair that was unnaturally blond, almost tinged with orange. He wore a light blue velvet coat, and a greasy smile lit his face.

I took a step away.

"Yes . . . ," I said.

"A golden shade of red," he mused. "The hair of our goddess, but the color Auster chose for their uniforms and flags. It's all a bit ironic, don't you think?"

"Not really," I said. "Salvala is Astraea's sister. They have the same coloring."

A young man, no older than myself, appeared behind the man in the blue coat. He looked like Billy Porter, Henry's cousin, and the thought wrenched my gut.

"What have I told you about keeping up?" the man asked pleasantly enough.

"Sorry, Mr. Genet," the boy said.

Mr. Genet leaned over and muttered, "George is just my assistant; ignore him if you like."

"You're"—I thought quickly—"a wizard?" North had been so warm and I had thought the same would be true for all wizards, but it wasn't as easy to identify them as I had thought.

"One of a few in the city, but the best of these parts— number one hundred twenty-two."

"One hundred twenty-two?" I asked helplessly.

Genet let out a delighted laugh. "What a simple girl you are! That's my rank in wizarding society. Out of over four hundred wizards, I am the one hundred and twenty-second most powerful. It's quite an accomplishment, you know. My magister, the great Alfred Ollman, fell over himself to accept my application for training when he recognized what a child prodigy I was."

I nodded, trying to move past him, but he blocked my path.

"You're a special one, aren't you?" he asked. "It took me a moment to realize it, but I felt it the moment I came out of my room. Join me for a drink downstairs?"

Genet must have misinterpreted my stare of open horror for awe, because my hand was suddenly in his, pressed to his droopy—and drooling—lower lip. I ripped it away.

"Sir!" I said. "Please!"

He reached for me again, catching my arm and pulling me back so hard I let out a shriek. His assistant took my other arm, and it was a long struggle among the three of us down the hall. I dug my feet into the wood and clawed at their arms, but once we reached the narrow stairs, I was wedged between Genet's protruding stomach and his assistant's sharp elbows.

I did it without thinking, though the moment my teeth bit down on Genet's arm I regretted it. He let out an awful shriek of pain, pushing me down the last few steps and back into the tavern. I landed hard on my knees, knocking into the feet of two tavern patrons.

"Have some respect, you stupid girl!" Genet howled, stumbling down the rest of the stairs. "Do you know with whom you're dealing?"

"Yes," I snapped, struggling to my feet. "A filthy pig!"

Genet raised his hand, and I squeezed my eyes shut, sure I would be receiving the worst backhanded slap of my life.

Genet froze and whimpered, but didn't back away.

"Oh, ho," said a familiar voice. "That was close!" I opened my eyes as North's free hand—the one that hadn't caught Genet's wrist—gently pulled my arm free. I pushed myself away from both of them.

"You interrupt my business?" Genet sputtered. "Do you know what this wench just accused me of being?"

"A filthy pig," North said good-naturedly. "But there's only one filthy pig allowed in her life, and the position's been filled."

Genet's eyes swept over the length of him, taking in the foot of height that separated them with cool indifference.

"Up to the room with you, Syd," North said under his breath.

"No, Syd, stay," Genet said.

"Stop calling me Syd!" I cried.

"She's agreed to come with me." Genet did not seem to notice the tavern had quieted around us. Even the barman was studying our exchange closely.

"I don't even know who you are!" I said. Genet grabbed for me again, but North was between us.

"I did not say that you could leave." Genet flicked his cloak back dramatically, revealing a multicolored rope hanging like a tamed snake at his hip. North looked as if he'd love nothing more than to strangle the other man with it.

"Who in the seven hells . . . ," I heard North mumble as he pushed me behind him yet again.

"I am Renald Stonewall Genet, wizard of the much esteemed patron Mr. Orvilley of Orvilley and Orvilley Sea Shipping, ranked one hundred twenty-two of all wizards. I'd prefer not to use my magic, so if you, young sir, would kindly wait here while I escort this young lady back to my residence . . ."

"Can't you do something?" I asked North desperately.

"Syd," North began warningly. "Don't—"

"You're a wizard, too, right? Make him—" I stopped, seeing the pained expression on North's face. That had not been the right thing to say.

"A wizard?" The smile crept back up the side of Genet's greasy face. "No wizard I've seen. Dressed as you are, I doubt you have a patron, but if you do, I would like to know his name as well, so I can write and tell him of your inferiority. I'll have to know your rank before we duel, as well."

"*Duel?*" I asked, looking back and forth between them. I knew about wizard duels; everything I had read pointed to bloodshed and destruction.

I looked around the tavern to faces that were both startled and intrigued. The man in the pale overcoat with a pipe had moved to stand near the door, as if anticipating the need to run—or perhaps just to get a better view of the fight. But the wizards couldn't fight here, not when there was a chance others could be hurt. North appeared to have a similar thought.

"You want to duel? Right now?" North asked. "Right here?"

Genet nodded, a smile stretching across his face. "Don't be frightened, friend; you get the first attack. It's only proper for the challenged wizard to go first. If you'd be so kind as to tell me your rank . . . ?"

"North!" I hissed. "Let's just go! Don't forget—"

North silenced me with a wave of his hand, smiling as though he were about to eat the other wizard whole. He stood like a statue, the perfect image of self-confidence. Genet looked just as sure, maybe even more so now that his braided whip was in his hands, the split tip dragging lazily on the ground.

"Hey!" the barman called. "I don't want none of this in—!"

I will never forget the sound North's fist made as it connected with the other wizard's skull. Genet's nose crunched sickeningly, and a large spray of blood flew up before he slumped to the ground, motionless. George rushed forward, dropping to his knees next to his employer.

North leaned over the other wizard's unconscious body. "I win."

"Did you kill him?" I asked as the tavern roared with laughter.

"Oh, *hardly*." North snorted. "I barely hit him, and he went down like a daisy."

I looked down at the unconscious wizard and shook my head in disgust. Genet may have been the scum of the world, but it didn't change the fact that North was little more than a drunken brute.

The crowd in the tavern showered him with applause and cheers, and North took it in like a conquering hero. He stepped over Genet's prone body and was welcomed back to the bar with a tankard of ale.

"Fine!" I said to no one in particular, and turned to go back up the stairs.

As I pushed through the crowd, a hand caught mine, and I felt the touch of warm, wet air against my neck. I tried to shake free. It wasn't North.

"That's not magic," a quiet voice said in my ear. "Watch closely . . ."

The man in the pale overcoat gave me a smile as he pulled away and lifted his hand to his lips. With a single breath, he blew a cloud of blue powder from his palm, which expanded and grew around me like a thundercloud. I saw the man's face flash before me, and for the first time I saw the horrible scars that he had kept hidden beneath his hat. The right side of his face looked as though some wild animal had mauled it—his eyelid had melted down his cheek, and the deep, red lines continued across his face to where his ear should have been.

His free hand took mine again, and I couldn't pull away.

"What—?" I choked out. I squeezed my eyes shut against the smoke. The air smelled of ash, of fire. I forced my eyes open again, but I was no longer in the tavern. I was in Cliffton, in the village marketplace. I recognized most of the faces as they ran past me, past the soldiers who were dragging families from their homes. Mr. Porter screamed for them to stop, to spare his house, but the soldiers threw the torch on the building's roof anyway. And I screamed, too; I screamed until I couldn't get enough air into my chest. The nighttime sky, usually so clear over Cliffton, was nothing more than a haze of orange. The world was dizzy and awful. I clutched my necklace in my hand, a wave of nausea passing through me.

With my free hand, I felt in my dress pockets for something sharp. A new blast of fire flew past my head and sent the strange man sprawling to the floor. That magic could only have come from a wizard.

"North!" I called, waving the smoke away from my face.

I felt a pair of arms wrap around me, but I wasn't about to be taken by a soldier that easily. I kicked and clawed at the fabric of his uniform, screaming, "Let me go!" I screamed again. "North!"

"I'm here!" he said, and I felt the arms around me tighten. "Stop, stop, it's not real!"

It had to be real—I saw my father and mother and Henry; I saw the swords and horses. The ground was shaking with the force of soldiers stampeding through the village. I couldn't force the smoke from my lungs or stop the pounding in my heart. I squeezed my eyes shut again, praying this was nothing more than a nightmare.

It must have been; I opened my eyes again, only this time it was to North's face and the sight of a clear sky behind him. Dellark, somehow I was back in Dellark—but the ground was still trembling and the roar that I had attributed to the horses was actually the sound of the stone buildings and bridges grinding against one another.

North used the fire, I realized.

"Wait here!" North shouted, dragging himself to his feet. I pushed myself off the ground, narrowly avoiding the patrons fleeing the tavern and surrounding buildings. The wizard pushed through them, heading straight for the quaking buildings. He ducked inside and emerged a moment later with our belongings. He threw them in my direction.

"We need to go!" I yelled, my voice still hoarse. "It's not safe!"

"Not yet—" North's jaw set in a line of determination, and I saw him ripping his green cloak from the others. He set it flat on the ground, pressing his hands hard against it. The green cloak faded into the street. I watched, mouth open, as the tavern and buildings around us stopped moving. It lasted only a moment. When the tavern began to move again, he dug his hands harder into the ground, with more insistence.

North caught my eye for a moment, then he nodded, once, twice, and the green cloak reappeared on the ground, caught beneath the loose rubble. I pulled the loom and my bag to my chest.

I scrambled to my feet, pushing my hair out of my eyes, and then North was behind me, pulling me toward him. I didn't have time to move; he wrapped his black cloak around us, up and over our heads, and blocked out the image of crumbling stone.

"What—?" I choked on my own words, my heart dropping again into my stomach. We were sliding sharply downward, the air buzzing and singing. The world went dark around us, but there was no more fear in my heart.

Ah, I thought, feeling the first brush of tingling warmth as we fell into the unknown. *Magic.*

CHAPTER THREE

I didn't have time for another thought. My knees bent to absorb the shock of the sudden contact, but the soft ground shifted beneath me, and I tumbled backward. North tried to brace us, but I twisted out of his grip and landed flat on my bottom with a gasp, our bags spilling out into the grass.

"All right?" he asked immediately, rubbing his eyes. No wonder he couldn't see straight—the ground was still shaking beneath us.

"What was that?" I whispered. "I was in Cliffton, I swear. . . ."

"It was dark magic," North said, "meant to toy with your mind, to trap you in your worst fears. Everyone in the tavern was affected."

"What did you see?" I asked. "How did you break out of it?"

He didn't answer. The deep grimace on his face was clear as he knelt beside me, though there was only a sliver of moonlight escaping the clouds. The ground wasn't shaking anymore, I realized, nor was I. It was *North* who was shaking. I could see his hands trembling.

"What's the matter with you?" I asked. "Why are you acting like this?"

North had gone deathly pale, and the night's shadows were heavy across his face. A thin sheen of sweat broke out across his brow. He was in pain, and he couldn't hide it from me.

The wizard didn't answer. His shaking hands fumbled around in the tall grass for something—a bottle—and he thrust it at me.

"Who was that man?" I asked. "The one with the powder? He was missing an eye and an ear." I watched an ugly expression take hold of North's face. "Do you know him?"

Once again, North looked away. "Take . . . ," he said past his clenched jaw. "Take this and the blanket . . . and go to sleep."

"Absolutely not," I said. "You obviously need whatever it is more than I do."

"Take it!" he said wildly, pushing the little blue bottle into my hands. "Take it, or by the gods, I'll pour every drop down your throat!"

"North—" I began, but he walked away to the small patch of trees and sat down heavily. He clawed at the knot of string around his throat, ripping his cloaks away from him and letting them flutter to the ground. I hadn't had the chance to fix them since the night before we had left, but I could see how badly they needed it. His back was to me, but I saw how he brought his knees tightly to his chest and pressed his face down hard against them. Something inside of me lurched at the sight, and eventually I got up to wrap his blanket around him. The one my mother had packed for me was thinner, but it was still a comfort. Eventually, I felt the insistent tug of sleep. But all night that little blue bottle lay somewhere between us, past my tired body and just out of reach of his low, muffled cries of pain.

*   *   *

I was restless under the unfamiliar sky. They were the same stars I knew in Cliffton, but the way they glared down at me now was almost mocking. I searched for the constellations, trying to figure out which way the wizard had taken us—east?

I sat up in the soft grass and felt my eyes inevitably drift his way again. He was so still, the rise and fall of his chest so subtle, that for a moment I was actually afraid. His face was cold to the touch, and when my fingers brushed the pale skin of his cheeks he cringed—actually *cringed*.

My head snapped back up, the weariness in my limbs and mind suddenly gone. Somewhere in the distance an animal let out a long wail, but it didn't mask the sound of breaking twigs or labored breathing.

The moon's full, creamy face gave off more than enough light, yet I saw nothing but the scattered patches of trees around us, just large enough for a man to hide behind.

"North," I whispered. When he didn't respond I tried again, this time with a hard shake. "North!"

His head lolled to the side, and I had to check once more to make sure he was still breathing. The sound I'd heard was most likely an animal, but there was no way for me to shake the image of the scarred man in the tavern or the crisp red uniforms of Saldorra's elite soldiers. It was impossible, though, wasn't it? For the man with the powder to have followed us all the way into the wilderness—how could he have begun to track us when we had left no footprints behind in our escape from Dellark?

Something touched my back. It lasted no more than a moment, but even half delirious from lack of sleep, I knew I couldn't have dreamed it. It was a warm pulse through the thin fabric of my dress, there and gone. Then again, and again, and again . . . like a slow heartbeat.

"North!" I said through gritted teeth, while searching the trees around me. *"North!"*

There was nowhere for us to hide. I couldn't lift him into the trees; I could barely climb up into them myself. But we weren't safe, not when whoever—or whatever—was out here and could hide itself under the cover of leaves.

I was proud of the way my hands didn't shake or tremble as they slipped under the wizard's arms. A warm flush seemed to wash through my body, and I was dragging North's prone form out into the open field, toward the small, trickling creek. I kept my eyes on the trees and my back to the water, but all I could see were the shadows the trees cast, skimming the ground, weaving in and out of one another as if in a game.

I left our bags behind. The rock in my hand would be useless against sword or magic, but it was the only weapon I had. The wind kicked my curls up around my face, but not even its slight push at my back could hide that second pulse against my shoulder.

I dropped the rock onto the soft ground and threw my hands behind me, then turned to see an enormous beetle. It hovered near North's prone form for a moment, its wings letting off a loud buzz. Its color was the strangest thing about it, a purple so deep I nearly mistook it for black.

"Get off! *Go!*" I said, waving the beetle off the wizard. It launched itself back up, caught a strong breeze, and disappeared into the night. I laughed then, shaking my head at the thought of being so worked up over such a small thing.

"I've completely lost it," I said, pressing my hands to my face.

*　　*　　*

I sat beside the wizard until morning, the gray rock still nearby. My dress was uncomfortably damp with the dew, and the morning was cooler than I expected and far quieter. When the sun was finally above us, when the shadows faded into something far less sinister, I was finally brave enough to stand again. North slept on, untouched by the relief I felt when I made out the familiar form of our bags. Everything, even the contents of North's bag, which had scattered the night before, was in the exact place I had left it. If the intruder had been an animal or a man, he hadn't been interested in a loom or glass bottles.

I looked around for what else might have fallen from North's bag, finding a small, nearly empty bottle and a worn-out, leather-bound notebook stuffed with loose sheets of paper and rumpled maps. I took one of the maps in hand as I walked back over to the wizard. The cold wind that whistled through the trees and tall grass tore the frail paper into two neat pieces, and I had to grab them before the wind blew them away completely.

I collapsed in a heap by North's side, pressing both fists against my eyelids. The exhaustion was back now, worse than before. Every bone in my body screamed for sleep, but my mind was still restless, turning itself in endless circles.

I turned my face toward North, hoping for some sign that he would eventually wake.

"North?" I asked, my voice thick. The muscles in his arms had relaxed, and his face was slack with sleep. He looked as though he was actually resting and would be for some time.

My body seemed to stand again of its own accord. I washed my face in the frigid water of the creek and filled our flasks. It was strange to see water running freely, winding through the countryside with perfect ease.

It was enough to remind me of my morning prayers. I was halfway through the ancient words when I felt something soft brush against my hands. The wind had carried North's loose blue cloak over to me.

I gathered the rest of the cloaks, separating them to get a better look. There were five in all, including the red one still wrapped tightly around his shoulders, and most were ripped and tattered. I had repaired only the yellow one in Cliffton.

Maybe, I thought, it wouldn't be so bad to have a few more minutes of quiet.

Some hours later, when the sun was almost directly above us and I was on my third cloak, North sat up suddenly.

"Syd!" he said, on his feet in a moment.

I glanced up from the green cloak. I had liked him much better asleep, tucked away in his silent dreams.

"My name is *Sydelle*," I said, snipping off an excess bit of thread. His lips parted slightly, as if surprised to find me sitting nearby. "Syd reminds me of some fat, lazy old man—I knew a Sid, and all he ever did was sit on his mother's porch and complain about the heat!"

"Was that the one who tried to give me his chicken?" North asked. "Had a perpetually dazed look about him? Too much time in the sun, maybe?"

I gave him a pointed look, which he returned with an annoying grin. Finished with the green cloak, I folded it neatly beside me.

"You—" he began, looking down. His hand came up and touched the red cloak, still hanging around his shoulders. "What are you doing?"

"I think it's fairly obvious," I said. "If you're done sleeping away the day, I was hoping we could move on before nightfall. If we take Wickerby Road, we should be able to find Prima, the road that will take us directly to Provincia."

The road that was one day supposed to take me into a new life far from home. Henry had said it would take me less than a day to find the road from Dellark, and if I stayed on its straight path, it would take only a month to arrive in Provincia, Palmarta's capital city.

"Why didn't you wake me?" North asked, dropping down next to me. "And wait—why are we over here?"

I thrust the yellow, black, and green cloaks at him. "I heard something last night, and I thought we'd be safer where I could see someone approach."

"And you didn't think to wake me?" he asked, suddenly angry. "What if it had been a wizard? What would you have done *then*?"

"A wizard like the one that attacked us last night?" I asked. The blue cloak in my hand was icy to the touch. "You knew him—not Genet, the other one."

North rubbed the back of his neck. "His name is Reuel

Dorwan. He's been tracking me for a while now—if I had noticed him earlier, I would have tried to find a way to end it once and for all."

For the first time in years, I pricked my finger on the needle.

"You want to kill him?" I asked slowly.

North turned his face away and took the blue cloak from me.

"You wouldn't understand," he said.

"Of course not," I said in a low voice. "I'm just a stupid little girl who's incapable of understanding anything."

North bristled. "There isn't much to say about him except that he's the vilest rot ever to have walked this world. That trick he did was pure dark magic, magic that's forbidden by wizarding society. Not that he cares, of course. He never did."

"His trick—was that what caused you to act like that last night?" I asked. "I tried everything to wake you up, and you still slept like the dead."

North shook his head and turned away from me. I drew in a sharp, angry breath at the silence that followed. He would have walked away if my voice had not caught him and held him there.

"I hope you realize that nothing will ever be right between us until you tell me—until you just tell me why you took me," I said, frustrated. "You keep everything to yourself, and I'm just supposed to accept the fact that you can create a gust of wind and stop the world from shaking and that you're surprised I can fix your rotting cloaks—"

"It's because most humans can't," he cut in, turning back to me. "What would you like me to say, Syd? It takes some degree of magic inside a person to repair a talisman and not have it lose its ability. *That* is why I was surprised."

He reattached the rest of his cloaks in a whirl of color.

"Are . . . you saying I have magical ability?" I asked carefully.

"Magic is inherited through families," he said. "You may have had a wizard in your family, but it was a long time ago. What power you have in you is weak and useless."

"Not useless," I said, giving him a hard look. "Not entirely."

"No," North agreed with a small smile, and for the first time I thought I finally had an answer to one of the hundreds of questions that poured through my mind. I bent to pick up my loom.

"Are you positive you didn't see anything last night?" North asked after a moment. "It's not like him to just . . . give up. . . ."

"I thought there might have been something out there, but it was only a beetle," I said, watching a strange look come over his face.

"A beetle?" he repeated.

"Well, it was rather large," I said defensively. "It was practically the size of a small animal!"

"And purple?"

I whirled around. "How did you know?"

"Please, *please* tell me you killed it. Tell me you took your boot and smashed it," North said, passing a hand over his face. He didn't wait for my response; he already knew the answer. The wizard moved quickly, throwing his bag over his shoulder and scanning the wide expanse around us.

"Stop moving!" I said. "Tell me what's happening."

"It was a rover beetle," he said, his mouth set in a firm line. "Time to leave, Syd."

He reached for my arm, but I pulled it away.

North blew out a frustrated sigh, but he knew what I wanted. "It's a beetle that can sense magic. They're trained to track wizards, usually by the Wizard Guard, but in this case, by our dear friend. And it means he probably knows by now where we are, unfortunately."

"I'm sorry," I said. "Next time I won't make the same mistake."

North let out a humorless laugh.

"There won't be a next time. There are a number of ways to find a wizard, and he won't use the same trick twice." He motioned for me to follow him. "We need to leave now. He'll be right behind us."

"What are we going to do?" I asked, keeping my eyes on the path his boots made in the mud.

"We have to stay off the main roads," he said, still a number of steps ahead of me. "He'll have a greater opportunity to find us if we stay out in the open for too long."

"But Wickerby is the fastest way to Provincia—"

"And if he finds us on it, he'll know exactly where we're going," North said. "I need your help, Syd. We have to find a different way."

"All right," I said. I reached for his black cloak, forcing him to stop. "If that's true, then I need to look at the map. If we're where I think we are, I can find us a route that stays close to Prima Road, but not on it. Are you sure we can lose the time, though?"

"We won't be losing it if it keeps us alive," he said. I pulled out the map I had accidentally torn, and we both looked it over.

"I still don't understand why Dorwan would be tracking us," I muttered. "I don't like feeling like a pawn in someone else's game."

"He wants to stop us from telling the Sorceress Imperial that he was the one behind the poisoning, not Auster," North said, tying something around my neck. I glanced down at the black cloak around my shoulders.

"It'll mask any remnant of the locating spell still on you," he said, answering my unspoken question. "I think. At least I hope."

"You *hope*?"

"It's the best I can do for now," he said. "I'm sorry."

And he was.

* * *

By the end of the week, North and I had developed a routine. It wasn't the best, and it certainly wasn't fun, but it was our routine, and we clung to it like a religion. I seized the maps and plotted our path through the maze of roads; I cooked, washed, and mended. North found us food and shelter. My anger toward him for taking me from my home was still there, but I could no longer ignore him or sit around waiting for my life to weave itself back together.

It was a strange experience to wake up one morning and find the leaves of the trees a muted yellow instead of their usual vibrant green. And with the change of colors came a change in the weather. The warm, sticky air was suddenly, at least to me, dry and chilled. It was days before I became used to it, and weeks before I realized that time was slowly marching forward. It was fall—a real fall—and it was beautiful.

I found a bundle of paper in one of the markets we had passed through and used the only gold I had to purchase it. I wrote letter after letter to my parents and Henry, telling them what cities we were cutting through so they would know where to reach me. There was no telling who would read them, or if the letters would even get through the line of Saldorran soldiers.

Was the village still standing? Were my family and friends all right? I was desperate for information, for any hint of their well-being. North dutifully mailed my letters—at least until we got so low on money that we could no longer pay for postage, since we had to conserve every coin we had. This presented a new problem entirely.

"We're going to have to stop for a few days," he said suddenly as we cut through a stand of trees. We were on our way into a small village I had found on the map, having seen no sign of Dorwan at all. "I'm thinking we'll need at least two hundred gold pieces for food and transportation."

"We haven't got the time," I said. "You wouldn't even let me stop to wash my face in the river this morning!"

"Without any money we won't be able to continue at this rate. Perhaps you feel differently, but I do enjoy eating real food and sleeping in actual beds. And since you *insist* on separate rooms, my poor little money bag has gotten considerably thinner."

It had already been over two weeks since our run-in with the wizards in Dellark. I didn't think we had time to waste, given that we had less than a month to cross the rest of the country.

I looked away, gripping the strap of my bag. "I don't think we should stop. I want to get to Provincia as soon as we possibly can. Maybe you wouldn't understand because you have nothing at stake—"

"Nothing at stake?" North let out a dry laugh. "If Auster takes over the country, do you honestly believe they'll leave everything as it was? That the wizards will have any place left? Who knows what they'd do to us?"

"So you're doing this because you're scared for your own life," I said. "How inspiring. Astraea would be ashamed of you. You're supposed to be protecting her people."

"Astraea can go rot," North said harshly. I flinched as if he had slapped me. "She doesn't give me food or find me a safe place to sleep at night. I do that myself."

"You're a wizard," I snapped. "Can't you just use magic to make your own food?"

"Ah, yes," he retorted. "Because mud pies are so very delicious and the wind fills empty stomachs quite nicely."

I gave him a long, hard glare before storming ahead. North caught up to me and blocked my path.

"Move," I said. "If you want to stop, then fine, I'll go ahead by myself. You can go wander off a cliff for all I care!"

"I'm sorry I said that about Astraea," he said quietly. I tried to step around him, but he moved with me. "I haven't been able to find any customers in the past few towns we've passed through, because opinions toward the wizards have changed. A lot of people blame the wizards for the king's death and the war. I'll be lucky to find a few jobs here and there to keep us going, but don't think, not even for a moment, that I've forgotten why we set out in the first place."

His face was so sincere that my body seemed to unwind on its own accord, loosening all the knots and frustrations.

"Well, have you ever thought of bathing?" I asked, turning away. "No one wants to hire a wizard who smells worse than their outhouse. And who knows what creatures are living in that hair?"

"Why do I need to brush my hair, anyway?" He lifted

his arm and gave a few experimental whiffs. "And I smell wonderful. All manly and whatnot."

Seeing my look of utter disgust, without another word, he wrapped an arm loosely around my shoulders, and the black cloak came up around us, and I was falling, falling, falling . . .

The moment my feet hit the ground, I pushed him away from me. North tripped over his heavy cloaks, stumbling backward until he fell onto the dirt with a startled curse.

"Don't do that without giving me some warning!" I cried, my head still swimming dizzily.

He grunted as he picked himself off the ground.

"All right, all right," he said. "Next time I'll warn you when I'm about to twist the magical pillars of time and the world."

"I don't know what that means," I said crossly. "But you'd better!"

"I thought you'd like twisting . . . ," he mumbled, picking leaves from his matted black hair.

"Twisting," I repeated slowly. "Is that what it is? Why can't we just twist to Provincia if it'll get us there faster?"

North let out a dry laugh. "Don't you think that if I was capable of doing it, we would already be in the capital by now? Twisting is extremely difficult for a wizard to do alone, let alone with someone else."

"How far can you twist us at a time, then?" I asked.

"A mile—at the *most*," he said. "And that's quite a feat."

I blew a stray curl out of my eyes. "Where are we now?"

"Our best chance for a job. Have a look."

Dellark had been far nicer than anything I was used to in Cliffton. But even at night, this city was *grand*, far grander than anything my imagination could have produced, and for an instant I was sure we were in Provincia. Its walls and towers reached toward the sky in columns of the purest white. I followed the line of purple flags on the towers down to the moat surrounding the city. From a distance, the walls glinted in a way that reminded me of the porcelain in Mrs. Whitty's shop at home. So smooth, like cream. It was *Fairwell*, home of master artists and their apprentices, the city that was to have been my first stop on the road to my future. I would take this chance to walk its streets, even with a reeking wizard at my side.

"Fairwell seems to have captured your heart as well," North commented, pausing only a moment to readjust his leather bag.

I nodded. "It's so . . ." I couldn't find the right word. Even I, a world away in my little desert house, had heard stories of Fairwell's fabulous glass sculptures. I had to find the green crystal dragons, and the blown vases large enough to fit a grown man inside. Henry would be incredibly jealous—in all of his travels, he had never once seen the white walls of Fairwell.

"Looks like they still haven't fixed the bridge," North said absently. In the distance, I could just make out a long, thin board that stretched over a waterless moat.

"Great Mother, what happened to it?" I asked. There should have been a drawbridge, or at least a stone entry into the city.

"Fairwell had an awful time with hedge witches a few years back," North said. His shoulders slumped slightly. "But you probably don't know what a hedge witch is, do you?"

"They take care of the gardening at the palace?" I tried.

"What we all wouldn't give if they did." The wizard chuckled. "They're rogue women with magical ability, shunned by the wizarding community for their practices. They usually live on the outskirts of cities and steal shipments in and out of them to survive."

"So there are no . . . male hedge witches?"

"No, we just call them rogue wizards or something of the like."

"Well, that hardly seems fair," I said. "Why are only the women singled out that way?"

"They got that name because for a very long time, female wizards were banned from learning most magic. It's not that way anymore, of course, and you're almost as likely to see a female wizard now as a male one," he said. "About two hundred years ago, after the last great war with Auster, there were few magisters left with the skill to take on apprentices. At the time, the Sorcerer Imperial decided that the male wizards would be the ones to receive schooling, so that the next children of children would have a selection of magisters to choose from. Many women were unhappy, to say the least, and left to create their own communities where they taught themselves and one another. Those women and their descendants never came back to proper wizarding society."

"What are the hedge communities like?" I asked.

"Tightly knit, highly secretive," he said. "Though I've never seen one myself. I've only come across one male wizard who grew up within a hedge community, and he wasn't forthcoming with details."

"Who?" I asked.

"Who do you think?"

I stared at him. "Dorwan . . . ?"

North nodded. "Explains quite a bit, doesn't it?"

"How do you know so much about him?" I asked. "He doesn't seem the type to share."

"I met him when we were both still young," he said. "Look, Syd, it's not something I'm proud of. I'd rather not talk about it."

"Did you train with him?" I asked. "Did he have the same magister?"

"*No,*" he said. "When I was with my magister, Oliver was the only other student he had."

"Who in the world is Oliver?"

North gave me an exasperated look.

"He's the current second-in-command of the Wizard Guard, ranked number two just behind the Sorceress Imperial, who is ceremoniously ranked number one. He hates tea, enjoys moonlit walks through Provincia's palace, and is a spectacular git," he said. "Now that we've played twenty questions, would you mind dropping it?"

The thin scrap of wood covering the moat could barely support our combined weight. It dipped dangerously beneath us as we crossed into the silent, dark city. There was no one around, save for the two guards on either side of the entrance. Both were fast asleep and snoring in high, extended wheezes.

From the outside, except for the demolished bridge, the city had seemed unspoiled, marred by age and hedge witches, but no worse for wear. Inside the walls, however, it was a very different story. The outer ring of buildings had sizable pieces of roofs and entryways missing, some completely torn away and left as rubble on the ground.

North led me through the streets, and slowly the buildings began to appear whole again. The sounds of actual life in the distance reached my ears.

"It won't be as bad once we get farther in," North said, as if sensing my thoughts. "The people here gave up waiting for repairs and just moved farther inside, where it was harder for the hedge witches to reach them. We just passed the streets with all the glass blowers."

"So you come here often?" Somehow, I wasn't surprised.

"It's gotten worse over the years," he admitted. "The king neglects—*neglected*—this part of the country for far too long, and now it's fallen into this mess."

If my mother had heard him say such a thing, she would have boxed his ears for being so disrespectful. I bristled on her behalf.

"I'm sure that wasn't the case," I said. "It might have been the fault of his *advisors*, but not the king."

After blocks of dirty, broken-down buildings and uneven streets, the light of the inner city was like a beckoning fire, a fire that became rowdier and louder and drunker the closer we got. One entire block was made up of pubs and taverns; we saw drunk patrons thrown out of one pub only to stumble into another right next door. There wasn't a place of worship in sight.

"We're going to get something to eat," North explained, as we stood beneath a wooden sign that read THE STUBBORN DRAGON. "I'm hoping my friend is here tonight."

"Please don't drink," I begged, but he didn't hear me. Instead, he pushed a path for us through the crowd inside. Someone was banging an unidentifiable song on an out-of-tune piano. Occasionally North would recognize someone and give a curt nod or a smile. He reached back to take my hand, but instead I slipped it into the pocket of my dress.

"Waaaaayland, I thought you had abaaandoned us!" a woman purred. "Where did you find such a precious little doll? Got a sitting gig?"

"Just a friend, Anna," North said in a smooth voice. "Speaking of friends, I heard a rumor that Master Owain has been around these parts. Has he been in tonight?"

"Why do you want to talk to *him*?" She pouted, sliding off our table.

North smiled. "Business. You know how it is."

"I'd know if you told me more about—" she began, but never had a chance to finish.

"If it isn't Wayland North, finally back to make an honest living!" came a voice behind us, a deep baritone. "That is, if you're really here for business."

The man was a great mass of muscles and stringy blond hair. He looked to be twice my age, with the beginnings of a beard, uneven and slightly darker than the hair on his head. A shirt of old, rusted chain mail covered his broad chest. He wore mismatched metal wrist guards that scraped along his side and snagged the frayed bottom of his wrinkled undershirt. When he grinned, his teeth gleamed in the faint light of the tavern like a wolf's. If his eyes hadn't betrayed how overjoyed he was to see North, I might have thought he was ready to devour us both whole.

"Honest is probably not the word I would have chosen, Owain, old friend." North clasped the other man's hand, and Owain pumped it up and down enthusiastically.

"Hah! So you haven't heard yet!" Owain crossed his arms over his chest. "I've gone straight. Only good, clean jobs for me now."

"So, in other words," North said, "you're living in poverty?"

"When am I not?" Owain scoffed. "Seemed foolish of me to try to live like a knight but not work like one."

"In that case, I'll have to buy you dinner," North said, motioning for him to sit down.

"Where have you been all this time?" Owain asked. "I thought about sending a few of my boys out to look for you, I was getting so worried."

North chuckled into his mug. "Here and there and everywhere, as usual."

"But your . . ." Owain made a strange gesture with his hands. "That's all right?"

North snorted, and I knew what Owain was referring to.

"So he gets to know what's wrong with you?" I asked bitterly.

"There is *nothing* to tell." North hid his face behind his pint. "Owain, meet my lovely new assistant, Sydelle."

"Pleasure, of course," Owain said. He took my hand and gave it a gentle squeeze. He leaned forward between us, so North disappeared behind his enormous frame.

"I sent that letter of application off," he said. "But I got this short piece in reply saying the Wizard Guard isn't in need of human services."

"I told you that before you applied," North said, and his voice was somehow stiff. "You're not a wizard. If you want a position as a steward in the palace or a post along one of the roads, you'll have to ask the most powerful wizard you know for a recommendation."

"But, lad, that's you."

"And that's terribly sad, my friend."

"Why?" I asked. "Why is it sad?"

"What if I don't want a do-nothing post?" Owain asked. "I don't understand why it's only the wizards that get to fight, even when a war is coming."

"I don't make the rules," North said. "It's the way it's always been."

Owain snuck a glance at me out of the corner of his eye, but before he could reply, a resounding bang cut through the racket in the pub. A large man had upended his table, sending drinks and cards high into the air. The thin man across from him sat perfectly still, arms crossed.

Owain dropped his hand to the hilt of his sword, but North only glanced over his shoulder.

"Rottin' wizard!" the first man yelled, seizing the other by his crisp collar. "Think you can cheat me?"

The thin man ripped himself away from the other's grip, retrieving his cane from where it had clattered to the floor. The entire length of it, right up to the ivory claw at the top, was wrapped with thick, yellow braiding.

"Think I wouldn't know a cheat when I saw one? Can't sucker me or my cards!"

The wizard raised his cane. The barkeep would have none of it.

"Out, you fool!" he hollered, throwing a bottle against the counter. "Didn't you see the sodding sign? *No wizards!*"

My eyes darted to North, my hands instinctively reaching for my bag.

The thin wizard didn't retreat; his slit eyes cast out over the length of the pub, searching for some ally or friend. North turned in his seat, watching the scene with a look of great amusement.

"*He's* one!" The wizard thrust his cane in North's direction, and the pub's attention immediately shifted. North raised a brow, and I wondered how the other man could have possibly known.

"Who, him?" the barkeep snorted. "That lad's been one of us since he was a boy, so walk that arse out, or Viktor will throw it out for you."

Seeing the other wizard's snarl, North held up his hands and shrugged innocently. But the wizard wasn't looking at him any longer—his eyes flashed to my face, half hidden by Owain. North glanced back, as if trying to figure out where his gaze had fallen. He missed the way the other wizard took a step forward. Toward me.

Viktor gave the wizard a hard shove that sent him sprawling into the scattered cards and drinks.

"I'm two hundred fifteen!" the wizard hollered as Viktor dragged him to the door. *"Two hundred fifteen!"*

North turned back to our table as the music started again. "If I was only ranked two hundred fifteen, I wouldn't be shouting it for the entire city to hear."

"What number *are* you?" I asked. North bit the side of his thumb.

"Two hundred fifteen outta four hundred twenty-seven

isn't bad," Owain said. "When's the next ranking?"

"Next spring, I suppose," North said. "If we lose wizards in the war, the numbers will shake up."

"Will the Sorceress Imperial lose her ranking?" Owain asked. "Can't imagine her being too pleased."

North snorted. "Whoever holds the title is number one, regardless of how many duels they win in the rankings. She'll be in power for a few years yet."

I leaned back into my chair, brushing my disobedient hair from my eyes. The way the wizard had looked at me— squinting eyes stretched wide and shining brightly, lips parted—had been suffocating somehow, setting the small hairs on my arms on end.

A word caught my ear.

"Dragon?" I repeated. "That's impossible. Astraea and the wizards destroyed them all with the giants ages ago."

Owain coughed lightly, but it was North who answered.

"Mostly, yes, but there's a small number still lingering here and there." Seeing my expression of horror, he added, "But the giants never existed, just the dragons."

"It's a few miles west of here in Farfield," Owain said. "They've promised a hefty reward for the first wizard who shows. Most of your kind have already moved on to the capital to prepare for war. The people are desperate, from what I hear."

"You have to destroy it," I said, and both men turned identical looks of astonishment on me. I turned to face North.

"It's your responsibility, the reason Astraea gave the wizards magic."

Owain let out an uncomfortable laugh. "This lass is one for the myths, then."

"It's not a *myth*!" I said, gripping the table, unable to stop myself now that I had started. "It's the reason Astraea inherited the world from her father, the Great Creator. She gave the gift of magic to her people, and it was only because of that that they were able to defeat dragons and all wicked things! It's why she has supremacy over her sister goddess, Salvala. You *have* to do it, North; it's your responsibility."

I knew the Wizard Guard had been established for that very purpose. When it became clear no common sword would be strong enough to cut through dragon hide, the wizards' mastery of the elements made them the only weapon the kingdom needed. North refusing to do it was like a slap in the face, both to tradition and to our faith.

"I would have rather had a sword," he grumbled, reaching for his pint. "The amount of magic this will take . . ."

"Then go worship Salvala!" I said, standing up so quickly that I knocked over my chair. I still couldn't shake the way the thin wizard had looked at me, like he wanted to eat me alive. It was too much: the heavy, suffocating pipe smoke, the stench of alcohol, the buzz of noise. I refused to sit there and let our goddess be mocked in such a way.

"Where are you going?" North asked. I saw his cloaks swirl around his feet as he stood.

"Outside, to pray for your black, withered heart!" I pushed North's hands away and picked up my things. "What do you care? Just leave me alone!"

"I'll go with you, then," North said, matching my glare with his own.

"I'm just going to find us a place to stay!" I adjusted my bag's strap on my shoulder.

"Would you do me the honor of allowing me to escort you then, lass?" Owain said unexpectedly. "Food won't be here for quite some time, anyway."

I didn't protest. I just wanted to get away from North's dark eyes.

Outside, Owain did most of the talking. He told me how he and North had met—an almost brawl when they had both been out of their minds with drunkenness—and went into even greater detail about the beautiful, fair-haired Vesta. It took me several minutes to work out that Vesta was a horse, and Owain was possibly in love with her.

"Finest girl a man could ask for, I tell you," Owain swore, pounding his fist against the stone wall. "Ever been on a horse, lass?"

"Once," I admitted. "The horse threw me."

Owain let out a long whistle but said nothing.

"Is there a place we could stay tonight?" I asked him. "I'd rather not go back in."

"Of course there is! Just depends on how much you've got." Owain leaned down.

"We don't have any money," I said, resting my hand against my forehead. "He came here looking for work."

Owain tilted my chin up with two large fingers, and his green eyes bore into mine. "I'll get him to take the dragon job, lass. I almost have him convinced. The two of you can stay with me for the night. Nice place—clean and safe. We'll all go slay the dragon together."

"I don't understand how you can be friends with him," I said.

"You mean Wayland?" Owain clucked his tongue. "Aw, lass. He's just like a stallion. Wild and kicking on the outside, but a heart as soft as satin on the inside. Just waiting for the right girl to break him in." As if the implication of his words wasn't enough, Owain gave me a big wink.

"Your friendship was built on ale," I reminded him, pulling my bag over my shoulder.

"And what a fine friendship it is!"

✻   ✻   ✻

The section of the inner city Owain took me to was several streets behind the row of taverns, and the blue building stood out like a flower among dead, rotting trees. I was surprised by the interior; fine carpets and flower vases were scattered around, brightening up an otherwise dark setting.

A small, old woman was sitting at a desk by the entryway. Owain introduced her as Mrs. Pemberly, whispering as we went upstairs that her kindness was the only reason he could afford his room. Apparently, there was some sort of trade between the two of them. He cleared out any "bad sorts," and she let him live there at an extremely discounted rate.

"Bless the lady's heart," Owain said, fumbling with the lock on the door. "Cleans my room and everything. You can go to her for anything you need, lass."

"Thank you," I said, dropping my bag to the floor. "Will you tell North where I am?"

"Course! Poor ol' lad is probably tearing out his hair with worry, thinking I've stolen you away for myself!" Owain laughed.

"I sincerely doubt it," I said, settling down on the corner of the small bed.

"Ahhhh . . . ," Owain sighed. He leaned up against the wall. "You know, lass, the reason I was surprised to see you was because I thought that a pretty, delicate thing like yourself couldn't possibly be there with Wayland North. He doesn't bring many girls round unless they're part of a job—but also 'cause his smell can sometimes kill kittens."

A laugh bubbled up inside me. Encouraged by this, Owain continued, "North kept looking at you out of the corner of his eye. It's not proper to speak with ladies if they haven't spoken to you first, or I would have asked you what you were doing with him."

"I didn't know that," I said, wondering where he could possibly have heard such a thing.

"I read it in my knighthood guide." Owain pulled a small book out of his pocket. It was old, maybe from the time of my grandfather. "Anyway, lass, if you're with North, you must be something special."

"I'm not with him by choice," I said, idly playing with the strings on my bag. "I'm only with him for as long as it takes to get to Provincia, and then I'm on my own, regardless of what he wants."

Owain laughed again. "That's good news for me! Maybe I'll steal you away when he's finished."

I had to smile at his enormous grin.

"All right, lass. I'll grab the wizard and bring him back here. Then we'll be off." He patted my head, and I was glad to have made him so happy.

"Are you a knight, Master Owain?" I asked as he reached the door.

Owain's face rearranged itself. For a single second, it was devoid of any of his former cheerfulness—a blank slate of fiercely withheld emotion. Then his muscles relaxed. "Perhaps in another life, lass," he said, shutting the door purposefully behind him.

CHAPTER FOUR

I didn't realize I had fallen asleep until I awoke to an unfamiliar ceiling above my head and a floral bedspread beneath my cheek. Blinking at the early-morning light, I wiped away the last remnants of sleep and said my prayers. My muscles ached from the cramped position I had slept in. The bedsheets beneath me were perfectly tucked in. It was as if no one else had been in at all.

I sat up straight. No cloaks, no bags, no boots—no men. I had been left behind.

A sharp knock on the door startled me from my thoughts. The small face of Mrs. Pemberly appeared in the doorway.

"Oh, bother!" She opened the door wider. She was carrying a heavy tray of food. "I thought for sure Owain had come back last night. . . ."

"He didn't come back at all?" I asked.

Mrs. Pemberly shook her head and set the tray down on the small table.

"Hungry, my dear? I wouldn't mind some company for breakfast. . . ." After not eating the night before, I was ravenous. As we chatted, I couldn't shake the image in my mind of Owain, hunkered down next to the little old woman, sipping tea and eating eggs. She asked me where I had come from and where I was going and, when the opportunity presented itself, counted off her ten grandchildren on her fingers, pausing when she momentarily forgot the sixth one's name. When we were finished, she went about her day, and I was left alone to worry.

There was nothing for me to do in Owain's room. I must have plotted and replotted our path to Provincia a dozen times, looking for the shortest way possible.

"Are you looking for something to do?" Mrs. Pemberly asked when I finally came downstairs. "I have a package that needs to be delivered, but I'm waiting for two of my guests to arrive—I would hate to miss them."

"Of course," I said. "Do you happen to know anyone else who might need help today? I need to earn a bit of money."

What I didn't say was that we needed to earn *a lot* of money, and I doubted North could do it alone. If he was going to leave me behind to fight a dragon—a dragon I would have given anything to see with my own eyes—then I wasn't going to have any qualms about taking the day for myself. Besides, I wanted to be able to buy my own food, to have some sense of independence while I was bound to the wizard.

The old woman rested her hand on her hip. "Emmaline Forthright, perhaps—though she can be a tough bird to haggle with. She's the one you'll need to deliver the parcel to. Let me just write a note to her."

Armed with the parcel in one hand and the note in the other, I passed into the bustling streets of Fairwell. It wasn't difficult to retrace the path Owain and I had taken to get to Mrs. Pemberly's inn; the only real danger I faced were the carts of pumpkins and enormous horses that had very little regard for the humans passing before them.

When I finally managed to cross Main Street, I found a small boy sitting beside the road with tears streaming down his cheeks. He had been struck by a wagon; I could tell by the bruise forming on his face and the way he clutched his arm against his chest. At his feet were piles of sand that had escaped from torn burlap sacks.

"Are you all right?" I asked. My eyes were focused on his small face, but my hands had found the piles of sand. *Cliffton.* I had thought I would never see or feel sand this rough again. I forced the images of fire and tortured faces to the back of my mind.

The boy nodded, but his breathing had become erratic.

"Your arm—is it hurt?"

This time he nodded, and when he spoke, his voice was

scarcely above a whisper. "I got kicked by a rottin' horse and dropped the bags. Mrs. Forthright'll slaughter me for messin' up her deliveries."

"Mrs. Forthright?" I repeated. I tried to salvage as much sand as I could into the bags that weren't badly torn. They were all labeled with the glassmaker shop names. "We'll have to talk to her about that then, won't we? I was just going to see her myself."

"Why would you want to do that?" the boy whispered. A few minutes later, when I handed the near-empty bags to the middle-aged woman, I understood why.

"And *what* is *this*?" she demanded. The boy cowered behind me. "I give you a *simple* task—"

"He's hurt his arm," I cut in. "I don't think he'll be able to deliver the sandbags today."

"And what a little genius *you* are," the woman practically snarled. Her fingers raked her dark hair out of her eyes. "What in the *seven sodding hells* are *you* doing here?"

I handed her Mrs. Pemberly's parcel and note and watched her sneer of anger turn to appraisal.

"So you're looking for work, then?" she asked. "Off home with you, Geoff! I'll be speaking to your mother tonight about this!"

The boy turned and ran as though the four winds were at his heels, leaving me the sole victim of scrutiny.

"I'll work the entire day for you," I said. "For a hundred pieces."

The woman let out a strangled laugh. "Do you have any idea how much that is?"

"I'll do every delivery, and I'll do them quickly, without a single complaint," I swore.

"Little girl, I *make* that much in a *month*!" she said. "You'll do all that for ten pieces."

"Sixty," I said. I was in the position to bargain. The city relied on glass to stay alive, and no glassmaker could make his creations without the sand.

"I can find another boy just as easily for twenty."

"And I can go faster and take more at once for fifty."

"With those weak arms? You'll be lucky to get four deliveries done. Twenty-five."

"Forty, and I'll mend the poor excuses for curtains you have in your store window and that dress you're wearing."

Mrs. Forthright caught her tongue at my final offer, glancing down at the frayed hem of her old dress. I gave her a hard look, already frustrated by how little I would make from such hard work.

"Forty," she agreed at last. "But if you drop a speck of sand on the way to any of the deliveries, you'll be gone without a single piece. And don't think I'll give you directions—*you* are here to make *my* life easier."

I fought to hide my smile. "Where would you like me to go first?"

*   *   *

The task was simple enough, but it didn't make carrying the bags any easier. I had helped Henry load his father's wagon with mud barrels hundreds of times, yet the distance we had been forced to walk with each bushel had been minimal. Fairwell's strange streets seemed to constantly double back on one another, and for the first time in my life, my sense of direction abandoned me. I wandered helplessly from one street to the next, relying on chance to find the shops I needed.

I had wanted to love Fairwell so badly, to take in everything it had to offer. Now I was ready to smash in the glass signs and sculptures outside each shop. When the sun reached its highest point in the sky, not even the rainbow of light they created could put the smile back on my face. Finally, after I passed the same glass shop half a dozen times, a little woman with an enormous grin stuck her head out her door to ask if I was lost.

I handed her the delivery slip on which Mrs. Forthright had hastily scribbled the address.

"You're nearly there," she said. "Two streets over—you'll have quite a battle trying to get through the crowds, I'm afraid."

"Why?" I asked, shifting the bag's weight on my shoulder. "Did something happen?"

"The men are leaving for the capital," the woman said. "They were summoned last night to prepare Provincia's defense. Just manual labor, of course, but the Wizard Guard needs the able bodies to do it for them."

"What about Fairwell's defense?" I asked.

The woman gave me a sad smile and patted my arm. "Exactly, my dear, exactly. What do they care so long as they're safe in their castle? In the past, we've suffered through years of fighting and destruction, but none of our calls for help were ever answered. There's a crime in that, you know, a real tragedy. I don't think any of our men should go."

But they did, by the hundreds. I found the large street not by her directions, but by the sound of smashing glass and humming voices. I abandoned the bag on my shoulder in front of the nearest shop and pressed my way through the crowds to the very front.

The children in front of me threw flowers, and petals showered down from above, but there was no way I could tear my eyes away from the broken glass in the road. Every now and then, a glassblower would present one of his or her creations, bending down to place it on the road. The men, dressed in everything from dress coats to torn trousers, smashed the figurines to pieces beneath their boots.

It went on this way for some time, until every piece of glass had been ground into a fine dust and mixed with the fallen petals. When the last man had finally passed, a group of women came along and began to brush the dust into bins.

"What's happening?" I asked the woman next to me. Her little girl chewed on the end of her braid and pressed her face into her mother's skirt.

"It's tradition," the woman said, patting her daughter's head. "You'll have to excuse her. She's never been without her papa for long."

"I'm so sorry," I said, looking down at the girl again.

"The glass and petals," the woman continued. "They're refired into new shapes and forms. It's meant to show that even if the city is set forth into ruin, it can always be built back up. We're a city of re-creators, you know. It's in our blood to start again."

I didn't know what to say to that, but it seemed some-how appropriate to me that we were standing on Restoration Road.

✳   ✳   ✳

With the deliveries finished and my money collected, I ran back to Mrs. Pemberly's inn. The woman caught my eye as I ducked back inside and shook her head. The wrinkles on her face deepened with her frown.

"They're still not here?" I asked, my fingers fiddling with my necklace.

She shook her head. "I'll send them up as soon as they get back."

The hours went by, and there was still no sign of either North or Owain. A dragon isn't an easy job, I reminded myself. But it was half-past six, and I was ready to start trav-eling again. We had wasted too much time already.

Half sprawled across Owain's creaky bed, I wrote a letter to Henry. I told him about the wizards, about the fight and earthquake in Dellark, the rover beetle, and Fairwell's destroyed bridge, but there was no way to explain the strange headache I had, or the hollow feeling at the pit of my stomach. Examining the letter, I saw that my words were disjointed and angled; none of my *o*'s were fully rounded, and I hadn't dotted any of my *i*'s.

I don't know what to do, I wrote. *I want to look for them, but I'm too scared to go outside. Does that make me a terrible person? One of them—or both—could be terribly hurt, and would anyone know? I'm not sure when I'll have time to write again, or if this letter will even find you at all. Write to me if you can, please, at this address! I miss you very, very much.*

I crossed it out hastily, guilt welling up inside me. I didn't want Henry to know any of it, but every word of the letter had been true, and seeing my heart splayed out in words made me feel only worse.

*   *   *

Several hours later, I found myself by the lonely window in Owain's room with my reassembled loom and ten rows of blue. Mrs. Pemberly had brought me dinner and even cookies, though they weren't nearly as delicious as the ones that emerged from my mother's oven. At that point I would have given anything—a finger, my best dress, my loom—just for a taste of her cooking. I would have devoured it, even if it had been coated with dust.

The room had darkened abruptly, and all I had to light my work were three candle stubs that were melting quickly. Still, once my hands began their usual routine, it felt like coming home again. When the rain finally started to fall, I opened the windows and listened to the droplets as they hit the roof and windowpane. For the first time in days, I felt like myself.

But just as quickly, a different storm blew in, one of hearty laughter and heavy stomping.

"I think I know which room is mine, boy!"

"Didn't know you could read!"

"How 'bout you read my . . . my . . ."

"Ha! Still a quick wit, I see!"

I dropped the thread without a second thought.

Thank you, Astraea, I thought, releasing a heavy sigh.

The door to the room banged open, and two figures stumbled in, laughing and wheezing. I turned to greet them, but the words died on my lips. They stopped midchuckle, their eyes wide. They had forgotten about me.

"Hullo, Syd!" North said brightly. He was leaning heavily on Owain, who looked only a little steadier on his feet.

"Are you hurt?" I asked. "When you didn't come back I thought that— Did you get the dragon?"

North tried to draw me into a hug, but I knew the warning signs now. Flushed cheeks, glazed eyes . . . and *the smell.* I took a step back, and he landed face-first on the bed.

I looked to Owain in disbelief, but he wouldn't meet my eyes.

"He's drunk—you're both drunk!" I said. "All this time, were you just drinking yourself to rot?"

"We did the job, lass!" Owain said quickly. "Job done, dragon slayed, all merry!"

"So tell me how the job entailed drinking yourselves into stupidity?" I demanded. "You should never have left me behind! I wanted to go!"

"But it was a *dragon*—too dangerous," Owain said, almost whining.

"I'll decide what's too dangerous for me from now on, thank you," I snapped.

Owain shook his head, and the rain clinging to his thick hair went flying. "Took us hours to ride out there on Vesta. North gave that dragon hell—never seen so much magic in my life. Whirls of ice, fire of his own! I thought he might be burned to a crisp, but he brought the red cloak down and there wasn't a burn on him. Then I climbed on the dragon's back and took my sword and—" He took a deep breath. "And then the villagers made us stay and feast, because that dragon had been around for a year and no wizard had been able to kill the bloody thing until him and me!"

I clenched my fists at my side. "So North, where's your pay?" I demanded. "If you killed this dragon, I want to see what the villagers gave you."

North had a piece of paper in his hands and was peering

at it closely. He blinked several times, trying to clear his vision.

"Henry Porter," he began, his voice slightly slurred as he read the name on the letter I'd written earlier. "Who is this *Henry*? Why do you keep writing to him?"

"That's my letter," I said, ripping it so brutally from his hands that it tore. "How dare you?"

"Why do you keep writing home, anyway?" North asked, rolling onto his back. "What do you tell them? How much you . . . you hate me and how stupid I am?"

My throat burned, but I couldn't speak. *He* was the one who had taken me far enough away that I could only imagine what was happening to my home—to my friends and family.

North continued playing with the ripped edge of the letter. "'S not so bad with me, is it? I take care of you. Not like your parents. Gave you up for a few drops of rain."

He wasn't even talking to me anymore. My throat clenched, and I felt the letter wrinkle in my palm. *Don't cry,* I told myself. *Don't cry, don't cry . . .*

And just as quickly, the ache in my heart gave way to a new one, only this pain was hot and burning. The tears dried up in my eyes before they had a chance to fall.

"You're better off with me, Syd," North said simply. "I'll take care of you and all."

"Well," I said, clutching my necklace in my fist. "Start taking care of yourself, because I won't be your problem anymore."

"What?" He lifted his head. "Don't be stupid, Syd—"

I tore out of the room, not letting him finish, and I stumbled down the stairs.

"Syd!" he yelled, his voice cut off as the door shut behind me.

I heard the door bang open again and the sound of a few heavy steps before a sudden crash marked the end of all further movement. "Syd, don't—"

But I just ran harder, past a startled Mrs. Pemberly and out into the cold rain.

*　　*　　*

If it had been a clear night, I would have been halfway back to Cliffton, but the rain was hard and unforgiving, so thick that I had to stop and shield my eyes just to see the street names. Lungs burning, desperate, I forced myself to keep running.

I came to rest against the beveled surface of a building, gasping for air. The wind howled angrily back at me, as if disappointed that I had given up so easily. The rain soaked straight through to my bones and caused my stubborn hair to cling to my cheeks. I took a deep, steadying breath. The more upset I let myself become, the worse the storm seemed to be. I needed a few moments to think, I told myself, bringing my hands to my face.

I had to go back to North. It wasn't a choice; no matter how many times I stormed away, it did not change the situation in

Cliffton. What was I running toward? Soldiers? A village that was no longer standing?

When I closed my eyes, I could see everything so clearly. The sun-bleached mud houses, the shadows the foothills cast over the valley, the mountains that scraped the very sky— those things were a part of me. I had spent so long dreaming about the day I would leave, but I had never imagined the world to be as it was. For so long I had thought of those mountains as nothing more than the barrier that kept me from my freedom . . . but the truth was, they had kept so much of the world's wickedness out. Times had been hard before the rain, but we had managed. There had been no angry crowds, vile wizards, or drunken brutes. There had been family and love.

But there hadn't been hope. There hadn't been a dream to keep me there. There had been only the same of everything I had known, and a suffocating familiarity.

I needed to escape the storm.

Across the street, a small OPEN sign hung on the outside of a great wooden door, clattering noisily whenever the wind brushed by. *Thank you, Astraea,* I thought, wiping the rain from my eyes. I struggled to pull the door open against the wind and barely managed to slip inside before the storm slammed it shut behind me.

It took me a few moments to gather my wits enough to recognize the shop I had wandered into. I had been in this particular building earlier in the day, making a delivery of sand to Mr. Monticelli, the glassblower. He had been so completely involved in his work that he hadn't even looked up as I dropped the sack of sand on the floor.

He was still working, hours later, though this time he did spare a glance in my direction.

"I see you have come back to me," he said, in a strangely accented voice. "Terrible storm we are having, no? Come in, come in."

I nodded, taking a few steps closer to his fire. The rain, dripping from my hair and clothes, collected in a puddle on the stone floor.

Mr. Monticelli's careful hands curled around one end of a large staff, expertly shaping a glowing ball of molten glass against a stone table. I stood there and watched as the shape of a cat began to emerge.

"You do it so perfectly," I said. "Sometimes it takes me three or four tries to get a blanket right on my loom."

He laughed. "I'll tell you my secret: steady hands, eyes always on the art, mind always on the art. No matter how many times I've done it. Steady hands, careful focus. Remember that."

I nodded, and Mr. Monticelli held up the small figurine for my inspection. There was still a faint pink glow at its core, but the edges had been pointed and darkened by ancient tools. A slant of light struck the glass figurines in the shop and set the whole place aglow.

"It's not so different from weaving," Mr. Monticelli said. I nodded. Focusing was so difficult when I wove; my hands knew exactly what to do, but my thoughts and emotions were usually somewhere else.

"Do you know any of the master weavers?" I asked. He took the cat back and held it up to the fire to examine it.

"Mr. Monticelli?" I said when he didn't respond. His thick black eyebrows drew together with his frown.

"Thinking, thinking," he said. "I am thinking."

There must not have been many master weavers in Fairwell if he couldn't think of even one. Maybe they had moved on to another, quieter city? I knew from experience that it was difficult to concentrate with the noise and bustle of the streets.

"Ah!" Mr. Monticelli slapped his hand down on the table. "We will go ask Colar!"

"Colar?" I repeated.

The glassblower lifted his heavy apron over his head and used it to wipe the sweat from his face.

"He is my sister's husband," he explained. "Bit of . . . how do you say . . . bit of air in the head. No, head in the air?"

I shrugged.

"Bah," he said, taking my arm. "Let me tell you, where I come from, a man who does not use his hands for his job is no man at all. Books! Bah! My sister must have air in her head, too, to marry such a man."

I looked down.

"No? Not even a smile for me?" he asked, studying my face.

"Not today, I'm afraid."

He patted my head fondly, the way my father sometimes did, and the knot in my stomach became unbearable. The only thing keeping me from tears was the confusion and anger I felt toward North. About the way he had treated me, about what was plaguing him, about why he had taken me in the first place.

For a moment I was afraid we would be heading back out into the rain, which was still coming down hard enough to flood the deserted streets. Instead, Mr. Monticelli led me through the maze of shelves and cases in his dark shop to yet another door. This one, however, he kicked open, taking obvious pleasure in the way his brother-in-law jumped at the noise.

Connecting shops, I thought as I stepped through the doorway and into a different world. Where Mr. Monticelli's shop had been dark and smoky, I had to squint my eyes against the sudden onslaught of brightness in Mr. Colar's shop. Gone was the smell of fire, replaced by the familiar, comforting odor of old parchment and leather-bound volumes and bookshelves lining every wall. A bookshop and a glass shop were not an obvious pair—but, then, neither were their two owners.

Mr. Colar had his back to us as we walked to his front counter; I heard the pages of his book rustle.

"I see my wife inherited all the manners in the family," he said loudly. We were standing right behind him when he finally turned around.

The resemblance kicked the air from my lungs. The similarly bent nose and square jaw, the light, receding hair—the man was a living double of my father.

"A refugee!" he said. "Well, come in!" he added, ushering me closer and ignoring Mr. Monticelli. "Terrible weather, isn't it?"

"I've never seen anything like it," I said. "It makes me miss the desert."

"I've been trying to get home for hours, but I can't coax my horse from his stable." He laughed. "You say you're from the desert? Not much of that in this country."

"Cliffton," I answered. "The very far west."

"Of course, of course," he said. "Terrible drought you've been having—do *not* touch that, Renaldo!"

Mr. Monticelli dropped the book back onto the counter with a noise that was halfway between a groan and a growl. "I see business has been slow."

"No slower than yours, I assure you," Mr. Colar said, turning back to face me. "Now what can I help you with?"

"This pretty young lady has asked about the master weavers," Mr. Monticelli said.

"Ah," Mr. Colar said again. "I'm very sorry to say you won't find any of them here in Fairwell."

"Why not?" I asked. "I thought Fairwell housed the guild?"

"Years ago," he said. "Most left when the hedges tried to take the city. Only one, a Mr. Vicksmorro, stayed and suffered terribly for it."

"I remember now!" Mr. Monticelli cut in. "They poisoned him like a common pig! This was before my sister and I came, you see."

"I'll tell the story, thank you," Mr. Colar said irritably. "Vicksmorro and many of the other guild leaders soon found themselves with raging fevers, horrible spasms in their bodies. Worst of all, their hands shook so badly that they couldn't practice their craft. Awful magic that was— and it was only *rumored* to be poison."

Disappointment washed over me like the cold rain— sudden and surprisingly painful. But just as quickly, a thought struck me as Mr. Colar described the weaver's hands. How many times had I seen North's hands tremble and his body shake with unexplained pain? It might be random similarity, but there was a possibility, if only a slight one, that I had accidentally stumbled upon the answer to his mystery.

"Do you think this rumored poison could affect a wizard?"

"My." Mr. Colar laughed. "What a question! I suppose we could look it up. I believe I remember how to spell the poison's name."

The water squelched out of my boots as I followed him through the labyrinth of shelves, running my fingertips lightly over the leather spines. There wasn't a gap or cranny a book hadn't been crammed into, red, brown, faded blue. They all looked like they were fighting to slip out from their constraints, to be open on a table or even the floor.

In all, Francis Colar had three hundred twenty-four books on magic, of which fifty had been written in the past thirty years, and only two were of any remote use to us.

"This one," he began, tugging at a clunky volume, "is a reference guide, covering every possible subject in every possible detail."

He opened the book, blowing out a small cloud of dust from its pages.

"Black ether . . . black ether . . . black—here it is." Mr. Colar cleared his throat. "'Black ether, a poison rumored to be developed by a hedge witch community outside of Provincia in the years of King Siegbright. Its contents remain a guarded secret, though its effects are easily recognized. Victims of this poison will display erratic, nervous behavior, severe cramping in abdominal muscles, uncontrollable shaking, and, most noticeably, crescent-shaped welts on the back and chest. Though the pain and welts can be treated with simple elixirs, there is no known antidote.'"

"Nothing about wizards?" I asked.

"Perhaps they have a cleverer way of counteracting it, but the effects would be the same," Mr. Colar said. "Not even a wizard is immune to poison."

"If the effects are the same, then any treatment . . ."

"Would also be the same," he finished. "But you heard what I read. There is no antidote."

I still wasn't fully certain that this poison was causing

North's strange behavior. It was a strong possibility, though, given the disgust that had rolled off him when he told me about the hedges.

"Remember that it was only *rumored* to be this poison," Mr. Colar said, snapping the book shut. "Although . . . if you're interested in antidotes and elixirs, I do have a book that might be useful to you."

"I would love to see it," I said. My eyes followed the line of books in front of me. *A Brief History of Casting, Casting Fire, Reign of Magic* . . .

He dropped to his hands and knees, digging through the books he had already cast aside. The book that emerged from the pile was also black, but it was soft and worn down. My eyes fell on the gold-embossed title: *Proper Instruction for Young Wizards*.

"It's what all the young ones use while apprenticing. Must have put out a new edition, though. I had a dozen old copies flood in a few years back. It'll tell you anything you want to know about elixirs and how to make them."

"This is perfect," I said, my eyes drifting over the pages. Seeing I was sufficiently distracted, Mr. Colar returned to the front to sweep out his brother-in-law and the rainwater that had flooded in beneath his door. Mr. Monticelli called out to me as he crossed back into his own shop, but I barely acknowledged him.

I leaned back against the shelf, paging through until I found an elixir that listed honey and lavender as ingredients.

Those were the two strongest smells I had been able to make out in North's bottles.

Sleeping draft, it read. *Mix one part honey, two parts lavender with essence of mandrake root. If ineffective and more restful sleep is required, grind and add a strong dose of rosemary and poppy. As is the case with many drafts, dependency may arise from misuse and ill care.*

That had to be it—the night of the battle with Dorwan, he had told me to take it and go to sleep. So why had he decided not to take the elixir himself?

I could be useful, I thought. I could mix the elixir for him. I had charged the air between us with anger and hate—I had seen him as a villain and nearly missed the fact that he was suffering.

The rest of the book was slightly less useful to me. Most of the sections discussed the proper concentration for casting spells, others were history lessons about great wizards of the past, and I was surprised to find a few outdated maps lining the covers. I was just about to close the book when a passage caught my eye.

Magical inclinations (humans)—often a rare occurrence of a wizard's blood being diluted by many marriages to non-wizards. Though they are unable to cast spells or break curses, they often make excellent assistants for their ability to mix powerful elixirs and, in some instances, repair a talisman.

All this time I had suspected that there might have been something else involved in North's choice of me. I would have read more had a large crash and a booming voice not broken into my small sanctuary.

"By the heavenly bosom of Vesta! It's a raging downpour out there!"

I leaned around the edge of the bookshelf, unsure of whether I wanted to be seen.

"It certainly is!" Mr. Colar said cheerfully. "Please come in. I already have one refugee!"

"Oh?" Owain said. "Any pretty girls with hair as red as roses?"

"About *this* tall?" Mr. Colar asked.

"Wearing a blue dress?" Owain replied. "Blue eyes?"

"Lots of freckles?"

"Just a bit on the nose and cheeks—smallish nose, a little upturned?"

"For goodness' sake!" I stepped out from behind the bookshelf. "I'm right here! You could have just called for me."

"Oh, lass!" Owain galumphed the entire distance between us, heaving me into a bone-crushing embrace. The mail across his chest was frozen against my cheek, but his hug was warm and inviting—even if he smelled like a wet horse.

"We've been searching all over for you!" he cried. "Going out of our minds with worry, running to the four corners of the world! I thought for sure our boy was going to break down in tears."

"You mean he sobered up enough to care?" I mumbled. Owain's large hand came up to stroke my hair.

"How could you doubt that?" he asked in a surprisingly gentle voice. "Poor sod's probably torn up half the city by now."

"And who is this?" Mr. Colar sounded hesitant.

"Thanks for keeping an eye on her," Owain said to him. "I think we'd best be going now. I hate to leave Vesta alone in this storm. . . ."

I tried to give Mr. Colar the book I had in my hands, but he shook his head. "Please, I insist. It sounds as if you'll need it."

"I couldn't—" I protested.

The old man merely smiled.

He really didn't look much like my father at all, I decided.

Outside, the storm had faded into a gentle relief that I hadn't felt since the day I left home. I held out my palm to catch a few scattered rain droplets. The streets may have been converted into rivers of white water, but watching them, I could see they were carrying the darkness and filth of the city down with them into the gutters.

"Looks like the rain's letting up, lass," noted Owain, squinting at the first tentative stars against the black sky. And I smiled, because it was.

✶   ✶   ✶

Mrs. Pemberly greeted us at the door, fussing over my hair and dress.

"Found her!" Owain sang out.

"Oh, my darling!" Mrs. Pemberly ushered me closer to her fireplace. "Can I get you something? Hot cider? Tea? Are you hungry? I just pulled an apple pie from the oven. . . ."

"I could use a little bit more water," I said, trying for a joke. Owain chuckled. I glanced around the room, surprised to find the parlor empty.

"He's upstairs," Mrs. Pemberly said. "He got back a little before you, and I sent him to change into something dry."

I didn't think North would be wanting to see me anytime soon, but I began to climb the stairs anyway. I held the book against my side, glancing through the thin crack of Owain's door. North sat on the bed with his back to me, his drenched cloaks still attached and his dark hair flattened against his head.

The door creaked as I pushed it open, but North didn't turn around. I set the books down on the table and came to stand beside him. The wizard's eyes were studying the abandoned loom, taking in the smooth rows of dark and light blue as he shuffled a red apple between his hands. I sat down next to him and forced myself to be still.

He nodded his head toward his old gray blanket, a short distance away on the floor, but I turned my face away from it. North's hands stopped moving, and he lifted the shiny apple toward me. I hesitated a moment before closing my hand over it. I took the apple, but only—*only*—because I was hungry.

Out of the corner of my eye, I could see that North was

still watching me, but whenever I turned, he would quickly look up to the ceiling. Still, I felt as if for the first time, he was really seeing me. He could see what his words had wrought, that I could and would leave if he pressed me too hard. And I think I saw remorse in the darkness of his eyes, but mainly I saw unmatched misery. I saw what I had done to him.

In the end, we didn't need to apologize. We understood.

CHAPTER FIVE

A day later, we were still at Mrs. Pemberly's, arguing over our next move.

"It makes more sense if we follow this road up to Andover and cut across the plains to Scottsby," I said, for what had to be the hundredth time. It was the route Henry usually took, and I certainly trusted his sense of direction more than North's. Yet even with the map smoothed out before them, the two men refused to listen. I was beginning to think I was going to have to knock their heads in and drag them to Provincia myself.

"Wiltfordshire Road runs right from Fairwell to Scottsby, straight as an arrow," Owain protested.

"But you'll have to cut around the lakes, and that'll take you—"

"Going to Andover first would be better," North cut me

off as if I hadn't spoken at all. "You and I can handle Wilt-fordshire, but it wouldn't be safe for Syd."

I sucked in a sharp breath. "Why, because I'm a girl? If that's the case, we'd better stay off *all* the main roads. There are hundreds of men heading up to the capital, and they're on every one of them."

North shook his head. "You may know the names of the roads and where they lead, but you don't know the kind of people that travel on them. Owain and I will sort this out. Go sit down and weave."

"That's rich coming from the wizard who can't tell east from west, let alone up from down," I snapped. "We'll go to Andover, but when it takes us a week and a half to get there, don't cry to me about it."

Owain was the one to break the tense silence that fol-lowed. "Going to Andover first, eh? I've never taken that route before, but I wouldn't mind trying something new. Never fear the unknown, Mother Bess always says."

We both turned to look at the fuming wizard.

"Fine," North said at last. "If we don't follow her, who knows what kind of trouble she'll get herself into."

I shook my head, rolling the map back up and handing it to the wizard.

"Are you sure it's a good plan to bring the lass with us?" Owain asked quietly as I sat back down in front of my loom.

"If I had my way, neither of you would have anything to do with this war," North said.

"But then it would be your choosing instead of ours," Owain said. "And there's nothing right about that."

I worked the blue thread through the warp, watching North, who was leaning against the wall, looking out the window. "I should just go alone," he said.

I was on my feet a moment before an earsplitting clap of thunder and a sudden downpour drowned out his next words. Mrs. Pemberly shrieked in surprise from downstairs, but the biggest crash of all came when Owain fell off the bed.

"How can you even suggest that?" I said. "What good would that possibly do?"

"As if you could ever understand," North scoffed.

I looked at him. With dark circles framing his eyes, an agitated curve to his spine, that ugly sneer: Who was this person?

Seeing that my words had done absolutely nothing to pull North from whatever depths he was clinging to, Owain did what came naturally. He smacked North upside the head hard enough to send him sprawling into the window. And when it seemed that North would turn around and return the favor, Owain hit him again, harder.

"What put this madness into that head of yours?" Owain asked. "Going alone, without any help, a mad wizard after you—you've lost it, lad."

As if summoned, the rain began once again, and with it thunder that seemed to make the walls of the building quiver. Owain returned to his bed, and I sat back down in front of the loom. I couldn't clear my thoughts, and my throat knotted itself as I looked at the outline of North's hunched shoulders.

The mirror on the far side of the room tumbled to the ground, sending a spray of glass onto the floor.

"Wretched thing," Owain said, standing to clean up the mess. "An unlucky sign, that is."

North remained exactly where he was. The feeling of disquiet that washed over me was as cold as the rain had been; its sting didn't ease until I disassembled the loom.

Owain and I had just climbed into our respective bedding when North finally spoke. It was only two soft words, but it didn't matter whom they were meant for.

"I'm sorry."

I bit my lip, wondering what I could possibly say. I couldn't even look at him.

Owain waved him off, turning over on the floor. "Go to sleep, lad."

And wake up your old self, I added to myself. *Please.*

"In a moment," he said, though he finally sat down on his own bedding. "I'm not tired."

Of course not. I twisted my blanket between my hands. He tried to hide it, telling me it was water or mead or some kind of ale, but I could always smell the honey and lavender on his clothes and breath. I realized I hadn't smelled it for some time.

I wasn't sure when I drifted off, but later that night I awoke to a fantastic show of lights, burning beneath my heavy eye-lids. Even after I opened my eyes, the vision persisted. All around me, a thousand threads of light wrapped around my body and fed into the ground. Red, blue, yellow, green . . . a pulsing rainbow that began at my heart and seemed to be sewn into every bit of my skin. It was a dream I hadn't had since I was a very young girl.

It would have been frightening had there not been the heavy shadow hovering just at the edge and the sweet sense of calm he brought.

"North?" I asked.

A hand, finally free of its glove, came to rest on my fore-head. It trailed gently down my face and softly over my eyes until they were once again closed, then over my nose and my parted lips.

"You're dreaming, Syd," he whispered next to my ear.

Of course I was.

* * *

"Sod it *all*!"

I dropped my washcloth on the floor, ducking my head back into the room. Owain was stumbling, half awake, to where North stood, letter in hand. I hadn't seen Mrs. Pemberly bring it to him.

"What—?" I began.

"We're under attack by what appears to be a wolf," he read

aloud. "It howls all night. The children think it's some kind of demon. The crops have been torn up, and not by the hands of an ordinary man. One child claimed that the wolf climbed into her window, and it was made of light."

"What does that mean?" I asked.

"It means we're leaving right now," North said. "For Arcadia. It's north of here, in the mountains. Two days of traveling, maybe more."

"What in the world is in Arcadia?" I asked. It was no place I had ever heard of, but Owain and North continued their conversation without me.

"I'll come with you," Owain said. "You'll need support if it's as bad as it sounds."

"No, if Syd and I are delayed for long, we won't make the treaty deadline," North said. "I think you should ride ahead to Provincia and try to get an audience with the Sorceress Imperial or even Oliver."

"And tell them what? That you've gone and gotten yourself killed?" Owain said.

North snorted. "I doubt they'll care about that. Tell them that I'm going after a rogue wizard."

"Who?" I repeated. "Dorwan?"

"Who else?" North dragged a hand through his matted hair. "I knew he had been too quiet; I *knew* he would bait me—but not Arcadia, never Arcadia."

"What's in Arcadia?" I asked again.

"A lot of innocent kids," he said.

I asked, "What if we don't take the bait?"

North shook his head. "If you think for one moment that Dorwan wouldn't hesitate to kill a child, then you've clearly overestimated his humanity. He's not bound by anything—by wizard law, by the ways of the hedges. He does what amuses him, and we've become his latest game."

"Why waste the days of travel?" I said. "If we don't go to him, won't he have to come to us?"

"I won't let him hurt one of the kids," he said. "If I don't help them, no one will."

✳   ✳   ✳

Within minutes, Owain disappeared before I could even give him a proper good-bye. We twisted as far as we could from Mrs. Pemberly's, but when the black cloak fell around us, I immediately knew something was wrong.

"You took us east!" I said, pulling out the map to make sure. "I said *north*!"

"I took you *north*!" he snapped. The wizard stepped away from me, but the moment I held up the map, his anger deflated with a harsh breath.

"You took us *east*," I said. "Twist us back and try again."

"I told you," he said, his hair hiding his face, "it's not something I can do on a whim—you have to give me a moment!"

"Then we'll walk," I said. "It seems a more efficient method of travel than to rely on your complete and utter lack of direction. How in the world did you make it all the way out of Cliffton?"

"I had a guide," North said, storming past me. "Does that make you feel important?"

"No," I said bitterly. "But it does make me feel useful."

North bit the side of his thumb, slowing so I could catch up to him. I reached out to put a hand on his shoulder, but pulled it back at the last moment. Something about him reminded me of Henry, and that made me wonder what my friend would say if he knew I cared about the wizard.

"I'm sorry," he said. "Arcadia means a great deal to me. Oliver and I spent a lot of time there while we were training with our magister. I thought it was the only safe place left in the world."

"It's not your fault," I said, but he only looked away.

✳   ✳   ✳

Many miles and muddy roads later, a grimace on North's face and a new limp told me it was time to stop for the night.

"Lift up your pant leg," I said, watching his features twist in pain as he sat.

"I'm fine."

"You can hardly walk, and your cloaks are a mess," I said. "I'll bet that dragon did a number on you."

North grunted, looking away. An ugly burn revealed itself inch by inch as he rolled up his pant leg. I took one look at the angry, puckered red burn and shook my head. The bandage he had tied around it was loose and dirty.

"All I have is an elixir for the pain," I said. "If we pass by a market, I'll see if I can find what I need to help heal the burn."

As North drank the remnants of an elixir I had made at Mrs. Pemberly's, the look of relief on his face changed to one of surprise.

"You made this?" he asked, smelling the empty bottle. "It's a wizard elixir, one of the strongest I've had. Where did you learn how to mix it?"

I traded *Proper Instruction for Young Wizards* for his ripped cloaks and sat down to mend.

"I haven't seen one of these in years!" He thumbed through a few pages. "And you're even reading it—great gods, why would you punish yourself like that?"

"I'm trying to learn, you know," I mumbled. "You never tell me anything. I have to find the information out somehow."

"Ask me a question about magic, then," he said. "Any question."

I didn't even have to think about it. "Why did you choose me?"

"I believe I said a question about *magic*, not my sanity."

"What do the colors on your cloaks mean? You have five of them, but Dorwan only had blue on his knife."

"I could have chosen one color for my talisman, but I wanted to be able to use all magic, not one," he said. "Dorwan stole that talisman from someone, by the way."

"Doesn't surprise me."

North pulled his green cloak free and held it up. "Each color corresponds to a type of magic. It's something the wizards invented for themselves, and it has little to do with the actual magic. The colors began as a courtesy in duels, so a wizard would know what world of pain he was about to visit. Now a wizard generally announces his specialty with the prevalence of any color."

"So why do you have black as your outer cloak, then?" I asked. "I thought that color was used just for traveling?"

North smiled mysteriously, rolling over on the ground. "Black is my color."

"Then why have all of the colors? Is that even allowed?"

"I use all of them equally," he said. "And of course it's allowed. Most just choose not to do it because it's difficult to have to carry so many talismans. Besides, my father used all the colors. I guess it felt right to honor him like this."

"So the . . . talismans," I said. "Each can only be transformed into one kind of magic?"

"Right, it's all about channeling the elements, changing the talisman into the one element each attracts. Magisters are the ones to choose the talisman for the apprentices, and depending on what element your talisman is best attuned to, that's your specialty."

"And the cloaks took to all magic?" I said. "That was lucky."

North laughed. "Yeah, but I wasn't exactly thrilled when

he handed me a piece of red wool on my fourteenth birthday, especially when he turned around and gave Oliver a sword. Oliver's never let me live that one down, even after I left them."

"Boys," I said, shaking my head. "Were you fourteen when you finished training?"

"Yes," he said. "Oliver went to Provincia to join the Guard, and I went anywhere but Provincia."

I started with the top cloak, his color, and worked my way in. The black—the cloak that twisted all of the elements together and allowed us to travel—had seen the most trouble and was split almost entirely down the middle. Next, red, fire, sorely torn almost down the middle. Yellow, air and light, untouched save for a singe that even I could not fix. Blue, water, missing a corner. Finally, green, earth, five gashes from top to bottom.

How many times would I have to repeat the same process? I had been with him for only a few weeks and already my stitching crisscrossed every cloak. Sewing wasn't the same as weaving, not even close. Weaving was the creation of something new, the coming together of a pattern or a scene that took on a life of its own. Mending wasn't anything more than an insult to battered fabric. It was a lucky day, indeed, when I had to do only one. Five of them were enough to cramp my fingers and strain my eyes.

"Would it be possible," I said, "to have one cloak able to channel all magic?"

North looked thoughtful. "I've read about it being done in the past, but I've never found a cloak with an equal amount of every color, and I've certainly never been in the position to commission one. But yes, I think it would be possible."

The green cloak slipped from my fingers and floated to the ground. That was the solution, wasn't it, to both our problems? A single cloak would provide him with all of his colors at once, rather than having to switch back and forth between the thin, ragged pieces of cloth. I could picture exactly how I would make it, with everything from woven dragons to shimmering grass and mountains. It would be sturdy and well made—to save his skin and my patience. As long as I kept track of how much thread I was using, it could work.

I looked at my loom; the moonlight seemed to be shining directly on it. It was a personal gift, but how many other times had I woven things for friends? Henry had at least three blankets; the other boys in the village had everything from socks to hats . . . so why did this feel different?

"Syd?" North mumbled, rolling over again to face me. "Put them aside for now. They're good enough."

I blew a curl off my face. "I thought you'd gone to sleep."

"Takes me longer to fall asleep these days," he said.

"I might have some sleeping draft in my bag," I said.

North made a face. "I just meant I'm not much for sleeping outdoors anymore."

I folded the cloaks. "Did you—in the past, I mean?"

He was silent so long I was sure he had drifted off, his gray blanket tucked around his body. I unfolded the blanket my mother had hastily packed. It was poor protection against the coming winter, but it was something.

"When I was younger, after I finished my training," he said quietly into the darkness. "I never had enough money to rent a room."

I watched his face closely, studying the way his dark lashes fell against his cheeks. I could see him years ago, wrapped in the very same blanket, lying there, on the cold dirt between the trees.

"Where was your mother? Your father?"

North's eyes remained closed.

"They . . . left me a long time ago." He turned back away from me. "It doesn't matter anymore."

"Of course it matters," I whispered, holding the braided metal of my necklace between my hands.

"Sleep," he said. "There's still a long way ahead."

CHAPTER SIX

The next afternoon, our shadows were long against the dying grass, spread out over the ground like one of my blankets. It was a strange shape, but one that was ours.

Which is why it was so disturbing suddenly to find another, unfamiliar shadow trailing ours.

At first I thought North had slowed, but the shadow was moving too quickly. It skimmed in and out of the grass, like one of Henry's little brothers in a game of go-seek-find. By the time I had enough sense to point it out, North had seen it, too.

"A neat little hedge trick," he said, seeing my startled look. "But it can't do anything to hurt you." He threw a stone, which struck the shadow and passed through it. The shadow scattered, falling apart into small pieces before pooling together again on the ground. It disappeared back into the blades of grass and did not reemerge, even after North threw another rock.

"Where did it go?" I asked. "What happened to it?"

"It's a messenger shade," North said. "It's going back to Arcadia to tell him we're coming."

"Then we should go after it," I said. "If he knows we're coming—"

"Syd, I *want* him to know," North said, taking my bag and putting it on his own shoulders. "I want him to know this little game is about to end. Come on." He pressed a hand to my back and urged me forward.

"How is it even possible?" I began, when we were a good distance away. "How can he play with shadows like that?"

North gave me a wry smile. "The next time I come across a den of hedge witches, I'll be sure to inquire for you."

*   *   *

A few days later, we were at the foot of a mountain path when he finally said the words I had been begging Astraea for. "I think I can twist the rest of the way."

"Are you sure?" I asked.

"Well, it's worth a try," he said, putting an arm around my shoulder. "If I miss and we plummet to our deaths, you can blame me."

We were falling once again. I clutched North's chest, hating the way it felt—as though my heart had sunk to the bottom of my stomach. Even the warm, tingling sensation that ran from my head to my toes couldn't quell my discomfort.

My feet hit the ground—*Wood*, I thought, *thank Astraea*—with a dull thud. When my eyes finally came into focus, I saw an old woman. She sat next to a small fire in a hearth, tapping her fingers in an impatient rhythm. North cleared his throat behind me. The woman merely clucked her tongue in disapproval, rising from her chair like a queen.

"You're later than I expected," she said. "Do you have anything to say to your patroness?" This woman was russet and deep wrinkles. Her skin was dark, well worn like soft leather.

My father once told me that you could tell the rank of a woman by the tone of her skin. Fine ladies never had to work outside and were therefore milky pale. However, despite being as translucent as a ghost, I was not included in this category; I was pink skin and freckles all over.

"Why, yes, I do." North gave an exaggerated bow. "You are looking absolutely lovely this evening, Lady Aphra."

"You have a patroness?" I whispered through clenched teeth.

"Oh, did I not mention that?" North let out a low, nervous laugh.

"No," I said, my hands tightening into fists. "Actually, you didn't."

Lady Aphra took a step closer to him. "I'm glad my letter found you."

His face darkened. "I came as fast as I could."

"I believe you," she said. "The wolf's been quiet for the past few nights. We're hoping he's moved on."

"Doubtful," North said. "It's a wizard casting a specter, I'm sure of it. It's a trick he's used before, but only when he needed to create some revenue—he terrorizes families with it and then sweeps in to act the part of the hero and earn a few coins in the process."

"Why would he come here, then?" Lady Aphra asked. "We don't have much wealth."

"He's here for us—for me." North's face darkened. "He lost us when we twisted out of Dellark, and the only way to call me out again was to threaten you. It's my fault; I'm sorry."

"Well," Lady Aphra said, finally casting her eye on me. "You'll be the ones to fix it."

✳   ✳   ✳

Lady Aphra provided us with North's usual room in her cottage, and we slept on rolled blankets stuffed with hay. It wasn't so much the sleeping arrangement or my bedding that had me waking nearly every hour—it was the cold air that seeped in through the floor beneath me and the small windows on the wall. Pressing my frozen fingertips under my arms and curling myself into a tight ball, I faded in and out of the darkness.

There was no hint of Dorwan that night. Instead, I dreamed again of the threads of light. They were still wrapped over my skin but had loosened enough for me to lift my arms and free my hands. My fingers groped for the edges, taking some of the warm strands and pulling them up from the ground. The ends fluttered around in the air above me; there was a spark of light as they touched, and they weaved among one another as though invisible hands were guiding them.

I sat up straight, cold dread settling in my stomach like a stone. My skin tingled with the memory of warmth, but my vision was splotched with black, and it took several minutes before my eyes readjusted to the dim light of early dawn. I pressed my hands against my face and breathed in the cool air. North was snoring in the far corner of the room.

The pieces of my loom leaned against the wall. I still hadn't begun North's single cloak—with all our traveling, the opportunity hadn't presented itself. Now, in the quiet, hours before the others would rise, I picked up the pieces of the frame and fit them back together.

The hardest part was deciding where to begin; I knew I wanted the edges to alternate between colors, framing the scene inside. But would he find it odd if I began with shades of yellow, of dust?

It was strange how easily I fell back into it. The colors came together fluidly and my fingers worked quickly. The usual daze of color and imagination came over me, and by the time I began work on the yellow-and-brown mountains of Cliffton, my thoughts were somewhere else, caught in the snare of the picture I would weave.

The window shutters clattered against a sudden light breeze. The air whistled through the cracks in the wall and caressed the branches of nearby trees. Everything seemed to fall into perfect rhythm: my breathing with the wind, my fingers with the branches. Mr. Monticelli's words floated up in my mind. *Steady hands, eyes always on the art, mind always on the art . . .*

I knotted, took up a different shade of yellow, began a new row and didn't stop until I felt a hand clasp my shoulder, breaking the spell the loom had cast over me.

North leaned forward to take a closer look at my work but didn't lift his hand.

"What are you doing up?" he whispered.

"I couldn't sleep."

"Why not?" he asked. "Was your bed too uncomfortable? I told you to take that extra blanket."

"It was a little cold," I admitted.

"Why didn't you wake me up?" he asked loudly, then dropped his voice. "You should have woken me up! We're up in the mountains now—I forget you're not used to colder weather."

I rolled my eyes. "Oh yes, I'm going to freeze to death while sleeping in front of a fire and under a hundred pounds of blankets. I said I was a *little* cold!"

"Do you want me to relight the fire for you?"

"No, I want to know where you're going," I said.

He looked pleased.

"I was going to put protective wards around the village," he said.

I finished my row and stood.

"What are you doing?" he asked.

"Coming with you, of course," I said.

"It's freezing out there," he protested.

"I'll bring a blanket."

"Why the sudden interest in my work?"

"It's not that sudden. Why the reluctance to let me come?"

North and I stared at each other, waiting for the other to back down. Finally, North chuckled. "I'll wait outside for you. Wear something warm, all right?"

The problem was that I didn't have anything particularly warm to wear, just a thin shawl. I did the best I could, layering my stockings and underskirts. I was sorely tempted to crawl back into the little warmth my bed provided.

Outside, North was sitting on the cabin's small stoop, his head tilted up at the remaining stars. The air had a strange scent, crisp and fresh, but . . . cold. It bit at my nostrils and the tip of my nose. The scent was unlike that of desert rain; it was unique and telling.

"It smells like it's going to snow," North said, as if reading my thoughts.

"Snow?" I gasped. "Do you think—? I mean, do you believe it's really going to snow? Is this what snow smells like?"

North looked at me in pure amazement.

"Right . . . ," he said. "Right, desert. No snow."

I felt childish, as if my excitement had somehow betrayed me.

"Well, I do hope it snows for your sake!" North said. We both rose to our feet, but North's hand caught me and held me back. He unknotted his cloaks, pulling the crimson red material from the pile. I thought for a moment he intended to create one of his balls of light, but instead the cloak fluttered down onto my shoulders. He stuck the tip of his tongue out of the side of his mouth as he tied it securely around my neck.

"There!" he said. "We're ready to go. Is that a little warmer?"

It felt like heaven, actually. I was warmed down to my very core.

"Don't you need this?" I asked, feeling a little bit guilty. He secured the rest of the cloaks back in place before taking my hand.

"No. Besides, it suits you."

"Red and red?" I sighed.

He winked. "My favorite color."

We followed the short path from Lady Aphra's cottage to the main village below. The thatched roofs were uneven from our vantage point, each small cabin seemingly built on its own hill in the valley. A small river ran along the far edge of the village, catching the early-morning light. Mist rolled off the mountain's tree-lined slopes like a swirling light stream.

"It's so quiet and peaceful," I said.

"Just wait until everyone knows we're here," North said, laughing. "You'll be singing a different song then."

Rather ungracefully, North scaled the fence surrounding one of the small homes. He pulled a slip of paper from his pocket and buried it at the foot of their stoop.

"What are you doing?" I asked. He handed me a slip of paper over the fence before bending down to bury another one. Written across the thick paper were symbols I didn't recognize.

"These should ward off anyone with ill intent," he said. "Including our friend Dorwan."

When I leaned over to get a better look, my hand slid against a sharp edge of the fence. I sucked in a quick breath, pulling it away. North snatched up my hand, a strange expression transforming his face as he watched the blood well up along the cut. He didn't move, but held my hand firmly in his own.

"North?"

He started slightly. "Careful, careful," he mumbled. He pulled a purple handkerchief from his bag. It was embroidered with his initials and the crest of Palmarta. He held it there until the bleeding was staunched, and only then did he pull away.

"I'll wash it," I promised, but he tucked it into the pocket of his trousers before I had the chance to take it back.

"Don't worry about it," he said, looking at the ground.

"Hard to believe, I know, but there was a time in my life when I had to do my own washing."

We moved down the main row of cottages. At each stoop, he would stop, dig a small hole, and bury the paper. After the fourth cottage, I realized he was mumbling to himself under his breath—something that sounded vaguely like a prayer. I added my own, rubbing the frozen metal of my necklace between my palms.

With all ten cottages taken care of, North and I settled on the side of the hill, halfway up the path to Lady Aphra's cottage.

"I didn't even know this village existed," I said. North reclined back on his elbows, his eyes closed.

"I'm not surprised," he said. "Lady Aphra actually owns the entire valley. She bought the land grant from the king himself."

"How did you meet Lady Aphra?" I asked. "She's an interesting choice for a patroness."

"Why, because she's not wealthy?" North asked with a teasing smile. I winced at the memory.

"No . . . I would have thought she'd be . . . much younger, and more attractive," I said.

North laughed. "So I only help attractive people? You realize you're flattering yourself."

"You're not helping me," I said. "I'm helping you, remember?"

"Yes, of course," North said.

"Good," I said, happy to be in agreement. "Now answer my question!"

"So nosy," he said, toying with one of my ringlets. "Magister Pascal and Lady Aphra have been . . . *friends* for quite some time. He used to bring Oliver and me up here all the time to help with building the cottages. After I left Magister, I stayed with Lady Aphra and offered my services."

"I thought wizards relied on their patrons to earn money," I said. "Do you have another one?"

"No," he said. "Some of us do odd jobs here and there to get by. You take a patron because you like them or because you're in for some gold. I chose the former."

Just then, a small figure came out of the school and rang a large bell four times. The sound echoed off the mountains and carried throughout the valley. North and I watched silently as one by one the door to each cottage opened and scores of children poured out, each followed closely by an adult. I counted thirty-four small heads lined up outside the school.

"Good morning," came a new voice behind us. We turned to find Lady Aphra descending the path, resplendent in a worn navy dress. A decorative clip pulled back her gray hair, but wild strands were already escaping. Everything about the way she carried herself provided evidence for North's story. When she reached the school, the children broke ranks and swarmed the old woman.

"She's a good teacher," North said. He was on his back, nearly buried in the long grass. His eyes were shut, and his gloved hands were loosely folded across his chest. The smile on his face must have been as wide as my own. I had never seen him like this before, and it was such a pleasant sight I almost didn't feel the cold.

I lay down next to him in the wet grass, feeling the dew and the new sun. A light breeze whispered through my hair and across my cheeks. And despite the threat of Dorwan and the ache of travel in the soles of my feet, there was little else but happiness in my heart.

*   *   *

Later that day, just as I finished the first quarter of the cloak, a young boy brought two letters up the hill to Aphra's cabin. North was at the schoolhouse asking a few of the older children about the wolf, so the boy handed the letters to me. They had been forwarded from Fairwell.

The shock that went through my system stole any coherent thought from my mind. Henry had *finally* written me back.

Turning the envelope over, my fingers brushed the seal almost reverently. There were small bumps in the wax. I brought it to my face for closer inspection. There, in the deep crimson sealing wax, were dozens of small granules of desert sand—of home.

Delle,

I hope you're safe and this letter finds you somehow. I'm sending a copy to various inns in the major cities, hoping you'll stop in at least one of them. I want you to know that I'm safe and that the Bailey brothers and I slipped out of Cliffton several days ago on your father's orders. He wants us to go to Provincia and have me help in the war effort in his stead, but I'm more concerned about spreading the news about Cliffton. When we left, most of the crops had been picked over by the soldiers, but no one had been seriously hurt. The few who tried to get out and were caught were beaten, but not to the point of death. Your family is fine— mine, too—though our mothers are a little worse for wear.

You'll get to Provincia before us, so I'll come find you. Stay safe until I can see you again. I miss you.

Henry

"Anything good in the post?" North asked. I pressed the letter to my chest and turned around slowly. He had a smile on his face, and it was such a rare sight that I almost didn't want to tell him.

"A letter from Henry," I said quickly. "You have a letter from Pascal."

"What did Henry have to say?" he asked. He leaned over my shoulder to get a better look, but I kept the paper close.

"That my family is safe and that he and a few others escaped," I said. "They'll be in Provincia a few days after us."

"How *very* convenient," North said. "It's really too bad we won't have time to drop in for a cup of tea."

"I'll have the time," I said.

"Don't be so sure," he said, and reached for one of my loose curls. "Maybe I'll keep you all to myself."

I pulled away, my stomach flipping. It was such a familiar touch, something that North had done a dozen times over the past few weeks, but it seemed so wrong for me to like it, to want him to do it again, when I had Henry's letter in my hands.

"Read your letter and leave me alone," I said, still unable to meet his eyes.

"Yes, my beautiful, beautiful darling!" he said. "As my beautiful, beautiful darling wishes."

When I finally had the courage to look up again, North's brows were drawn together.

"Bad news from Pascal?"

"He's the same as always, the old grump," he replied distractedly. "Still treats me like the seven-year-old he took in."

"You only trained with him for seven years?" I knew only so much about wizarding education.

"Yes. I lived with him until I finished training at fourteen and was supposed to be ranked." North glanced up from the letter. "Why are you looking at me like that?"

"You aren't ranked?" I asked.

"I thought you knew," he said. "Is that a problem?"

"But all of the other wizards are."

"I'm nothing like the other wizards," he said. "Nor do I intend to be. It . . . just wasn't the right way for me."

"I'm surprised you had a magister then," I said, a page of the wizard book floating up in my memory. "Isn't that the whole point of being trained—to be ranked and join the Wizard Guard? The unranked wizards are usually . . . like Dorwan, right?"

North narrowed his eyes, obviously offended. "Are you comparing me to the hedges?"

"No! Well, a little—but not really," I finished lamely, watching the expression on his face darken.

"You aren't ranked," I tried again. "And you left, wandered, and . . . er, I'm sorry?"

The corner of his mouth twitched up. "I suppose you're forgiven—as long as you write a letter for me."

"I'm sure you can write your own letter," I said. "Or is it one of my duties as your *assistant*?"

"Actually, I only asked because your penmanship is much nicer than mine. Magister is fond of telling me that my handwriting looks like the scratches of a blind chicken."

I sighed, pulling a small writing quill and a fresh sheet of paper from my bag.

"Dear Magister," North dictated. "Thank you for your help. I do think you're correct in supposing that the ingredient should work, but I've tried once to little effect. I don't believe I will try again, not for lack of curiosity but for lack of propriety. Also, I'm quite glad that your wheat fields have finally picked up again. As if there was any doubt that you could fix them yourself—keeping up, Syd?"

I cursed under my breath and crossed out where I had written, *Keeping up, Syd?*

"Yes," I said, sighing. "Keep going."

"I have the information I need, though I'm not sure my very dear friend will hear me out," North continued. "Yes, I am aware of what has been going on with Oliver, though I haven't received a letter from him in quite some time."

"What's going on with Oliver?" I asked, looking up.

"Nosy today, aren't we?" He smiled.

"Fine, fine," I said. "Keep going."

"I've sent him numerous messages, but he seems too enthralled with his newfound power to listen. I'll try to write to him again, but I can't trust the post with these things. Magister, I know you wanted to see us, but I won't be coming to see you with my beautiful, beautiful darling—!"

"Stop it!" I said, crossing out the last three words I had written. "You are so ridiculous!"

"Here, I'll finish it," he said. He pulled the paper away before I could protest. I thought it was strange he didn't want me to see what he was writing—and I did try to look, but his magister had been correct. He wrote like a blind chicken.

There was only enough time for him to seal the letter with wax before one of the village boys burst into the cabin.

"It's here," he said breathlessly. "We saw it through the schoolhouse windows—down by the stream."

North and I stood at the same moment, but his arm lashed out, stalling me.

"Stay here!" he said. I took a step forward, but he would have none of it.

"Right here!" he said. "For once in your life, do as I say!"

The cabin door slammed shut behind him, but it didn't stay that way for long. The last time North had gone off like this, he had come back with burns from a dragon. I wasn't going to be left behind, not again.

The afternoon air cut through my thin dress as I ran, following North down the long hill. And when he and his cloaks finally got so far ahead that they were out of sight, I followed the trail his boot prints had left behind.

At the first sign of the specter the children had been drawn inside, and the bell inside the school's small tower was still ringing. I was sure I heard someone call my name, once, maybe even twice, but I kept running. My hair flew around my face as I made a sharp turn straight into the forest.

The sound of the bell died slowly, just as I lost the trail of North's boot prints in a clearing. I glanced around. He must have twisted—it was the only explanation. That, or he had climbed up into the trees.

I moved to the other edge of the clearing. Nothing. Not even a rabbit or bird.

There was, however, the strangest sensation at my feet. Even through the leather of my boots, I could feel the brush of cool silk against my skin. The mist from the mountains had rolled down into the forest, hovering around my ankles in a pool of white.

Yet when I moved, so did the mist. It swirled without the aid of wind, gathering into large pockets between the trees. A breeze lifted the hem of my dress and sent my hair flying.

I took a step back. My skin felt ready to crawl off my bones.

The hand that latched on to my bare arm felt frozen to the touch, and that alone was enough to make me scream.

"Miss Mirabil!" Lady Aphra said in a rush of breath. Her face had lost all its robust color. "Do you not understand the concept of danger? Or is there so much dust and dirt crammed up in your ears that you can't listen to the warnings people have given you?"

"Did you see?" I gasped. "Did you see it?"

"I saw nothing but a foolish girl, running out into the woods to get herself killed!"

The old woman's fingernails dug into my skin like claws and didn't release me until we were halfway up the hill to her cottage. When I did look back, I saw nothing to be frightened of except the suddenly empty air.

*   *   *

I was tempted to escape the confines of Aphra's cabin more than once, and the desire grew with each passing hour—each minute—North was gone. I forced myself to stay inside, alternating between weaving North's cloak and playing with those few potion ingredients I had left. My mind was too restless to settle.

After a few hours, Lady Aphra shut the door quietly behind her and set a small basket beside me on the floor. I looked, surprised to find it full of more plants than I could identify.

"They go to waste in my garden," she explained, her voice low and rough. "I don't have the patience for such things. I suspect you'll need them more than I will."

"Thank you," I said. It wasn't an apology for the way she had scolded me earlier, but it was likely the closest thing I would receive. I poured the pain elixir I had just finished into an empty jar.

Lady Aphra walked over to the small window. Her eyes were cast out over the valley below, but I knew exactly what they were searching for.

"He'll take care of it," I said, trying to sound confident.

"I'm sure. I am getting a little concerned, however," she said. She wiped her hands on her apron. "He'd better be back before dark."

"Are the children still inside?" I asked.

"We've kept them in the schoolhouse all day, but they won't stand for it much longer," she said.

"I'm sure—" I began, but her body tightened like a spring, and she shot toward the door.

I jumped to my feet and followed her outside. I hoped that with the day's work done, North would be open to the idea of traveling that night.

But when North came into sight, it was clear we would not be traveling.

"What happened?" Lady Aphra demanded.

Supported on either side by a villager, North was barely able to keep his own head up. Several of his cloaks had nasty gashes or were missing pieces entirely. His dark pants and shirt were spotted with dirt and blood. He had a shallow cut on his face, and his dark eyes were closed.

"North . . ." At my touch, he blinked.

"Hullo, Syd," he mumbled as the men lifted him up the steps of the cabin and onto the nearest pile of bedding. His breathing was low and hard—I couldn't understand what he was trying to say.

Seeing the grimace of pain on his face, I lifted the jar of pain elixir to his mouth and helped him to drink it.

"If you have something for sleep, you'd better give him that, too," Aphra said in a low voice. I retrieved another jar from my bag, and North drank its contents just as obediently. I lowered his head back onto the bedding.

Lady Aphra rose and signaled for the other men to follow her outside.

"What happened?" I whispered. "Are you all right?"

"He got away . . . ," North breathed, succumbing to the sleeping draft. "He . . ."

I leaned back, finally releasing the anxiety and fear I had been holding inside of me all day.

"It's all right," I said, though I knew he couldn't hear me.

I began unlacing one of his boots. "We'll get him. We won't let him stop us."

Beneath the leather were the shreds of a sock, a sock that may or may not have been red at one point in its miserable life but was now a faint pink. A sock that was gaping open at the heel and sliding down North's ankle, completely stretched out.

"I guess I'll have to forget about the cloak for a while," I said, covering my mouth and nose with my free hand. "Socks it is." In his sleep, North seemed to snort in approval. I peeled the sock away, holding it in front of me like a rotten piece of fruit. I held my breath while I used my free hand to open the window and drop the sock outside.

The other boot was laced tighter than the first, and I had a terrible time picking apart the knot with my stubby fingernails. As a weaver, I prided myself on being able to untangle the worst of knots, but this one was almost impossible. North didn't help me much, either; he kept shifting away from my hands. I held him firmly in place, giving him a look that I wished he had been awake to see. I was practically screaming in frustration when the worn string finally gave. I ripped the boot off his foot none too gently. Another worn-out sock came with it, leaving a large, reeking, perfectly black foot in my lap.

I'm not sure how long I knelt there. My first ridiculous thought was that the foot was just black with soot and grime, but not even the water from the room's small basin could wash the color away. The entire foot was solid black, right up to the ankle. North was practically kicking me with it now. Somehow, even in his sleep, he knew that I had unwittingly unwrapped one of his secrets. And he was powerless to stop it.

I lifted his other foot, noticing for the first time the edge of black on the two smallest toes. I pulled away his thick gloves and threw them across the room. The little finger on his left hand was black, and the next two were tinged a marble gray. His right hand was still—mercifully—his own, with spots of mud and dirt beneath his nails.

I brought his hands to my forehead and released the breath I had been holding in a low sob.

"So now you see what's been before you this entire time."

Lady Aphra came to kneel beside me, setting down a bowl of clean water. She took one of North's limp hands in her own, her thumb running over his exposed skin.

"No wonder he never took those stupid boots off," I choked out, trying to swallow the lump in my throat. "What's wrong with him?"

"It's a curse," she said. "I don't quite understand it myself, but I do know that the man I see now bears very little resemblance to the boy I knew."

"I don't understand," I said.

"After his father died and his mother sent him to be trained by Pascal, he was sullen, as any boy ought to be after losing someone," Aphra said. "But after a year with Pascal, he was happy, clever, a smart aleck, and a complete monster when he wanted to be. Then the curse struck him, and he's never been the same. His old smile and humor come in flashes, but the pain he feels and his anger toward the curse steal them away more and more as the years go by. This war has put him in an even worse place than before."

"Is there a cure?" I asked. "Some way to ease his pain at least?"

Aphra placed North's hand in my own. "No, Miss Mirabil, there is no cure. Wayland has spent his life looking, as his father and his grandfather did. Pascal refused to take on more apprentices in order to search for a way to help him, but there was nothing to be found."

"And so, what? He'll suffer from it his entire life? He'll drink his pain away, or rely on sleeping drafts?"

Lady Aphra shook her head. "He'll die long before then."

I gripped North's hand. "You're— You can't be serious."

"His father died at the age of thirty-five, while serving as the Sorcerer Imperial," Aphra said. "Pascal still hasn't recovered from the loss of him, and the thought of losing Wayland the same way has left us all helpless."

I looked down at North's face, still young and handsome in sleep, free of any sign of discomfort. He looked like a different person to me, and the thought alone was enough to bring tears to my eyes.

Lady Aphra stood, her knees cracking from the effort. She smoothed the hair back from my face.

"The curse only affects the sons in the family line, probably with the intent of ending the family line entirely," she said. "But you'll need to get the full story from him."

"Is there really nothing I can do for him?" I asked. *"Nothing?"*

Aphra turned in the doorway. "Love him," she said. "For someone who has grown up hating himself and fearing that there's nothing for him in this world but pain, there is no greater gift. Do you understand?"

I nodded, but I didn't say another word. Not while I tucked the blanket up around his chin, not while I brushed his hair from his face, not while I relit the fire. Lady Aphra's words echoed in my mind, but I forced them out and focused on nothing but the way the shadows played across North's face.

I had half of North's story now, but I knew the other half of it wouldn't come as easily. The secret of his pain ran deeper than I could have imagined. Who was Wayland North, I thought, and how many layers would I be forced to peel away before I actually found him?

*   *   *

I was fairly ravenous by the time one of the older girls brought in dinner. It was only sandwiches and milk, but I was so hungry I practically inhaled the contents of the plate. When I finished my own, I drank North's milk as well, surprised to find it still so cool after being next to the fire.

I thought about mending the threadbare fabric of his cloaks, but the events of the day had relit my desire to complete the single one, still unfinished on the loom. North deserved so much better than his ugly, battered cloaks—I wanted something to show the story of his life as I had seen it, without the gaping holes and tears that constantly ate away at him.

As I wove near the fire, its flickering light cast moving shadows over my loom. My eyes drifted over to North, watching the steady rise and fall of his chest. It was useless—I couldn't focus on the strands of blue that I was binding together; and I could hardly pay attention to each drop of rain I was forming around the shape of the dragon. When I looked at my hands again, the blue yarn seemed to glow in my hands.

I dropped the yarn and pushed myself away from it. The entire cloak seemed to blur in my eyes, a mass of color and light.

Falling to my knees again, I took up the spool of red thread and began blending it haphazardly with the blue. As the fire of the dragon came to life, so did the fire in the hearth. It crackled and hissed, billowing out for a moment. In his sleep, North began to mumble.

The thread fell from my lifeless fingers. I breathed in the cool air of the cabin, but the heat inside me was too much; there was little I could do but crawl toward the bedding, trembling and crying as I wrapped myself in its heavy layers.

* * *

It was only a short while before I woke again, my mind hazy with sleep and something else. The room was darker than before; the fire had died down to mere touches of warmth and light. My hands and feet felt stiff and cold. I brought my knees up to my chest and tried to rub some feeling back into my limbs.

Cold, I thought. *Cold, cold, cold.*

*　　*　　*

I woke several more times after that—or maybe I wasn't even awake, I couldn't be sure. The world around me felt like a feverish dream. Everything was slow and so, so painful. I sat up and dragged my bedding loudly across the wooden floor until it was directly in front of the fire. I picked up a log from the small pile, but it fell through my hands and thudded loudly against the floor. There was no feeling in my fingers, my palms, my arms. I braced my side against the wall and slid down, forcing my knees to stop straining and aching.

*　　*　　*

The rest was a blur of sound and agony. I must have pushed the log into the fireplace and sparked something, because the next time I woke, it was to Lady Aphra frantically calling my name and pulling me out of the fire I had started.

"Sydelle!" She was shouting. *"Sydelle, wake up!"*

I tried to open my eyes, to let her know how badly I hurt all over, but all I could mumble was "terrible, terrible cold" because it was all I could feel and think. Hundreds, thousands, millions of needles pricked my skin, and I let out a cry of anguish. Worse than breaking my arm, worse than falling onto fire-hot rocks. Worse than anything I had ever felt.

"Wayland!" she yelled. *"Wake up!"*

North's face hovered above me, but there were black blotches floating in my vision. It wasn't until he took my face between his hands that my sight momentarily cleared. Eyes, nose, lips, cheeks, gloves. Gloves. He had put his gloves back on.

"Syd," he said. His voice sounded much closer, and I was beginning to feel his hand rubbing hard circles on my chest, over my heart. My eyes closed, too heavy to keep open.

"What did she have?" North demanded. "What did she eat? Drink?"

"It was just milk and a sandwich," Lady Aphra said. "The healer is coming; it's taking her a while to get up the hill with the storm."

"She doesn't have time to wait," North said sharply. "Go get me some of the thyme and heartroot from your garden. Get my bag and find me a bloody bowl, please!"

"The snow—" Lady Aphra began. Yes, the snow, the snow. My mind clung to the word deliriously, even as my entire chest constricted with immeasurable pain, and I cried. The snow . . .

Something hit the ground beside my face. I felt it shake the floor, but the voice that accompanied it was much harder to distinguish.

"Pale . . . pulled her out . . . hands . . ."

A pair of strong arms pulled me up from the floor, though my limbs were dead weight. I was a lump of skin and bones, lifeless, freezing. Something warm wrapped around me, something red that I could sense beneath my closed eyelids.

I felt North before I heard him. That same tingling warmth that I associated with him seeped under my skin, even if just for a moment. My back was pressed against his chest, and his tall frame completely enveloped me. I felt his heart racing.

"N . . . Nor . . . ," I cried. "Please help me, please, it hurts, it hurts. I can't breathe. Please . . ."

"You're going to be all right," he said fiercely. "I've got you, I've got you."

There was pounding and screaming all around me. For one horrifying moment, I thought that the shrieking was coming from me, but my throat and voice were frozen. I couldn't breathe—I couldn't breathe.

"Shut . . . door . . . here!"

"Storm . . . help . . ."

"Get over here!" North barked. His face turned next to my ear, and I could feel his hand rubbing my chest for a brief moment. "Just breathe, Syd. I'm here. I know it hurts, but you have to breathe, you stubborn girl. . . ."

I was gasping, willing my hands to lift from my lap to pry

off the imaginary fingers that had encircled my throat. Everything was lethargic and cold and dark except for North's glove and its hard, uneven circles. That glove and the slowing beat of my heart.

"Mix the heartroot in now; just squeeze out two drops or it'll kill her—can you possibly go any faster? Give me the bowl; just let me do it—here, now put it over the fire—have you never made a kulde antidote before?"

"Wayland! Don't . . ."

". . . the storm . . . get more . . ."

"The girl . . ."

". . . Sydelle . . . look . . . she's not . . ."

"Be quiet, both of you!" North thundered, and the room was silent once again. North's body was shaking erratically, and he was breathing against my ear, breathing hard as if for both of us. He grasped my jaw gently and forced it open. Something hard was pressed against my lips.

"You have to drink this. I'm sorry, I'm so sorry," he whispered. "Please drink it, please."

The warm liquid went down my throat, even as I coughed and sputtered against it. Disgusting. It tasted of death and dirt.

North held me the entire time, forcing me to drink all of the bowl's contents. Every single burning, foul drop.

I felt . . .

I felt nothing. And then everything.

This time I knew I was the one screaming. Beneath my

skin, everything burst back to life with a roaring blaze that consumed me, pushing its way through my veins and forcing out the tolerable numbness behind my eyes. My head was thundering in pain.

Then North was holding the same bowl under my face, whispering in my ear, rubbing warm circles on my back.

"You have to spit it up—you have to get it out of you, Syd," he said. "Throw it up!"

If I had been myself in that instant I might have been embarrassed, but I did exactly as I was told. I threw up until there was nothing left in me but dry heaves and thick tears.

Somewhere a door shut, but all I could hear was North's voice; all I could feel was his warm breath on the back of my neck.

"That's my girl," he said. Sensation was tingling in my toes and fingers, but I still couldn't move, paralyzed by the pain the cold had left behind, by its last grip on my body.

That, and the solid, undeniable warmth that was North.

The wizard fell back against the wall in exhaustion. He held me against him gently, as if I was glass—as if I could shatter and fall away from him at any moment and leave him breathless and alone once more.

"That's my girl . . . ," he whispered, resting his cheek against my shoulder.

CHAPTER SEVEN

When I was a child, no older than five, I came down with an illness that left me bedridden for weeks. I have very few memories of that time. Flashes of my mother's pale face, the wide rims of the doctor's glasses. Mostly, I remembered the pain: the heaviness of my limbs, my head too weak to move.

It was exactly how I felt upon waking to the sun shining in my eyes and the sound of shuffling against the floor. The noise wasn't very loud at all, but it worsened the pounding between my ears.

I blinked. My limbs were as heavy as stones; I strained my neck, trying to see what was making the noise.

A bald old man was rummaging through North's leather bag. The sun outlined his profile, but I could still make out the deep wrinkles on his forehead and the tight line of his lips as he dug through the empty bottles. When his hand reappeared, he was clutching North's stained purple handkerchief.

Whoever he was, he didn't belong in North's bag.

My voice came out a rough whisper. "*Hey*."

The scrap of fabric fell from his fingertips. From beneath my layers of bedding, I glared.

"So you're awake," he said. He stood slowly. "Aphra!"

The old woman appeared instantly in the doorway. I felt the soft, worn material of her skirt as she knelt beside me and placed a hand on my forehead.

"How do you feel?" Her voice was the softest I had ever heard it.

"Hurts," I confessed, closing my eyes. I heard the floorboards strain and creak beneath the man's boots as he walked past me. There was the sound of bedding being pulled away, and a grunt from the corner of the room.

"Up, you bag of bones," the man growled. "I let you go back to sleep earlier, but now you have no excuse."

"Magister?" North groaned. "Gods, I was hoping that was a nightmare."

"Nightmare?" he scoffed. "You're lucky I came. It's not an easy trip."

"I didn't ask you to come, old man," North said. "In fact, I seem to remember telling you I wasn't coming to see you, either."

"And yet here I am to knock some sense back into that thick skull of yours," he said. "How very lucky you are."

"Wayland," Aphra said. "You're disturbing Miss Mirabil—may I suggest you do what your magister says?"

"She's awake?" North asked, kicking off the rest of his blankets. He squatted down beside me, a bright smile on his face.

"Hullo, my beautiful, beautiful darling," he said. "Feeling better this morning?"

I smiled back weakly. "Not really."

He chuckled. "It might take a few days. The poison has to leave your body."

"Poison?"

"Pascal, give them a moment," Aphra said, nodding her head toward the door. "I'll need your help to clear the snow off the path."

The old man clucked his tongue in disapproval, but he went.

"Snow?" I whispered.

"It was quite the storm last night," North said, brushing a stray curl off my face.

I swallowed hard, catching sight of the loom out of the corner of my eye. "Was it me?"

North brought over the pitcher of water and helped me sit up long enough to drink.

"Was it me?" I asked again, my voice stronger. "Did I cause the storm?"

North's brow furrowed. "What gave you that absurd idea?"

"The threads," I explained, but it was useless. North shook his head.

"When you're feeling up to it, I'll take you outside," he said. "I'll try to get a letter off to Owain to tell him we may be a day late."

"No," I said in horror, trying to sit up again. My head throbbed. "I can go now . . . we can't get farther behind."

North shook his head. "It'll be a day or two before you're strong enough to travel. I promised you that we'd get there in time, and I have no intention of going back on it."

"I'll hold you to that," I said, trying for a smile. North only looked away.

"I need to tell you something," he began, his voice tight. "That poison—that was the same poison that killed the king."

"But how did he . . . ?" My head spun. "You saved me. Why did he have to die if there were wizards there?"

"Because only I know who made the poison," he said. "And because I'm the only person to have seen him make the antidote. It's a hedge poison."

"Dorwan? Are you sure?" North gave a curt nod, but his eyes betrayed his feelings. Had he known this entire time? Was that the real message we were taking to the capital?

"I was with him for a little while, when we were both boys. The only reason I met him was because I was snooping around, looking for information around one of the hedge camps. He showed me . . . He showed me a lot of these poisons and tricks that he thought I would like," North said. "He thought we were alike, and that I would appreciate knowing them, I guess. It was a long time ago."

"And it's the same poison?" I said.

"It was the perfect plan," North said. "No one recognized the poison, so they assumed it was foreign—"

"And that it came from Auster," I finished. "He fooled everyone. How could something like this happen?"

"It happened because I didn't stop him years ago, when I had the chance," North said angrily. "I underestimated how much hatred he has . . . to do something like this . . ."

"It's not your fault," I breathed, my eyes drifting shut. For a moment he didn't say anything, but I felt his dry lips press lightly against my cheek.

"Rest, Syd," he said. Another dreamless sleep washed over me.

*   *   *

After sleeping for so long, I sat up slowly, my limbs stiff and aching. I knew another day had passed us by—a day we could have been traveling.

I felt surprisingly alert as I glanced around the room. The cool air was a welcome replacement to the unbearable warmth of the blankets.

"North?" I whispered.

I heard a muffled crash outside. My legs buckled beneath me as I stood, but I forced myself over to the window. I pushed it open, thrusting my head into the freezing air.

It was barely light outside, but the wizard and his former

student were standing side by side, knee deep in a blanket of snow. Around North lay dirt and grass in stark patches of brown, but for the most part, the snow remained undisturbed and piled high.

I reached through the window's opening, barely able to contain a grin as I scooped up a handful of snow and let it fall between my fingers. It clung to my skin in a way sand never would have, and it was soft. I brought my lips together and blew. A thousand little specks of white flew off the window ledge, floating to the ground.

Under the cover of snow, small, smoking chimneys were the only parts of the roofs visible to me in the valley. I missed the endless sea of billowing green grass, but there was something beautiful here as well. I turned to look for my boots and a blanket in order to go outside, but Pascal's voice stopped me.

"If you want to track him using magic, you have to be willing to open yourself up fully to the magic."

"But doing that is agony," North said. "I can't hold on to it like the others can—how am I supposed to track him when I can barely hold myself up?"

"I know, Wayland, I do," Pascal said. "I know how difficult it is for you, as it was for your father and his father before him. But you must try."

North knelt in the soft dirt, pressing a hand to his face. "I see a line of red, pulled tight . . . and . . . a ribbon of white, hot to the touch . . ."

"Keep going," Pascal said. "You mentioned he specializes

in ice—see if you can find a gathering of blue. He'd be calling that magic to him most strongly."

"I can't." North rubbed his face.

"Don't be afraid," Pascal said. "You're holding yourself back by anticipating the pain."

"Does it ever go away, even just the slightest?" North asked quietly. "I don't remember my father ever being so weak."

"You're just as strong as your father was," Pascal said. "Weldon was only better at hiding the pain."

I shut the window, feeling as if I had already heard more than I should have. He had only brought up his parents once—and that was enough for me to see how deeply he felt their loss. Resting my forehead against the glass, I watched the two figures circle each other, North's cloaks flying around him. As always, he wasted precious time untying and retying each cloak. More than ever, I realized how important my work could be to him.

The loom was still waiting for me, its rough wooden frame balanced carefully against the wall. I sat down in front of it, pulling my bag toward me. My mind was fully absorbed in every detail of the cloak, straying only once to acknowledge the sunlight filling the room.

*　　*　　*

I was halfway done with the cloak before I forced myself to stop and relight the fire. Sometime after I finished the castle walls of Fairwell and before I had begun the green of Arcadia's mountains, the embers had died out completely. The wintry air that saturated the room had stiffened my fingers to the point that they could no longer move.

I must have watched my mother light the kitchen fire a thousand times with an ease and fluidity brought by constant practice. But she had let me try only once, and that one time—with the spilled stew and ruined pot—was enough to convince her that I had no place in the kitchen.

I ground the hard, thin piece of wood against the other, softer piece with as much strength as I could, but all I got for my effort was tired arms. I was working so hard, was so busy praying to Astraea for just a small spark, that I didn't hear the footsteps behind me.

"Girl," Pascal said. "If you were out in the wild, you'd pass out and freeze to death before you saw even a hint of fire."

I blew my unruly hair out of my face and glared up at him. He gave a dry laugh as he knelt beside me.

"May I?" he asked. I passed the wood to him, watching in frustration as he used magic to light the fire. "Now, coffee?"

He disappeared into Aphra's room and returned with a kettle, two beautiful teacups, and a little burlap sack.

"Where's North?" I could already smell the coffee, and my empty stomach twisted in anticipation.

"Out prowling for Dorwan, I assume," he said gruffly.

I looked down at the cup in my hand, studying the little blue flowers.

"Why are you training him again?" I asked when the silence finally became unbearable.

"Wizards have ways of detecting others of their kind," Pascal said, pouring the coffee. "It's a difficult technique, but one he needs to learn regardless of whether he wants to stay a step ahead or seek Dorwan out."

"It looked like he was in pain," I said.

"He was struggling with himself," Pascal corrected me. "Over the years he's become more and more convinced that magic is nothing more than pain and destruction. It's hard to persuade him otherwise, especially after all that's happened to him and his father."

"I don't understand," I said slowly. "Don't you use Astraea's teachings in your lessons?"

"Those are the myths," Pascal said. "The reality is that magic is little more than a curse."

"They are not myths!" I said.

Pascal held up his hand. "You may believe whatever you choose to believe, but understand this, Miss Mirabil: magic is a responsibility, a burden, a duty. You are a slave to your faith and country. You don't choose to have it. Very few of us would, given the choice."

"Some wizards seem to enjoy having power," I said.

"Dorwan?" Pascal said. "I've often wondered if it isn't a weight for him as well. From what Wayland's told me, he wasn't allowed to participate in the ranking tournaments due to the circumstances of his upbringing. He didn't fit in with the hedges as a grown man, but he certainly couldn't join wizard society. He was trapped between what he wanted and what he could actually have. Perhaps that's why Wayland stayed with him as long as he did—they were both outcasts.

"They must have been together for six, maybe seven months before Wayland decided to leave. Dorwan disappeared, only to show up again a few years later at Provincia, demanding a meeting with the Sorceress Imperial. She refused to see him, by all accounts."

"How long ago was this?" I asked.

"Two years ago, I believe," Pascal said. "Right after the Sorceress Imperial had taken her oath of office."

I shook my head. "I can't believe North would ever choose to associate with Dorwan. They're completely different wizards."

"Different upbringings, different choices," Pascal said, rubbing his forehead. "You may not get to choose whether you're born with magic, you may not get to choose the people you're born to—but how you conduct yourself is entirely up to you."

I set my empty cup down beside me, unsure of how to ask my next question. "Do you think that magic can exist in someone without them knowing it?"

"There are always possibilities. Take Oliver, for instance. He never would have recognized the ability within himself if Wayland hadn't come across him in town and begged me to train him."

"But it is possible that a person, even without train-ing, could use magic?" I pressed. "Has that ever happened before?"

Pascal gave me a curious look. "I suppose it's possible, though it would be extremely difficult to control it. Magic exists everywhere, all the time. It never abandons us, though it can punish and compel us if we don't learn to master it. It is a tool, much like your loom."

Pascal glanced over at the unfinished cloak. "You are the wizard, and you can use that loom to shape the thread to create colors or shift patterns," he finished.

Something in his words struck me deeply, and I was on my feet before I even realized it.

"Where are you going?" he asked, startled.

"Just outside for a little bit," I said. "I want to walk around in the snow before it's gone. Will you tell North where I am?"

He nodded. "Don't stray too far from the house—and watch your footing. It would be extremely irritating to have to dig your body out of some snowdrift."

"I'll keep that in mind," I said dryly. I picked up a blanket from the floor and wrapped it tightly around my shoulders. With my boots on and my hair pulled back, I stepped out into a world of white, the likes of which I had never seen before.

I had things to do, but more important, things to think about.

✳   ✳   ✳

Later that day, as I helped Lady Aphra mix elixirs and drafts, I tried to shake Pascal's words from my mind. *You are the wizard, and you can use that loom to shape the thread to create colors or shift patterns.*

"I'm surprised you learned so many mixtures in so short a time," Lady Aphra said. "What made you decide to learn?"

"In the beginning, it was because I wanted to know what North was hiding," I admitted. "But I like it. It's something I can do without him, something that comes easily to me."

"I'm sure Wayland appreciates it," Lady Aphra said. "He never was very good at mixing them. If you're interested, I have a more in-depth book. It's fairly old, but it's served me well. I'm not sure there's much else I can get from it."

I nodded. "I would love it, if you're sure you won't need it."

She tapped her forehead. "I have it all up here now. That's what age does to you."

Back outside for a walk, my feet had a miserable time against the patches of ice, and dirt caked the wet hem of my dress. I stayed out for only a short time and shut the door of Lady Aphra's cottage behind me silently, feeling the warm air prick my frozen skin, a delicious relief.

"Does it matter?" North's voice carried from the other room. "I told you I tried, but it didn't have any effect—none whatsoever."

"Did you try with a fresh sample?" Pascal asked. "I don't think this will do anything. It's lost its potency."

"Once, and it was enough to realize the amount I needed would be fatal," North said.

"This may be your only chance," Pascal said. "You didn't seem opposed to the idea when you first wrote to me about it."

"Things have changed," North said tightly. "I'm not so sure the journey to Provincia will be worth it now—if they find out about the jinx, it will all be over."

"The choices will be death or subjugation," Pascal said. "You might as well use it now."

I stepped into the doorway, but the wizards didn't look up. They were huddled close to the fire, bent over empty bottles, herbs, and North's stained handkerchief.

"What are you talking about?" I asked at last. My voice sounded loud to my own ears. "What are you doing?"

"Nothing," North said. "We're leaving. Take your things."

"Now?" I asked.

"This instant," he said, casting a hard look in the direction of his magister. "We've wasted enough time here already. Owain will be waiting for us."

"He won't be the only one," Pascal said as I carefully unstrung the cloak and took apart the frame of my loom. North waited by the door, holding my bag.

"Wayland," Pascal said. "You must do it *now*, before Dorwan catches up to you, before the battle begins."

I hastily tied the wood together, feeling North's eyes burning into my back.

"There won't be a battle if I can help it," he said sharply. I came to stand beside him, gently prying his fingers from my bag. Pascal remained on the floor, kneeling by the fire.

"I won't lose you like I lost your father!"

"If you really think I'm capable of such a thing," North said, "then you already have."

"Wayland!"

North pulled me in front of him, ushering me out of the small cottage and slamming the door shut behind us. We didn't stop long enough to say good-bye to Lady Aphra. I tried to glance back, but he wouldn't allow me to. He led me down the long hill, and I felt the familiar warmth of his fingers as they threaded through mine.

"Are you all right?" I asked. "What happened?"

His dark eyes were fixed solely on our joined hands. "I'm going to twist us as far as I can, but we'll have to go by foot some of the way."

"What were you fighting about?" I asked, gripping his arm with my free hand.

"Something that's in the past now."

He pulled the black cloak over us, and the mountains of Arcadia disappeared from sight.

CHAPTER EIGHT

F or the first time, our landing was actually painful. We hit the ground too fast and at a strange angle, coming to rest in a tangled heap. I was still weak and sore from the illness, and North's weight knocked all the air from my lungs.

"If you're done getting comfortable," I wheezed, "now would be a great time to let me breathe."

In a single, fluid movement, North rolled off me and was on his feet.

"Sorry," he mumbled as he helped me up. He didn't look back toward the mountains. "I thought I could go farther."

I pulled the map from my bag and let North hover over my shoulder as I considered our options.

"We can pick up a wagon in Middleton," I said, showing him on the map. "It's a short distance by foot from here.

If we can cut through the mountains near Sapienshire, we should be in Provincia in no time."

North tugged on one of my loose curls, though his smile was somehow sad. "What would I do without you?"

"Are you worried about Dorwan following us?" I asked.

"He'd follow us to the seven hells if he knew it would prevent us from getting to Provincia," North said.

"Is he still working with the hedges?" I pressed.

"Even they couldn't stand him." North made a slicing motion with his fingers. "Who do you think took his eye and ear?"

I shuddered.

"The Wizard Guard needs to do something about him," I said.

"He's unranked," North said. "There was never a trace spell put on him because the Guard refused to admit him."

"Because he didn't have the proper schooling?" I asked.

"Because he had *dangerous* schooling," North corrected me. "I think he once really did want to prove himself everyone's equal, but now I think he *wants* Auster to destroy the wizards."

"What will he do?" I asked. "Won't he be destroyed along with the rest?"

North took my hand in his own and helped me navigate the rocky path. "Let's not find out, shall we?"

*   *   *

We heard the groan of the wagon's wheels long before we saw the two boys come around the bend in the mountain path. They were wearing plain clothing and their faces were surprisingly young. North held out an arm and drew me closer to him as the wagon slowed. The horses still had snow in their manes, but it was the word carved into the side of the wagon itself that caught my attention: ARCADIA.

North brought a hand up to his eyes, squinting against the setting sun's light. "Well, if it isn't little James and little Peter, all grown up and making the deliveries!"

The young man with blond hair waved, a huge smile on his face. "Mr. North! Didn't realize you'd left!"

"Just an hour or so ago," he said. "Where are you headed?"

"Mariton," the other boy said. "If you're going our way, we'd be happy to take you."

North looked at me, and I looked at our map. "Are you taking this path down to Mariton Pass, by any chance?"

We would be able to pick up Prima Road from there, and then it would be about a week until Provincia came into sight. North must have been thinking the same thing, because he favored me with a smile.

"We sure are," James said. "Hop in back. You might need to do some rearranging."

I saw what he meant. The wagon was filled with burlap sacks of apples and bundles of newly sheared wool. North pulled himself up first, piling the bags of fruit onto one another until there was enough room for both of us to sit. The wagon trembled to life, and while it felt good to be off my feet, I doubted we were moving any faster than before.

In front of us, the two boys chatted amiably, looking back every once in a while when they thought North or I might not notice. They quieted down as night came and the chill settled in, but I could still hear them whispering about us. I almost wished we were walking, both to get away from them and to warm my stiff, cold limbs.

"I was thinking," North whispered. I blinked my eyes open, rubbing them tiredly. He was looking at the half-eaten apple in his hand. "That once we got to Provincia, I would find you a nice place to stay while I take care of things."

"You don't have to do that for me," I said, sitting back up. "I want to be with you. This is really important to me."

"I can tell you're unhappy, you know," he said. "Please, I just want to do something nice for you."

"You did something very nice for me the other night, remember?" I said pointedly. The two boys chuckled.

"Oh, grow up!" I said. They simply waved me off, not even bothering to turn around.

North snorted with laughter, letting his heavy arm fall around my shoulders.

"You should rest," he said, his fingers threading through my hair. "We have a very long day tomorrow."

"I'm not tired," I said stubbornly, trying to shake off his arm.

"Well, I am!" North said, removing his arm. Before I could say a word, he had his head resting in my lap and his eyes squeezed shut. I wondered if he was waiting for me to hit him.

One of my hands came down to rest on his forehead, and all the lines of worry and tension seemed to give way. He was warm to the touch, as always.

"Gonna sing him a lullaby, now?" James asked.

North's foot lashed out, missing the younger man's back by mere inches.

"Oi!" North growled. "You're wrecking my peace! Just be quiet and drive!"

I swatted him on the forehead.

"You're being ridiculous," I sighed.

He turned slightly, as if trying to get more comfortable. "I need to feed you more, you're awfully bony."

"Go to sleep," I warned him, "before you say anything else and I decide to drop you off the side of the wagon."

He grasped the hand resting on his forehead and entwined his fingers with mine, pulling them down to his chest.

"What were you and your magister fighting about?" I whispered. "You were so upset."

"About whether," North said, "any man or wizard has the right to be selfish enough to want to save his life."

"Of course they do," I said. "It's only human to want to save your own life."

North dropped off into a heavy sleep, and there was no waking him after that. I sat straight up, watching the dark landscape roll by and trying to recall every word of their conversation. The only unfamiliar word had been *jinx*, and North had spat the word out so heatedly that it had goaded my curiosity.

Carefully reaching for my bag, I retrieved *Proper Instruction for Young Wizards* and flipped it open to a list of words in the back.

Jinx, I read. *A man or woman able to exude magic, as opposed to conveying it, said to appear once a millennia. Jinxes are very dangerous. Their inability to harness their magic is seen in their ability to cause, but not control, storms as they interrupt the natural balance of magic that exists in the world.*

The book slipped from my hand, thudding against the wagon bed. North shifted in his sleep. I felt shocked, almost as if the book had burnt my fingers.

"All right, lady?" Peter asked, looking over his shoulder.

I nodded my head. "Yes, I'm fine."

It was a long while before I could touch the worn leather binding again. By then, the words had settled into some dark recess of my mind, hanging there until I acknowledged them. I opened the book and realized there was still a bit left to the entry: *However, no records of jinxes reside in the capital, and many believe them to be nothing but popular lore.*

"A man or woman able to exude magic?" I mumbled. And able to cause a storm—like a snowstorm, or a rain shower? No. This definition didn't fit me at all; it didn't touch on the strange threads of light. *Exude magic.* From everything I had learned, wizards could only channel magic, not create it.

It wasn't possible—it couldn't be—because Astraea never would allow it. Never.

I snapped the book shut on the impossibility of it all, tossing it down into my bag. But the words weren't banished from my mind, and it was nearly sunrise before I was tired enough to rest.

I never had the chance to drift into sleep. The wagon came to a sharp halt that threw me forward, and James turned around and shook North awake.

"I think we have a problem," James said, as North and I stood for a better look.

Standing at the opening to the valley, hands shoved into his pockets casually, was a wizard, and his smirk was visible even from our distance. North shook my arm roughly to get my attention, but I couldn't tear my eyes away from the flashes of sunlight against the other wizard's long dagger.

CHAPTER NINE

I've been waiting for you, Wayland," Dorwan said.

Both boys turned to look at North, but he only let out a disgusted snarl, jumping over the side of the wagon.

"Take her back up to Arcadia," he said in a low voice. "Tell Pascal what's happened."

The boys nodded, and before I could protest, the wagon began to turn around on the narrow path. *He's leaving me behind again,* I thought. Watching him walk toward Dorwan, I felt sick, but not paralyzed.

I climbed out of the wagon, and Peter reached for my arm. I pulled away.

"Go back to Arcadia and tell them what's happened," I told the boys. "I need to stay with North. Lady Aphra will understand. Tell Pascal."

I waited until the wagon had cleared the pass before I took

a deep breath and walked toward the two wizards. Dorwan's eyes bore into mine, just as penetrating as I remembered.

"Why are you here?" I asked, already knowing the answer. My hand came to rest behind North's back.

"To see you again, of course," he said. Oh, that disgusting smile, that thinly layered malice. "I was so sorry to lose you in Dellark."

"Sorry enough to poison me," I said. I looked at North, but I couldn't read his expression.

"The poison wasn't meant for you," Dorwan said in his quiet, silky voice. "An unfortunate mistake. If he had taken it, we could have been together without this trouble."

North finally moved, blocking me from the other wizard's view. "You'll have to find your own assistant, Dorwan," he said.

Dorwan clucked his tongue. "Assistant? I take it she doesn't know, then?"

"Know what?" I asked.

"If I had your affliction, I would have experimented, too," Dorwan said, crossing his arms over his chest. "Though I don't think I would have stopped so short of a cure. Your magister had the right idea."

"You don't even know what you're talking about!" North's voice exploded through the pass. I winced.

"So you deny that you took her because you wanted to study her?" Dorwan peered around North's shoulder.

Don't believe that, North's look seemed to say. But why couldn't he just say that aloud? What did he mean, *study* me?

"Sydelle, you'd better come with me now," Dorwan said. "It would be a shame for you to witness what I'm going to do to Wayland if you don't."

"You disgust me," I spat. "I'd lie in a bed of snakes and spiders for all eternity before leaving this place with you. We're going to Provincia to stop this war, and there's nothing you can do about it."

"Are you honestly stupid enough to think you have a choice?" Dorwan said. "There's no stopping the wheels of chaos now that they've been set in motion. It's a glorious time to be alive in this world! I've seen to it that the wizards will be destroyed in this war, and you, dear girl, will help me to establish the new regime."

North's fingers tugged at the knots holding his cloaks in place, and time slowed around us. All of the cloaks fluttered down silently, ripples of color in the air, landing in a puddle of fabric between the two men.

"What are you doing?" I cried.

"What makes you believe I'd ever agree to a *wizarding* duel?" Dorwan's smile made my skin crawl. "Those rules are antiquated and useless to me."

"But you love a challenge, don't you? You'd love nothing more than a chance to use whatever dark magic you've created to end my life," North said. "If you give me time to take Sydelle to safety, that's the only rule I need."

Dorwan nodded, obviously reluctant. "There's no room for nobility in battle, Wayland. You're too soft."

"If I win, you'll leave us be. You'll never look at Sydelle again, or think about her, or try to stop us from going to Provincia," North said.

"If I win," Dorwan said slowly, looking straight at me, "the same terms apply, only I demand the surrender of your talisman as well."

"Fine," North said. "Are we in agreement, then?"

"Don't you request my talisman if you win?" Dorwan asked, seemingly confused.

"Why would I ever want such a piece of rot?" North said. "No, thank you."

Dorwan was silent, pulling a long, thin dagger from its sheath. Its hilt, worn with use, was wrapped with blue string; one long braid of strings, ranging in color from midnight to sky blue, hung down from the hilt.

Dorwan opened his hand, letting the dagger fall on top of North's cloaks. A palpable buzz of energy filled the air, touching my skin with a slight shock. When the sensation finally faded, Dorwan bent to retrieve his talisman.

"I'll let the two of you say good-bye," he said, and turned, walking back into the sunlight.

✳　　✳　　✳

"Great gods," North grumbled as soon as Dorwan was out of our sight. "Oh, bloody fantastic! I hate that rotting misericord, and he knows it!"

I stared at him helplessly.

"The mercygiver?" he clarified. "The dagger? Used by sodding tricksters and sneaks because they can't fight with a real weapon? Great. Oh, bloody great."

"You're worried about . . . the dagger?" I asked incredulously, wondering if I had misunderstood him. He shrugged his shoulders slightly. "Are you insane?" I said. "You just challenged him to a duel! What's gotten into you? We have no time as it is!"

"It was the only way to make sure he stopped chasing us," he said, stooping down to pick up his cloaks. "I didn't see another choice." He shook out the cloaks to clean the dust from them.

"Besides," he continued, "I'm much stronger than he is. He just doesn't know it yet."

"What good is strength if you have no sense?" I asked. I grabbed his forearms. He took the opportunity to wrap the black cloak around us; when it fell away, we were back at the head of the mountain pass.

"No!" I said, turning to run back into the pass. "I won't let you leave me behind, not again!"

"Syd!" he said, catching me in two strides. "Listen to me— you have to get away, all right? Stop!"

"No!" I said. "I won't!"

North gave me a hard shake, forcing me to look him in the eye. "Just for a little while," he said quietly. One of his arms wrapped around me, and his other hand came up to touch my hair. "Until the fight is over."

"What was he talking about?" I asked him. "When he said you took me because you wanted to study me?"

"Because . . . ," he began.

"Don't lie," I warned. "There's something you're not telling me. After hearing you and Pascal, and now Dorwan—"

"You can't believe a word he says, Syd." North pulled away. "He's full of deceit."

"Then why would he want me?" I pressed.

North dropped his bag unceremoniously over my shoulder. "Keep this safe for me, will you?"

"It's not because there's . . . something unnatural about me? About my magic?" I asked.

"There is *nothing* unnatural about you," he said sharply. *"Nothing."*

I nodded.

"Just wish me luck and let me go," he said.

I looked down. "You don't need luck."

He laughed, bringing my hand up to kiss it.

"Try to find a place to hide, or get as far away as you can," he said.

"What about you?" I said.

"I'll find you, as soon as I possibly can," he said, wrapping a loose curl around his finger. "You're a bit hard to miss, you know."

He backed away, pulling his cloak up and leaving me trembling and alone.

* * *

The path we had taken down the mountain wasn't difficult to follow, and the walk back was made easier by the fact that I had left our bags and my loom in the wagon. I was supposed to be with them, of course, but I didn't care what North wanted—I wasn't going to sit there and wait for him to return.

Jinx, my mind whispered.

A terrible boom echoed through the air, and I ran. A blast of wind blew my skirts up around me, and fist-sized rocks began to rain down. My boots threatened to trip me up against the loose rocks and soil, but I kept running. Another loud crash echoed through the pass, ringing out so loudly I thought it would consume me.

Someone screamed—a man's voice, strained and distorted. I saw a cloud of red fire cut through the sunlit opening of the pass, followed by a man shouting, *"Come on, you can do better!"*

I couldn't tell who it belonged to, and that scared me more than anything.

The slope was steep; I fell at one point and scrambled the rest of the way up on my hands and knees. The ground shook with the force of their spells.

The pass had brought me out far above where we had entered with the wagon. I could see the wizards throwing around blasts of fire, light, earth, wind, and ice as if it was the most natural thing in the world. The only source of shelter I could find was a gnarled tree, brown and barren. I was about halfway up the slope from them, but I could hear and see as clearly as if I was beside them.

Dorwan thrust his dagger onto the ground, and a vein of black ice sprang up, solidifying around North's heavy boots. North shattered it easily, kicking free. He didn't hesitate longer than a fraction of a second before he pulled up the red cloak and a line of fire shot through the air. It wrapped around Dorwan, and North yanked the other end, dragging his opponent to his knees.

Dorwan's dagger came up and cut cleanly through the cloak, severing the magic. He frantically patted down his shirt, which was still smoldering from the effects of North's spell.

North swept his hand across his brow, wiping away sweat.

"Don't tell me you're tired already," Dorwan said.

"Not too tired to burn that smirk off your sodding face!" North snarled. His fingers rested on the edges of his cloaks, poised to choose the next one.

"I have all the time in the world," Dorwan said, throwing his talisman up into the air.

Water poured from the sky, knocking both North and me off our feet. The trembling of the ground was more pronounced now; small rocks bounced past me from above, and the dirt shifted beneath my feet. North's next explosion of rock and soil from the ground missed Dorwan completely. I saw Dorwan's sleeve pull back and the horrible lines of scars that ran along his arm.

"What's the matter with you?" Dorwan complained. "You're distracted."

"Shut up and fight!" North growled, shaking his head.

Dorwan thrust his dagger in front of him. A million fragments of ice raced toward North, their tips aimed directly at his chest.

North instantly countered, bringing up his yellow cloak. The icicles hit a wall of wind and air and were pushed back. Dorwan's unmarred eye narrowed at the force of the spell, and his face twisted into what I thought was supposed to be a smile. The scarred skin of his face shone in the sunlight.

There was something graceful about the way North pulled his cloaks up in wide, sweeping circles. If the pace of the fight picked up, he would have only a moment to grasp the colored fabric in his hand, or to wrench it up to shield his face. At first glance, it all seemed effortless.

Dorwan moved fluidly with his dagger, twice shallowly slicing through North's skin. But North still had him—was moments away from finishing it, perhaps. He launched one spell after another, beating Dorwan down to his knees. I watched as Dorwan disappeared into a wall of fire, before pushing himself through, dousing himself with the water of his own spell.

It was then that Dorwan showed what he was truly

capable of. He cast one spell after another in rapid succession, ignoring North's turns and shouts. Clouds of smoke and ice wrapped around North, and Dorwan flashed about, moving so quickly it seemed he was everywhere at once. He followed every spell with a swipe of his dagger, catching North's clothing and skin until blood flew into the air.

One spell after another, and then another—it was too much. A spike of ice shot out of the earth beneath North, knocking him clear off his feet. He lay there, panting and shaking.

"Get up!" I whispered desperately, clutching my necklace. "Get up, get up!"

North pushed himself onto his elbows, and I thought he would take his chance to rally. He shot off a poorly guided blast of ice that Dorwan swatted away with his bare hand, his boot connecting with North's head and sending it back down into the mud.

I couldn't do anything without revealing myself or distracting North even more. My vision blurred with tears, and blood pounded in my head. Control was slipping away from me, and I couldn't stop trembling. North still hadn't gotten up, and now Dorwan knelt beside him.

"This is pathetic, you know," he told North. "I guessed it wouldn't be long before you burned yourself out, little fire."

"Sod . . . off!" North said, lashing out with his arm. Dorwan let it strike him before pushing it away.

"Tsk, tsk." The wizard shook a finger. "Stay down, dog."

My heart was hammering in my chest. It felt as if the world was sliding out from under me.

"That curse of yours . . ." Dorwan paused, dragging his silver dagger against North's chest. North kicked Dorwan with as much strength as he had, and the blade disappeared into North's chest lower than the other wizard had intended.

The cry of agony that escaped North would not be contained—and neither would mine.

Dorwan twisted his wrist, and it sounded to me as if something deep inside of North cracked.

"She did stay around, after all!" Dorwan said, sounding delighted. "I suppose she really did mean it when she said she'd never leave you. This is far better than I could have imagined—so much fun to be had!"

"Stop!" I begged, stumbling down the road to them, tears streaking my cheeks. "Please, I'll do anything, *anything*—just leave him alone!"

Dorwan's dagger pulled clean from North's chest with a sickening gurgle of blood. North raised his arms, warding off another blow.

"Please . . . ," I sobbed.

I fell to my knees beside North, ignoring the rocks that had begun tumbling around us. His tunic was heavy and warm with blood. *This can't be happening,* I thought. *No, Astraea, please!*

"Don't—don't—Syd." There was urgency in his voice. "Calm—calm . . ."

A roar sounded above us, and everything quivered with the force of my fear and desperation. Watching North like this, feeling his blood soaking between my fingers, I felt as if I would burst.

"Great Mother," Dorwan whispered. Not even the scars could hide the shock on his face. "It is true. . . ."

The earth shook, as if a great shock had run straight through its core. A cloud of dust exploded into the air. Then the ground was shaking so hard my teeth chattered, and a river of mud, rocks, and dead trees surged down the mountainside.

"Dorwan," North said over the bellowing landslide. There was no trace of pain or any other emotion in his voice. He waited until the wizard was looking directly at him. "My move."

A burst of fire erupted from North's palm, and he slammed it into Dorwan's face. The other wizard staggered back, screaming.

I felt North's arm come up behind me, pulling me in closer so he could wrap the black cloak around us. I squeezed my eyes shut against the wave of mud that fell over us just as we vanished.

When I reopened them, there was grass beneath my hands instead of rocks and dust.

North pushed me off him none too gently and brought the cloak back up around him. By the time my hands reached for him, there was nothing but empty space to grasp.

✳   ✳   ✳

"North!" I screamed, stumbling to my feet. *"North!"*

I didn't know where I was. I whirled around, looking for a way back to the mountain, or a village that could help me. There was nothing but tall grass and hills, not even the thatched roofs of a little village. But I recognized the area around me; North and I had passed it on our way down the path. Instead of taking me away from the mountain, he had twisted me back up, toward Arcadia.

I began to run back down the mountain—but it wasn't only my footsteps that thundered against the ground.

"Sydelle!" Pascal shouted, drawing his horse up short. His smooth, hairless head glinted with sweat, though the weather was brisk. On his horse, he looked taller than he was in person, more muscular and powerful, and younger as well. There were several young men behind him, all on their own horses.

"North—he—the mountain—the duel!" I gasped for air.

"It's what I was afraid of," Pascal said. "We saw it from Arcadia. Gorman, take her back to Lady Aphra and make sure we have bandages and ointment!"

"I want to go with you!" I said, reaching for his saddle. Pascal looked at me and sighed.

"Where are your things?" he asked.

"I left them in the wagon with James and Peter!" I said. "It doesn't matter! Let me go with you!"

Pascal's mouth was set in a firm line. Turning to two of the young men, he barked, "Spread out and keep your eyes open!"

Pascal hauled me up behind him and wasted no time nudging his horse into a gallop. The tall grass that grew alongside the path whipped our legs, and the wind kicked a cloud of dust into the air. The snow-covered fields disappeared into piles of mud and loose dirt. The deadly combination of the wizards' duel and the avalanche that followed had all but destroyed the mountainside.

"Is this where the duel took place?" Pascal asked.

"He couldn't have twisted far," I said. "There are limitations—"

The boy on our right let out a sharp cry, jerking his reins back so hard the horse nearly threw him. "Here!" he called. "He's here!"

Pascal slid down from his saddle, and I was right behind him.

"North!"

He was facedown, his arms thrown out at a strange angle, as though he had tried to brace himself. I rolled him onto his back, calling his name over and over until my voice was hoarse. Pascal knelt beside me, but I couldn't hear anything over the buzzing in my ears. I pressed both hands against his wound, feeling the sticky warmth of his blood, not caring as it seeped into my dress.

One of the young men pulled my hands away from North,

tending to the wound. It was Pascal who forced me to my feet and took me in his arms, pressing my face against his chest so I wouldn't have to see the deathly pallor that had spread over North's face.

"I'll do what I can here," the boy called, pulling open North's shirt. "We have to get him back to Lady Aphra—he'll be needing some of her elixirs."

I squeezed my eyes shut. *My bags,* I thought. *Why did I leave my bags in the wagon?*

"Why isn't he moving?" one of them asked. "Is he . . . ?"

"No!" Pascal cut in harshly.

"I'm nearly finished." The young man didn't look up from where he was stitching North. "He's lost a lot of blood. I'm not surprised he passed out from the pain."

Pascal told two of the young men, "Get the stretcher and tie it between our horses. We can take it slow and steady."

I watched them lift North as gently as they could onto the stretcher. It sagged beneath his weight, but the thin fabric didn't rip. I helped Pascal with shaking hands as we tied the rope around him, hoping that was enough to keep him still and safe until we made it into Arcadia.

CHAPTER TEN

With North swaying between them, the other horses couldn't keep up with Pascal and me. We continued on the dirt path back up to Arcadia, the harsh wind kicking up loose snow from the valley above us and showering us in a coat of white. Closer now, I was finally able to make out the familiar, snow-laden roofs of Arcadia.

"Aphra!" Pascal called. She was waiting for us in the center of the village, a look of horror on her face.

"Get a bed ready," he told her. "Wayland's going to need it."

Lady Aphra guided me through the crowd and up the hill. "Come along," she murmured, pulling me inside. I looked back, searching for any sign of the other horses. "Rest yourself a bit; you look halfway to death." She went to work at once, pushing the table and chairs to the far end of the room. She went into her bedroom to retrieve the blankets North and I had slept on for the past few days, and I watched, completely numb, as she unrolled them again.

I should help, I thought, but my body refused to move. I sat on the bedding until she came back with a bundle of bandages and rags, as well as water. She set the basin down, and I scrubbed the mud and dust from my skin. I tied my wild hair back into a loose braid, knotting the string so tightly I nearly snapped it.

The door to the cottage slammed open, and Pascal and another man carried North inside the room. The doctor fussed beside them, red in the face and panting hard as they set North's unresponsive body down on the bed. I searched his face for any signs of life or changes in his condition; the moment my hand touched his pale, dirty skin, he let out a horrible moan.

"Away—just—go—no one—!" His voice broke off in a tortured groan. "I don't want you—"

"North," I said. "Can you hear me? Can I get you anything?"

"No!" he yelled. "Nothing—alone!"

"Don't be a fool," Pascal said. "I'll get you a pain and slumber elixir. This is the curse, not just your wound, Wayland! You need to take them!"

"*No!*" North thundered. "I won't . . . I won't take it . . . Make Syd . . . Make her leave!"

"Not on your life, Wayland North," I said sternly. "I'll get you the elixir myself. You're too out of sorts to make a decision like that."

"*I SAID NO!*"

I stood there helplessly as he turned and buried his face in the bed.

"Just go . . . Just go . . . ," he whispered brokenly. "No one . . ."

I felt Aphra's hands on my shoulders, but I shrugged them off.

"All of you," I said, my voice surprisingly clear. "All of you, get out."

"Let me help," Pascal pleaded. North shook his head as if stuck in some fever dream. He didn't want anyone to see him like this, not even his magister.

"I'll need my bag," I said. "I have my own elixirs he might be willing to take."

"I have it," Lady Aphra said, her face pale in the candlelight. "Pascal, come with me."

"And what gives her the right to stay?" he demanded. "She's known him for two months—I've known this boy his entire life!" I had a sudden vision of Pascal's younger self, putting a small, dark-haired boy to bed and staying beside him through long nights of pain. This had been his role. His were the hands that had soothed away the ache and the vulnerability in North.

I took his hands in mine.

"I'll take care of him."

Pascal shook his head. "No, it's not your place."

"It is now," I said firmly.

Aphra took his arm and began to lead him from the room. The door closed gently behind them.

I sat back down on the bed. My lips pressed lightly against the pallid skin of his forehead, brushing his hair back away from his face.

"Syd . . ." His voice shook. "I don't want . . ." It looked as though he would rip the pillow between his hands in two.

"I made more of the pain elixir. Remember how much better you felt after you took it last time? I have some sleeping draft, too." I rubbed my hand along the length of his arm. I nodded to Aphra as she left my bag just inside the door.

"No," he grunted. "I don't want—!" He took in a great breath, holding it in. "You're not allowed to see . . ." A barely contained cry. "Please, please just leave me. . . ."

I felt his body shaking against mine; he was deathly pale, and a thin sheen of sweat spread across his face. He brought his hands up to clench his hair, pulling as hard as he could. A guttural scream escaped his lips.

"North!" I said. "Look at me. I'm right here."

His tortured breathing slowed long enough for me to seize the moment. I pulled him up and slid beneath him. With his head and shoulders resting in my lap, I had better leverage on his arms.

Unfortunately, not his legs. A new flash of pain overcame him, and he kicked wildly. I pulled him farther up against me, wrapping my arms around him. He groped blindly for my hands, squeezing until I thought every bone in them would break.

"Hush . . . shhh . . ."

He turned in my embrace, pressing his face against my shoulder. *"Gods,"* he cried. "Gods, it hurts . . . please . . ." He pressed himself even harder against me, as if struggling to hold on against a bone-crushing current.

I kept talking, stroking his back, running my hands through his hair. I kept a careful eye on the bandage, watching for any new stain of blood. The young man had stitched him up well.

North brought his legs up, curling into a ball. I felt a small dampness seeping through my dress, and I didn't have to look down to know that he could no longer contain his tears. My hand came down to rest lightly against his cheek, wiping away at his clammy skin until it was smooth and dry.

"It hurts . . . ," he said, trying to pull away. "I want it to . . . be over . . . all of it . . ."

"No, you don't," I said, not moving. "You don't mean a word of that, and you know it."

"I feel . . . I can't breathe . . . ," he choked out. *"Gods!"*

I forced him to sit up again; he was shaking beneath my hands. His breath came out in short punctuated gasps, almost as if he was laughing. But I knew he wasn't.

I slipped away long enough to retrieve the small bottles inside my bag. Giving him both the pain elixir and the sleeping draft would put him under for days, I realized, but mixing a portion of each and adding a few leaves of lavender might be just enough.

"Syd?" North called weakly.

"Right here," I said. "Will you take this for me? Please, I promise it'll help."

He turned his head, pressing his lips together until they were a thin, white line.

"For me," I whispered. "Please, take it for me. . . ."

I brought the bottle to his mouth, my hand shaking. Finally, his lips parted, and he swallowed the elixir in slow, steady gulps.

I held him until his tremors ceased and his breathing became slow and heavy. Only then did I untangle myself from his grasp, sliding down to the floor in exhaustion. I leaned against the bedding and finally allowed myself to cry.

Almost as if he had sensed it in his deep slumber, North turned over to face me, our faces so close they were nearly touching.

"*Sydelle . . . ,*" he breathed out, reaching for me.

*   *   *

I carefully mixed a large batch of the sleeping draft. When I was sure I had the right consistency, I set it aside and went to find the others.

"How is he?" Pascal was sitting outside the door, as if

standing guard. Hearing his voice, Aphra appeared from her room and crossed the small hallway.

"Sleeping," I said. "He didn't want to take the elixir."

"I should wring that boy's neck," Pascal said. "Of all the times to refuse it . . ."

I closed my eyes and exhaled deeply. I couldn't banish North's tortured face from my mind's eye.

"I'm going to Provincia," I told them.

"Out of the question," Pascal said firmly. "It's not safe for you to travel alone, especially now with all the men and wizards heading in and out of the capital. Prima Road is dangerous enough without the extra crowds."

"I can take care of myself," I said. "North isn't in any condition to travel. If you're concerned, then you can come with me—if we go by horseback, we should be there just in time."

"Wayland said Owain's gone ahead," Pascal countered. "He can bring the information to the Sorceress Imperial."

"Do you honestly believe they'll take his word for it?" I asked. "North has proof; it's in his notebook. If I can get that into the right person's hands, it'll be far more effective."

"You can drop that mad idea right now," he said. "I won't leave Wayland's side until he's healed, and as for you going out, without any kind of protection—"

"Then give me a sword!"

I was shaking with anger now. To have come all of this way only to have North nearly die because of my own stupidity—I had to do something. All I could see in my mind was Cliffton burning, crumbling, North falling under Dorwan's magic. Everything was coming down around me, and I was powerless.

"Pascal," I begged. *"Please."*

"Don't ask me again," he said in a rough voice. "You'll go when Wayland is up to it."

With that, he pushed past me and forced open the door. He didn't say another word, but I heard the door shut behind me.

I stood, barely able to contain myself. How could he not understand that we didn't have time to waste? Lady Aphra hadn't said a word during the argument, but now she placed a hand on my shoulder.

"Are you willing to be brave?" she asked me in a low voice.

"Of course," I said. "Anything."

She smiled. "I was hoping that would be your answer."

*   *   *

The next morning I was intently studying the little map of Palmarta inside the cover of *Proper Instruction for Young Wizards* when North let out a groan, his eyes blinking open. Pascal had gone out, sent by Lady Aphra to help the men of the village clear the remaining snow. The old man had gone out grumbling but finally gave up his position by North's side.

"Syd," North said. His voice was so weak I had to lean down to hear him. "Where . . . am I?"

"Arcadia," I said. "Pascal and some of the boys carried you back up."

He nodded and swallowed hard.

"Why did you go back?" I asked. "What were you thinking?"

"Wanted to kill him . . . too dangerous," he said, rubbing his face. "He was gone by the time I got back, but I couldn't twist all the way to Arcadia. . . . Pretty embarrassing, huh?"

I let out a weak laugh, and he tried to smile.

"Not at all," I said. "Can I get you something?"

"Water?" he asked. I poured out a glass, and he drank it down greedily, wincing as he pulled his stitches.

"My head feels . . . like it's going to split . . . in two," he said, falling back against the bed. He shut his eyes.

"Why didn't you want an elixir or a sleeping draft?" I asked, resting my hand lightly against his. "I had to force it on you."

North shook his head. He looked so slight on the bed. The dark circles beneath his eyes stood out plainly on his ashen skin. "I'm so sick of it. . . . I can't even stand the taste of honey. It's been a while since the pain was this real."

"North . . . ," I began. "You don't have to keep this from me, not anymore."

"It's an ugly, dark part of me, and . . ." His voice was bitter. "You have no idea how disgusting it is . . . how shameful . . ."

"No part of you is dark or ugly," I said sharply, squeezing his hand. "Not to me, not ever. Do you understand?"

North turned his head away from me, toward the faint light from the window. "I inherited the curse from my father, and he from his father before him," he said. "Do you remember . . . what I told you about the hedges?"

I nodded. "But I thought they were at the outskirts of towns, in the wilderness?"

"My grandfather was a Wizard Guard." He paused. "The king sent him to disband a hedge coven outside of Andover. Most of the wizard knights he brought with him were killed . . ."

"But not him," I finished.

"No, not him. They held him hostage for over a fortnight, and when he finally escaped, it was with this . . . lovely gift."

I ran my hand through his hair, waiting for him to continue.

"It eats away at my magic," he said in a hollow voice. "Rips through my blood and body. When I was younger, I could spend hours practicing magic and only feel the slightest discomfort—but now . . ."

"I know," I said softly.

"The black skin is an indicator of how much of my body has been corrupted by the hedge's curse. I don't understand why it's worse now than before. . . . It's happening *so quickly*. I use less magic now than in the past, but it hardly matters."

"And no one's been able to figure out a cure in all these years?" I asked.

"Hedges are dangerous because they're unrestricted." He was hoarse again, but he refused more water. "They experiment with horrors you can't begin to imagine—curses, killing spells. They're fiercely protective of their knowledge, even from each other."

"Is the hedge who did this still alive?" I said. "Couldn't she reverse this?"

"Dead from all accounts I've heard. Even my father searched for her for a time. From the sound of it, the old hag didn't have an apprentice to pass her secrets to."

I pulled the gloves from his hands, studying his skin with new understanding and a heavy sense of dread. It was important for me to touch him.

"Your hands are so soft." His voice sounded far away. I was losing him to sleep again.

"North, if it hurts you, if it's going to eventually kill you—why do you still practice magic?"

"Because," he said, his eyes drifting shut again, "who am I without it?"

*   *   *

Lady Aphra found me in the same position, perched beside North's bed, hours later. She silently set a bundle of clothes down at the foot of the bed and went out of the room to allow me to change. I had no idea where the brown pants and white shirt had come from; they were certainly nothing Aphra would ever wear.

She was waiting for me in the hallway, hands on her hips.

"Is it enough?" I asked her.

"You need a hat to hide that hair," Aphra said, pulling a knit cap from the hook on the wall. She tucked my hair inside it and pulled it down low on my face. I turned to look in the mirror hanging behind me.

It was dangerous to travel as a woman, but not nearly as dangerous for a young man. As long as I kept to myself, I could make the journey in peace.

"I'll distract Pascal," she said. "You'll need to move quickly. I can't give you one of the horses without his catching on."

I had never ridden a horse on my own before, and I didn't think now was the time to try.

"It's a five-, six-day walk to Provincia from here," I said. "If I leave now, I can still make the two-month deadline, but it'll be close."

"Then you'd better go now," she said, squeezing my arm. "Good luck."

I waited until I heard the door close behind her. My bag and dismantled loom were resting at the foot of North's bed, but what I needed was in his bag, not mine. I felt around the bottles for the small leather notebook and was just about to tuck it into my own when his quiet voice startled me.

"Syd?" I turned, expecting to be pinned in place by his dark eyes. But they were closed, and he whispered my name again as if in a dream. He couldn't be awake. I had given him the strongest sleeping draft I had made in Arcadia.

"I'm right here," I said, touching his arm. His face turned toward the sound of my voice, and it was nearly impossible to swallow the lump in my throat. "I won't leave."

I slipped the silver chain from around my neck, missing its comforting weight the moment it was gone. But North needed Astraea's help far more than I did.

"Protect those who are weak in the world," I whispered, the familiar prayer meaning so much more now than ever before. "Guide those who think themselves lost, for as long as you are above, all paths will be straight and all hearts will be strengthened. . . ."

I pressed the braided circle into his open palm and closed his blackened fingers around it, then picked up my bag and loom.

The lights in the homes still shone out through their windows, but I slipped through the shadows unnoticed. I thought I heard Aphra's voice somewhere behind me, but I didn't turn around. My sights were fixed firmly on Provincia.

The road was dark, but I knew the way.

CHAPTER ELEVEN

I walked through the night, resting an hour at a time in the tall grass until I finally reached the base of a mountain. With the air suddenly much colder and the now recognizable scent of snow in the air, I realized what a mistake it had been to leave North's blanket behind and how hard it was to carry my loom myself.

A hush had fallen over the countryside. I thought of Henry and his father, driving their rickety old cart up the same road I was walking on. I would need to find Owain first, to make sure that he had gotten through to the wizard leaders.

And then, would I find Henry? A week ago, the prospect would have thrilled me no end, but now the thought of seeing him only brought dread. I wasn't sure what I would say to him, but I certainly couldn't tell him about coming to Provincia alone. He wouldn't understand why I had put myself in danger, and if I knew Henry, he wouldn't let me out of his sight again. It would be back to Cliffton and the old way of life, and I wouldn't be able to get in a word of protest.

Somehow, it had come down to a choice between the two, and I wasn't ready to make that decision.

Over the next four days, more men and even a few families began to appear along the road, passing me in long wagon caravans. I tried vainly to keep up with some of the friendly-looking groups, but after nearly four days of walking, my body refused to let me. I had stopped for a moment, just to catch my breath, when someone shouted from behind me.

"Well, whadda we have here? A lad on his own, and with a bag full of food?" an older man asked, his head crowned with gray. Behind him were two stocky boys—his sons, most likely—and behind them was a cart loaded down with bags and weapons. The younger son seemed to be pulling it along single-handedly.

My stomach flipped in panic. I pulled my hat down farther over my head.

"Walk with us fer a bit," one of the sons said. "I'm thinking we're gonna be fast ol' friends."

The father laughed heartily, wrapping an arm around my shoulder. "Came up from Mariton fer the war; gotta help build trenches and the like. You gonna go, too?"

I nodded again, wondering how long I could go without having to say a single word.

"Then we're gonna get there together," the first son said. "Fast friends, it's like I was saying."

We walked in uncomfortable silence, the father never once removing his arm from around my shoulder. *He knows,* I thought, and the fear shredded my insides. *He knows.*

But if that was the truth, he didn't show any other indication of it, and his hands didn't wander anyplace they didn't belong. If anything, he was more interested in sneaking glances into my bag, and it was with a horrible start that I realized the numerous bags weighing down their cart had probably not belonged to them.

I focused my eyes firmly on the wild grass along the road. *Think,* I told myself, *think.* I could run—I was fast when I needed to be—but the father's grip on my shoulder was unyielding, and a small knife had appeared in the younger son's hand. He gave a nod to his brother, who circled back around me. We were slowly moving off the road, onto the grass fields. Another hand touched my bag, began to untie the knots that held it closed—they could have the bag, they just couldn't have North's notebook.

I twisted down and out of the father's grip, but one of the sons still had a tight grip on my bag and wrenched me to my feet. The small knife was back, this time digging into my side.

"Seems like our boy doesn't want to be friends," the father said. He placed a hand on my head, pulling it back to get a better look at my face. "Didn't take you fer a fighter. So what's hiding in that bag?"

I watched the sons out of the corner of my eye as they tossed the books and yarn out of my bag. North's notebook was thrown down carelessly into the dirt, spilling out letters and loose papers. Their hands stilled only when they touched the cool glass of my bottles.

"Drafts?" one asked. "All you gonna give us is drafts?"

"Not just any draft," I said, my mind working fast. "Special drafts—a delivery for the Wizard Guard."

The father's hand relaxed slightly on my hat. If he had pulled it any harder, my hair would have come tumbling out.

"Special draft?"

"I'm a wizard's assistant," I said. "He was hired to create a strengthening potion for the wizards to use in the war."

"Do you take us fer fools?" a son spat. "Only four bottles fer hundreds of wizards?"

"It's so potent you need only a drop or two," I said. "I'm not supposed to even say what I was carrying, it's so powerful!"

A grin flitted across the father's face, and I knew I had him.

"It'll make you unstoppable—invincible—strong enough to lift a horse," I continued. I wasn't scared any longer, but it was easy to feign the same panic I had felt only moments before. "Please—oh, *please,* don't take it! I'll never be able to show my face at home again! My wizard will beat me black and blue if I don't get the draft to the capital!"

"We'll be taking what we want!" the father said, jerking my arm. "Those wizards won't be keeping it for themselves this time. With something like this we could take all the wagons and gold pieces we want."

"And we're gunna want a lot," one of the sons added. "Imagine what would happen if we each took a bottle."

"No!" I yelled. "Don't! Please, *please*!"

I almost laughed when they toasted each other in triumph, tilting the bottles back at the same moment.

"This tastes like—" the younger son mumbled. I held my breath as his knees buckled beneath him and he tumbled to the ground. The other two men collapsed into heavy sleep a moment later, their bodies disappearing into the tall grass. With the amount they drank, they would be dead to the world for at least a day.

I searched through their things, hoping to find something that would be of use. They had bent forks, several knives, an apple core, but only one musty and stained blanket among them. I wasn't about to take anything that smelled of urine and ale.

"Idiots," I mumbled, gathering up everything they had tossed from my bag. I flipped North's notebook open to the front, tucking the loose sheets of paper back inside. He had written his name on the first sheet—the writing was practically illegible and looked as though a child had scribbled out the letters. He probably was a child, I realized as I scanned the first few pages. They were filled with notes on spells and simple elixirs—I laughed at Pascal's angry face, sketched between blocks of messy scrawl and numerous lists of ingredients.

The next few pages were void of even a stray mark of ink. When his writing appeared again, it was small and cramped.

The hedge settlements of Mariton and Andover were cleared. The Guard burned all of their huts and books—lit the women's hair on fire and left them to die. The boy that I spoke to seemed to believe the curse began as a kind of poison and would need the hedge's blood to make any kind of antidote. He agreed to come with me to see if we can't find her together. He knows more about them than I do, than even Father did.

The man at my feet stirred slightly, but it was enough to wake me from my trance and make me close the book. I would have to finish reading later—for now, I had to keep walking.

The road was empty for miles ahead, which was fine with me. I didn't stop until the sky had begun to darken, and I found a small clearing in the grass. The remnants of a fire were encased in a circle of stones, but there was no wood left—no trees or branches or even bushes for miles around me.

I sat down heavily, drawing my knees to my chest. Once I was down for the evening, I knew I wouldn't be able to get back up again. What little bread I had was almost gone after five days of walking. I wasn't even sure of when I had last stopped. Two days ago? Three?

I unlaced my boots, allowing my sore feet some relief against the frozen ground. I had two painful blisters, but they were nothing compared to the ache in my back. Stretched out on the dirt, wrapped tightly in my thin shawl, I tried to sleep.

But hours later, it was clear there would be no rest for me; not while the cold air was trying to overwhelm my body with a thousand stinging needles. I reached for my necklace, only to remember I had left it with North.

I stood, pacing around the clearing, trying to get my blood rushing through my veins again. My feet were clumsy with fatigue, and rubbing my hands and arms did little more than turn them a brighter shade of pink. I needed fire, I thought, squeezing my eyes shut against the night air.

My loom lay in pieces nearby, bright in the moon's strong light. I could do it, I thought, but what would that mean for me? For many years, that loom had been my entire world, my constant companion and source of happiness. But now, the loss of the future was more painful than the past. To do it now, to use the loom in such a horrible way, would mean not having the chance to finish North's cloak, to tie it around his shoulders and see his face.

But nothing would ever be more important than the bundle of North's work in my bag, than bringing it to the capital.

I folded the unfinished cloak and placed it in my bag before turning my attention back to the loom. The wood broke apart with surprising ease, snapping to pieces beneath my weight. I wiped the tears from my cheeks.

This is what I had wanted, wasn't it? To be on my own, to live my own life the way I wanted to, away from my family, from the desert, from everything I had ever known. But I had never taken into account how very alone I would be.

I rubbed two pieces of wood together furiously, as hard as I could for as long as it took—which was nearly an hour. My body came alive, flooding with warmth, but the burning behind my eyes had nothing to do with my effort. I ground the sticks again and again, until sparks finally fell onto the pile of wood like a thousand little stars.

A cloud of white smoke twisted itself up into the sky. The fire ripped through the dry wood, crackling and popping. I collapsed on the ground beside it, my arms aching, and watched the gold and red flames whip against one another.

It was not my first sacrifice, and I knew it would not be my last.

*   *   *

The next morning, the fire had settled down into embers. I scattered them with my foot and left the circle of stones for the next traveler. I felt noticeably lighter as I took to the road again, finally rested enough to continue.

Soon Hertford, the last small village on the way, came into view. It wasn't more than a resting stop, with a few taverns and beds for travelers. From there, it would be a full day on foot and then Provincia.

The village was unremarkable. A thin layer of frost and ice covered the dark stones, forcing me to watch every step I took until I reached the black doors of the nearest tavern.

I stepped inside the warm room—and immediately tried to walk back out.

"*Sydelle.*"

I let out the breath I had been holding, allowing the door to shut behind me. Sitting at the nearest table, his chair turned to face the door, was Wayland North. His arms were crossed over his chest, and his face was set in a furious expression.

"You shouldn't be here," I said. The wizard still looked deathly pale, and there were dark, heavy circles beneath his eyes.

"You're right," he said. "*I* should be in bed in Arcadia, and *you* should be at my side, nursing me back to health!"

"Stop it!" I hissed, taking the open seat at the table. "Don't turn this into a rotting joke!"

"I'm not joking," he said. "How could you be so careless as to go off on your own like that? You know that Dorwan is still out there, wounded or not. What do you think would have happened if he had—if something had—?"

"You were in no condition to travel," I said sharply. "You *still* aren't in any condition to travel! The whole reason we're together is to bring Provincia your report! If you couldn't bring the news, then I was going to do it in your place. I want to stop this war as much as you do—I thought you would understand that."

North's face softened slowly, and he reached across the table and pulled the hat from my head. My hair tumbled down around my face.

"You foolish girl," he muttered, now looking more relieved than angry. "You really are too much."

"I would have made it, you know," I said, pulling a piece of bread from North's plate. "I had everything planned out."

North leaned back in his chair. "You made excellent time for being on foot."

"Why, thank you," I said. "But how in the world did you get here before me? I only stopped a few times along the way."

"A horse!" he said. "I don't know why one wasn't part of your cunning plan."

"If you were on a horse, how long have you been here dawdling?" I asked. "And why did you not see me on the way?"

North suddenly found his gloves to be very interesting. I didn't miss the way his cheeks colored.

"You got lost?" I asked. "North, it's a straight road all the way to Provincia!"

"I might have taken one or two—or four—wrong turns trying to leave Arcadia," he said.

"You're hopeless!" I said with a laugh. "And besides, you shouldn't have been riding with your injuries."

"Yes, but how else was I going to keep up with my beautiful, beautiful darling? A wizard can only twist so far."

I rolled my eyes.

"How did you get away from Pascal?" I asked. "He seemed intent on keeping you in Arcadia until you were completely healed."

"He'll be staying with Aphra for a while," North said.

"He's angry about the entire situation, and I'm sure we'll both be receiving a few scathing letters from him. But for now, he recognizes that Arcadia needs protection, at least until Dorwan's been dealt with."

"There you two are!" The table shook as Owain's massive form sat down across from us. I wasn't sure who was more surprised—North or me. He reached over and took one of the rolls off North's plate and tore it apart with his teeth.

"What are you doing here?" North said.

"I've been skulking around here the past three or four days, waiting for the two of you to show up," Owain said.

"You couldn't wait until we were in the city?"

"That was a rash promise I made," Owain sighed. "They threw me out of the Wizard Command before I had a second to catch my breath. Not interested in the word of mere humans, I suppose. Figured I would wait until you got here to try again."

I cast a sidelong look at North, but he didn't seem surprised.

"We'd better head into the city," he said. "They close the gates at nightfall."

"I've got Vesta and a wagon ready, though I feel bad about making her haul the three of us," Owain said.

"Not to worry," North said. "I've got a horse we can hitch up. It's tacked up around the corner, brown with white spots. Go ahead. We'll catch up in a moment." North nodded in the direction, and the larger man set off.

I had just enough time to change my clothing before Owain came to find us again. North took my bag as we walked out into the daylight. The wagon that Owain had scrounged up was covered with a patched sheet of linen, but the wood of the bed looked distorted and cracked.

North set our bags inside the wagon and turned back toward me expectantly.

"Your book is in my bag," I said. "I didn't lose anything, I swear."

"No . . . I know you wouldn't," he began. "But where's your loom?"

"I had to use the wood for something else," I said, forcing a smile. "It's . . . all right. I don't think I'll have much time to weave in Provincia anyway."

North held my arm; the expression on his face perfectly mirrored the pain in my heart.

I hauled myself up into the back of the wagon. North climbed in stiffly, dropping onto the floor next to me. He took the book from my bag and placed it in his own. But when his hand emerged, there was a small velvet bag resting in it. He extended it toward me, unable to mask the slight flush of color high on his cheeks.

"Open it," he said.

"What is this?" I asked warily. The wagon lurched forward.

"You aren't one for surprises, are you?" asked North, exasperated. "Just open it!"

I gave him one more suspicious look before I untied the drawstring.

The three blue crystals slipped easily from the bag, attached to a small silver chain that coiled in my palm. *A bracelet,* I thought. The round crystals glowed like tiny stars.

"When did you . . . ?" I mumbled. My mind had turned to sap. "I don't . . . Why . . . ?"

North scratched the back of his head, looking away from me.

"Do you like it?" he asked hesitantly. "I've had it for a while, but I was waiting for the right time to give it to you. This isn't the right time, but I'm not sure what's going to happen over the next few days."

"Why are you giving this to me?" I brushed my fingers along the silver chain.

"Partially as an apology," North admitted. He smoothed the hair away from my face. "I know it won't replace your loom, but I swear I'll build you a new one even better than your last."

"This is too nice for me," I protested. "It must have cost you so much. . . ."

"May I?" he asked, opening the clasp. When he fastened it around my wrist, an overwhelming feeling of warmth raced through me.

"Thank you," North said. "You are the only reason I've made it this far."

"That's not true at all," I admonished him. "You probably would have run into much less trouble without me."

"See, that's the funny thing about trouble," he said, grinning. "It tends to find you when you go looking for it, and I'm always in the mood for a little."

Exhausted from the journey, I fell asleep in spite of the constant jarring of the wagon. When I woke again, the sun was setting, and North was sitting up front with Owain.

"I'm glad I almost punched you in the face that night for stealing my ale, lad," Owain was saying. "Lost an ale but gained a friend. I'm sorry I let you down in delivering the message."

"No, it was unfair of me to ask you," North said. "I knew they'd be difficult. I'm sorry."

"Nothing to be sorry about," Owain said. "Think about how unexciting my life would have been without you. No adventures, no dragons, only catching petty thieves here and there to stay afloat."

"Well, we should be there in just a bit," North said. "I can smell the Lyfe from here."

"Have you told her yet?" Owain asked. "Warned her, I mean, about the other wizards?"

North shook his head but said nothing.

"You know, lad," Owain said, snapping the reins, "finding girls as brave as dragons and sweet as flowers ain't so easy anymore. I thought Vesta was the last of them. Clever, generous—"

"Stubborn, *frustrating*," North finished.

"Ah, then, a perfect match," Owain laughed. "She's the only one I've ever seen kick that sorry bottom of yours straight. Promise me you're not going to let her slip away."

North glanced over his shoulder. "I won't."

CHAPTER TWELVE

I don't know what I was expecting of Provincia, but now that I was standing directly in front of its famous walls and four high towers, I was wholly underwhelmed. Even the tallest spires of the castle were smaller than I had imagined.

The city, and the castle within it, sat on a small isle near the shore of the great lake, the Lyfe. A stone bridge stretched over the water, providing the single point of entry aside from the shipping gates. I pulled back the flap of the wagon's cover to see the large wooden ships docked at the famous south gate, but the tents and fires were the first things to catch my attention. There were hundreds, maybe even thousands of tents in every shape and color on the mainland, just out of the lake water's reach. The surrounding forest seemed to have been recently cleared away to accommodate them. I asked Owain what they were doing there.

"It's where they've put the lower-ranked wizards and the humans that were conscripted to help fortify the castle," he said. "The humans will be sent home before the fight begins, whether they like it or not."

The freezing rain started the moment our wagon wheels touched the bridge. We joined an endless line of people making their way into the city, their carts and trunks dragging sullenly behind them.

I leaned between North and Owain, trying to get a better view of what was ahead, as North moved quickly, untying his cloaks and stuffing them inside his bag.

"What are you doing?" I asked, startled.

"I have to be a man in this city," North said as we rolled through the elaborately carved gate. Astraea's stone face watched us impassively from the top of the arch, sending a tremor through me. North kept his head down, but I didn't understand why until one of the guards, an impossibly large man, stopped us.

"Man or wizard?" the guard asked.

"Man," Owain said. "Here to volunteer."

The guard snorted, then turned to North.

"Man, of course," North said. "Harrington Marshall."

The guard gave me an appraising look.

"My *wife*, Sarah," North ground out. The guard merely clucked his tongue in annoyance. Another guard came around the back of the wagon, lifting the flap to look inside. Seeing it was empty save for our bags, he signaled to the guard up front.

"Head in, then." The guard stepped out of the horses' way. "Curfew starts in an hour."

"What was all that about?" I whispered once we were past.

"They would have made me sign the Wizard Registry," North said. "It doesn't matter that I'm unranked. They want to keep track of all the wizards going in and out of the city, and I don't want to alert people to my presence just yet."

We didn't have to fight any crowds once inside, though the rain did seem to be coming down harder than before. I caught my first real glimpse of the royal palace through a heavy downpour.

After the horses were boarded for the night and Owain gave Vesta a very long, tearful promise to return in the morning, North led us to the Good Queen. I was so miserably wet and cold that I didn't bother to see if there were any other taverns to choose from.

It was painfully obvious that there was something wrong with North. He kept his head down during the entire meal and barely spoke.

"Are you going to meet with the Sorceress Imperial tomorrow?" I asked.

"I was hoping to look for her tonight," North said, his finger tapping against his knife. "But tomorrow seems a little more realistic."

"And what about Oliver?" I asked. "He's a member of the Guard, isn't he? Could you talk to him about this?"

North sat perfectly still as the group of men behind him roared over some unheard joke.

"Of course I can talk to him about it," North said, "but I don't particularly enjoy the thought of his laughing in my face."

"In any case, you two will have to manage without me," Owain said. "I'll be down in the undercroft of the castle, helping to secure the gates."

"Lovely," North muttered. "Down there with the rats."

"North," I gasped.

"What are you implying by that, *lad*?" Owain asked severely.

"It's exactly what I told you before," North said, leaning across the table. "The Guard isn't going to look on you as anything but that. You should have stayed out of this like I told you. It might have saved you some loss of pride, at least."

"Don't confuse how folks feel about me with how they feel about you," Owain said. "I'll do everything I can to help protect my country, whether I have to knock in a few wizard skulls or not."

North leaned back in his seat, a dark expression crossing his features. Owain's hand dropped to the hilt of his sword.

"That's enough out of both of you," I said. "It's obvious we need to rest if we're already at the point of drawing blood."

"Fine," North said, pushing back his chair. "I'll go check the availability of rooms—"

The sword thrust down so quickly, I didn't have time to even gasp. The blade cut straight through North's bag, pinning it to the floor.

North fell back into his seat, looking annoyed but unsurprised. The dark-haired man sitting directly behind him, proudly wearing his black leather armor, leaned back in his seat with an infuriating smile on his face.

"I think," he said, "you'd best come with me instead."

North pulled the sword up from the floor, tossing it back to the other man in disgust, and examined his torn bag. "That was *completely* unnecessary!" he said. Owain's hand had returned to his own sword.

"You have a lot of nerve coming here," the other man—wizard—said. "It's unfortunate for you that I know this is the only rathole you stay in."

North clucked his tongue thoughtfully. "So I suppose you're here to arrest me, then, for evading the registry? It's a little sad they've forced you to stoop to this—I'm sure you have *far* more important things to do with your time. Drinking wine with the court, for example, or writing pretty letters. However did you fit me into your day?"

"If you take him, you'll be going through me first," Owain warned. "Don't think I won't break that pretty face of yours."

The wizard favored him with a look of annoyance, but Owain didn't back down.

"I'm here to tell you that the Sorceress Imperial wishes to

speak to you," the wizard said. "Though I have no idea why she continues to waste her time with you."

North chuckled. "Maybe she just likes me better than you, Ollie."

This is Oliver, I thought, the very same one I had been hearing about for so long. His dark hair was perfectly trimmed, and he was shorter and stockier than North. With that uniform and loud voice, he had seemed much older at first glance. But now I saw the way his teeth ground together when North spoke and how his hands were fidgeting with the red fabric braided into the hilt of his sword.

"This routine of yours ceased to be amusing when we were children," Oliver said. "You'll come with me and avoid making a fool out of yourself in front of your kind."

"I'll go with you, but only because I have something to say to her as well," North said. "Owain, will you take Syd upstairs when you're done? I'll be back a bit later."

I opened my mouth to protest, but North was faster.

"Go with Owain," he said to me in a tight voice. "I'll make sure she understands."

I stood, grabbing my bag in defiance. North looked as if he was about to reach across the table and give me a hard shake.

"Lass," Owain said slowly. "The lad will be all right, and we can get a good night's rest."

Oliver was staring right at me, his eyes burning. When he spoke again, his voice was hard and unyielding.

"Bring the girl, too."

✳   ✳   ✳

North refused to look at me as we left the Good Queen, but he took my arm as we stepped out into the dark, emptying streets. His cloaks were once again tied around his neck.

Instead of going through the inner gate of the castle, we made a sharp turn toward another building at the far end of the street. It had been styled in the same ancient way as the castle, with dozens of columns lining its grand entryway.

"I thought she'd be in the castle," North said to Oliver.

"In case it slipped your mind, Wayland, there is a war going on," Oliver said sharply. "While you've been prancing around the countryside, we've been preparing for it."

"I'm trying to feel sorry for you, really, I am," North said. "If you wait just a moment, I'm sure the tears will come."

"Oh, shut up!" Oliver burst out. He started to whirl around but seemed to catch himself. His hands clenched in fists at his side, and he picked up his pace.

Quite the temper, I thought. My eyes drifted down once more to the red hilt of his sword before I glanced at North. "Where are we?" I whispered, gazing up at the statues of Astraea lining the roof of the building.

"The Wizard Command," North said. "The center of operations for all of the world's wizards, including the island nations."

"And the Sorceress Imperial is in charge of all of the wizards?" I asked. I wasn't sure why I had thought her command was limited to the wizards of Palmarta. North simply nodded, his eyes falling to his black boots.

"Listen, I'm sure you know this, but the Wizard Command has always served under the royals as their protectors and servants," North said in a low voice. "But there've always been a few high-ranking wizards who believe that the Command should function independently and be granted full control over military affairs."

"Why are you telling me this?" I asked. Oliver glanced back, as if to make sure we were still following him.

"So you'll understand why this isn't going to be easy," North said. "I think the Sorceress Imperial sees the queen as an easy target. Queen Eglantine is young and inexperienced, and this is the best opportunity the Command has had in years to bully a royal into becoming a puppet, rather than a leader. To shift the balance of power, possibly forever."

"I understand," I said.

"What are you two talking about?" Oliver called. His eyes flicked back and forth between us, and I saw that his left hand was fiddling with the hilt of his sword again.

"About how lovely and wonderful you are, Ollie," North said. Oliver's face colored, and he turned on his heel. I shot North a look, but he only shrugged his shoulders and followed him.

Passing a small crowd of wizards, we came through an elaborately carved entryway of statues and murals. The wizards' heads were bent in serious discussion, but a few glanced up as we passed.

A long line of wizards was waiting in front of a desk set up in the middle of the chamber. Each looked more miserable than the next. Despite the crowd, the wizard at the desk did not appear hurried.

"Your assignment is *ground soldier*. You will report here at dawn every morning for further instructions." The man crossed the name from the list. "Next wizard!"

We walked past the line and continued down the long hall. North tried to keep his face hidden, but I had the sneaking suspicion that we were gathering more and more looks as we proceeded. Oliver seemed to relish it, taking long, confident strides down the marble floor.

How can he have such a high position, I wondered, *and at such a young age?*

"It's a ceremonial position," North replied, and I realized I had spoken aloud. "At eighteen, there's almost no chance he'd be ranked as number two, but he was given it when the Sorceress Imperial appointed him to that position. She's grooming him to succeed her."

After passing a dozen or so doors, we came to a stairwell carpeted in lush, crimson velvet. There was an enormous stained-glass window on the landing, depicting famous wizards throughout the ages. The upstairs hallway was a mixture of portraits and more stained glass, but North and Oliver were walking so quickly that I couldn't stop to examine them.

Another stairwell. There was only one door at the top. Oliver raised his hand and gave a sharp knock.

"Come in, please," called a woman's voice. Oliver opened the door and strode in. When North didn't move, I gently pushed him forward.

"*Now*, Wayland," she said.

North gave me a quick look. "Don't hate me," he said. "I'm nothing like her, I swear. I didn't tell you before, because I didn't want you to think even *worse* of me. She may be my blood, but there's no love lost between us."

"What?" I followed him inside, closing the heavy door behind me. A few scattered candles cast a halo of light around a desk, but otherwise the room was as dark as the night sky. A woman with long, dark hair stood by one of the open windows. She was wearing a stunning robe of dark purple with a mantle of gold over her shoulders. There was a small smile on her face—one that seemed vaguely familiar.

"Well?" she said.

Oliver stood off to the side, smirking.

"Hullo, Mother," said North, looking down at his boots.

*   *   *

"She seems surprised."

I stood rooted to the ground, unable to move even if I had wanted to. The Sorceress Imperial's brow wrinkled into deep creases and she seemed to go into a trance. I flinched away from her hand, my breath caught somewhere in my throat as her warm fingers came up to gently brush my cheek. At the touch, the spell broke. North stepped between us and gave her a disbelieving look. Even Oliver looked surprised.

The woman recovered from her strange daze, and the severity in her eyes quickly returned.

"He told me you were dead," I said.

Oliver let out a short laugh.

"I did not!" North said.

"You said that both your parents had left you, or something!"

"Yes, well, *left* doesn't always mean dead, you see," North said. He turned back to his mother. "Just a misunderstanding."

"In that case." The woman held out her hand. "My name is Hecate Aisling."

"Sydelle Mirabil," I said weakly, shrinking away from her tight grip.

She clucked her tongue at North, walking back around her desk. "I suppose you've come to see if you could fight?"

"I've brought you information to *prevent* the war," North said. "And what's with Aisling? You've forsaken Father's last name?"

"Don't take that tone with me, Wayland," she said. "I've only recently finished reviewing the complaints filed against you by Mr. Genet after that little stunt you pulled in Dellark."

"So is it jail or a written apology this time?" North asked petulantly.

"Was it necessary to '*savagely brutalize*' Genet in your duel?" Hecate asked calmly.

"Well, he was rather annoying," North said, as if that explained everything. "You would have hit him, too."

"Your behavior is shameful and inexcusable," Hecate said. "Yet again you've proven yourself to be more of an animal than a wizard."

I took a step forward, but North's hand stopped me. "This *animal* has brought you information," he said.

He reached into his bag and removed the envelopes tied with yarn from his book. Hecate held out her hand for them, but he threw them on the desk. She shook her head as she ripped the envelopes open, holding the paper close to the light. Oliver tried to read over her shoulder until she waved him away.

"Reuel Dorwan was the one to poison the king. I don't think Auster was involved at all," North said. "It's an old hedge witch poison, not something out of their kingdom. He wrote it and the antidote down for me years ago, when I was traveling with him."

"I suppose you thought this was going to earn you favor?" Oliver asked, disgusted.

"No," North said. "But I would have appreciated a little respect."

"Is that why you brought me this information?" Hecate asked, finally passing the sheets of paper to Oliver.

"I brought it to help convince you that there's no need to fight, and to warn you that dozens of villages like Cliffton have been invaded and set up as camps for Saldorran and Auster armies," North said, placing both hands on her desk and leaning forward. "Though something tells me you couldn't care less."

Oliver let out a bark of laughter. "Dorwan? That loon who was in here, making all kinds of threats after the Guard refused to rank him? That's rich, even for your imagination."

Hecate shook her head. "Are you truly naïve enough to think we'll believe this? That I'll just take your word on the poison? I know you spent time with him when you were younger. He told me that much when I met him, but I sincerely doubt he has the ability to mix that kind of potion. You'll need a better excuse than that."

"The negotiations won't end for another day," North said. "If you tell them it was a mistake and recall the declaration of war—"

"The negotiations never have and never will take place," Oliver said, throwing the papers down on the Sorceress Imperial's desk.

"What are you saying?" North asked.

"The information you brought us, if any of the commanders will believe the word of an *unranked* wizard, will, perhaps, force some of the other countries to consider coming to our aid. But this war will be fought regardless of your hedge rubbish," Hecate said. "Our plans have been in place for weeks now. You are the only one who does not want to see this through at last and rid ourselves of the threat from Auster once and for all."

"And what about the queen?" North said. "What does the queen have to say about your *plans*?"

"The queen needs to sit up in her chambers and mind what I say," Hecate said, "as her husband should have done."

"So you'll let them invade the country," I said, my voice trembling, "and destroy all of the villages, the towns, the homes and families—"

"Control your pet, Wayland," Oliver said. "No one speaks to the Sorceress Imperial in that tone."

"If you must know," Hecate said. "We've already been presented with this information by Cliffton's proxy, who arrived three days ago. He received the same answer you did. There is simply nothing else to discuss on this matter."

"No!" I said. "We didn't come all this way for you to tell us you never intended to seek peace in the first place! What kind of leader purposely sends the people of her country to their deaths? Don't you understand what we went through to give you this information? Can you even imagine what my family has been going through every day since you failed to stop the Salvalites from invading?"

Hecate clucked her tongue, studying me with cold eyes.

"Mirabil, was it?"

I nodded, swallowing hard.

"That's the name of the elder from Cliffton, is it not?"

"He's my father," I said, crossing my arms.

"Have you ever stopped to consider what use Cliffton is to this country?" she asked. "So far west it might as well be in Saldorra—no commerce, nothing but sand. You came here for purely selfish reasons, to save a village whose loss would be a necessary sacrifice."

"That's out of line, even for you," North said coldly. I was too furious to speak. "What will it do to those people when they discover they're considered by the wizards to be nothing more than a wall of bodies, an inconvenience for an enemy army to cut through? Don't you feel any compassion for them at all?"

Hecate's gaze on her son never wavered.

"This is our chance to assert some control over the leadership of this country," she said. "Finally, after years of subservience to human kings, there's a chance for us to exert our own policies."

"Oh? And how do you plan to enforce this policy when the Guard is overwhelmed by Auster?" North asked. "Are you going to send dozens, maybe even hundreds of wizards to their deaths just so you can speak up at the Elder's Council?"

"Better to die than to live under an Auster king!" Oliver shot back. "You don't understand because you have loyalty only to yourself!"

"I have loyalty to the people of Palmarta, and I'm loyal enough not to fight a war to satisfy the greed of the wizard leaders!" North yelled. "What's the matter with you? Magister would be disgusted by what you've become!"

"Take that back!" Oliver shouted, his hand on the hilt of his talisman.

Hecate stood, slamming both hands on the surface of her desk. The two wizards broke apart at once. "Commander Swift, go tell the palace officials that Miss Mirabil and my son will be staying there for the next few nights under my jurisdiction."

"Absolutely not!" both wizards shouted at once.

Hecate pointed toward the door, the air around her heating dangerously with magic. Oliver shot an irate glare in North's direction before storming away and slamming the door behind him. North whirled back around to face his mother, his cloaks billowing out behind him.

"We're leaving the city tonight," North said stubbornly. "I've given you my information. I'd rather go back and defend the *sacrifices* than stay here and watch you get yourselves killed."

North took a step back just as Hecate reached for him.

"Don't," he told her, and her hand fell away. "Just . . . don't."

"You have no choice," she said firmly. "They're closing the gates and restricting access, in order to set up the city's defense. I have other plans for you and your friend."

North didn't say a word—just picked up the wooden chair beside him and threw it against the ground. My lips parted in surprise.

"How very mature of you," Hecate said calmly. She sat down again, folding her hands atop the desk.

"I'm not ranked, so you have no control over my magic," North seethed. "You won't use either of us!"

"You should have thought about that before coming into the city," she said. "If you won't listen to me as the Sorceress Imperial, then you will listen to me as your mother."

"You haven't been my mother in twelve years," North said. "Not since Father died."

She didn't even flinch. "You have no idea how difficult this has been for me, Wayland. This title and position weren't handed to me. I had to fight my way up every single day to bring honor and power back to our family. Funny how living with your magister all those years has caused you to forget that."

"I'm sure Father would love to have seen you like this, destroying the country he cherished to take more power for yourself," North said cruelly. "What a waste—just like it was a waste that he died saving me, correct? Just like I'm a waste, because I haven't been ranked or done anything with my life. Isn't that the real reason you've been fighting so hard to bring honor back to the family?"

"I knew it was a mistake to send you to Pascal," she said, shaking her head. "I shouldn't have honored your father's request. I should have kept you here, where I knew you'd be raised properly."

"We're not staying in the city," North said again.

"You will, or I will throw you *both* in jail," Hecate said. "You won't take a step out of the city with that girl before I send every wizard at my disposal after you."

North looked murderous. "Is that all?"

Hecate sat back down at her desk, picking up a piece of paper. "I expect to see you at the castle tonight for dinner, Wayland. Find Oliver to see where you'll be quartering."

"Yes, Mother," North said mutinously.

He took my hand in a crushing grip and pulled me along after him. I glanced back over my shoulder, unsure if I should say something. I saw Hecate press her hand to her eyes just before North slammed the door shut behind us.

We practically flew down the hallways. I now knew why the wizards around us stopped to stare; it wasn't simply because of our appearance or the anger radiating off North. It was because North was the son of the most powerful wizard in Palmarta. Everyone knew his story—his past, his failures.

Everyone but me.

I let North lead me outside and around the building, through a small back alleyway, and into a small, neglected garden. There were marble benches and statues, but the fountain in the center of the small enclave was dried out and filled with dirt, and the flower beds around us had withered to brown.

He sat down heavily on the nearest bench and finally released my hand. For a moment I was too stunned to do anything other than watch the labored rise and fall of his chest. I wished I could see his face, but it rested in his hands.

"Forgive me," he said through his fingers.

I knelt beside him, gently pulling his hands away. "What's there to forgive?"

"I never should have brought you here," he said. "If I had been thinking clearly, I would have kept you somewhere safe."

"And you think I would have stayed there willingly?" I gave him a look of disbelief.

North shook his head. "Of course not. What was I thinking?"

"I wish you had told me about your mother sooner," I said.

"And what would I have said?" he asked. "Mummy dearest is the Sorceress Imperial, she likes to drag others around by their hair, her husband died as Sorcerer Imperial and left her a powerless widow, and she hasn't talked to me since I refused to be ranked and join the Guard?"

I shook my head. "You were only a little boy when you finished your schooling!"

North made a face. "I wasn't a *little boy.*"

"You were fourteen. She should have supported you, not disowned you!"

I sat back on my heels, studying his face. He wasn't angry anymore, but there was an unmistakable look of grief about him. Resignation, too.

"I didn't want that life," he said. "I didn't want any of this. I hate this city *so much*. Everyone here looks at me and thinks that I'm some sort of pathetic degenerate, that I can't hear them when they talk about how I'll never be my father, not now, not ever. Can you imagine someone with this curse becoming the most powerful wizard? Everyone respected him, everyone mourned his death. I promised him that I would look after her when he was gone, but she won't listen. She can barely even *look* at me."

I rested my hands against his knees, looking up at him. "Then let's leave," I said. "I'll protect Cliffton any way that I can."

"We can't," he said tiredly. "You heard what she said."

"Since when does Wayland North give up?" I asked, grabbing his hands. "There must be a way."

North shook his head. "Syd, I've been in jail before for disobeying her, and it's not something I ever want you to have to imagine, let alone see."

Dread was twisting my insides, wringing them out until there was nothing left but fear.

"You'll be safe," he said. "I won't let anything happen to you."

"I don't care what happens to me," I cried. "I'm worried about you!"

North shook his head again. "Listen to me," he said. "We'll both be all right."

"What about the war—?"

"I won't stop trying," he said. "I won't ever stop."

He ran his fingers along the bracelet he had given me.

"Are you ready?" I asked.

He nodded, his face turned toward the long shadows of the castle.

CHAPTER THIRTEEN

By the time we finally passed through the castle gate, the throngs of people gathered in the courtyard were overwhelming. North took my hand after a moment, when it became clear he might lose me in the crowd. We were heading toward the castle's enormous marble entrance when North caught sight of a familiar face.

"Owain!" he called.

"Made it out of there alive, eh?"

Some heads turned, and several voices leapt to greet him at once. North's face brightened when he realized he was among friends.

"Why is everyone out here?" I asked, standing on my toes.

"The queen went down to address the wizards on the banks," Owain said. "It's her first state outing now that the mourning period for the king's death is over. People are curious to see her."

Another wizard took North's arm. "All that rot aside, tell me straight, North—is what Owain told us true? A wizard poisoned the king?"

"Yes," North said, and a few of the other wizards began to groan and mutter. "Not that it matters. I tried to give the information to Oliver and the Sorceress Imperial, and they practically threw it back in my face."

"What in the seven hells for?" the other wizard demanded.

"They've wanted to fight the war all along, to grab power from the queen," North said, crossing his arms over his chest.

"I don't know who's worse," someone else said. "Our leaders or Auster's."

"The Sorceress Imperial is taking advantage of the situation," said North. "Of the queen and all of the Salvalites."

"I was wondering if it was just a coincidence that they want to invade this year," the first wizard said.

"What do you mean?" I asked.

"This is the year the worshippers of Salvala believe the goddess will return," North explained. "I've read their scripture and so has Hecate. When they 'align the tribes to destroy the heathens,' they're supposed to be granted a 'great weapon' to take the world back from Astraea. That's what Auster is counting on in this dispute: help from its goddess."

I turned toward him, surprised and curious. "Does it really say that?"

Why does it always have to come to this? I wondered. Time and time again the differences between the sister goddesses had been fought in wars, most of them unnecessary. Would the goddesses themselves have wanted that, and would they have kept up their rivalry if they had known how long its consequences would last?

North opened his mouth, only to be cut off by three loud knocks and the great groan of the gate's doors as they were dragged open. An instant hush fell over the crowd. Four guards rode out in front of the ornate white carriage, followed by another four at the rear. The horses were brought to a halt just short of the stairs; Oliver and the Sorceress Imperial seemed to materialize out of thin air, making their way through the courtyard to greet the queen on her return.

Two attendants appeared and announced, "Her Majesty, Queen Eglantine."

My heart was racing with so much excitement I thought it was in danger of leaving my chest. I stood on my toes, leaning forward to catch a better glimpse of the queen. North held out his arm to steady me.

The Sorceress Imperial met a prim-looking man as he came down the marble stairs. He was a lean man, well into middle age, his expression as sharp as the tip of his nose.

"That's Pompey, one of the queen's human advisors,"

Owain whispered to me. "He's the head steward of the castle."

Oliver opened the door to the carriage, offering his arm to the queen.

All girls, at one point or another, have fancy dreams of becoming princesses, but few have the poise and grace required for such a title. Queen Eglantine's enormous, diamond-studded dress didn't weigh her down in the slightest, and it seemed to me that she glided rather than walked, almost floating past the crowds. She held her head impossibly high, and her silky golden hair—so fair it was practically white—shone in long tendrils down her back.

She didn't even glance our way. Her eyes were on the ground as Oliver leaned over to whisper something in her ear. The wizard looked pleased with himself, with the queen's arm tucked beneath his own as he led her along.

At the stairs, she turned around, looking as if she wanted to say something to the crowd. Instead, the Sorceress Imperial took her other arm. She, Oliver, and the queen spoke in low voices as they began their ascent, turning only at the top of the staircase to look back over the crowd.

"Ah, it seems that you've been noticed, lad," Owain said.

He nodded toward the stairs. Oliver and the queen were both staring in our direction, heads bent together. Oliver was speaking into her ear—I didn't miss the way his hand rested intimately on top of hers—but the queen said nothing. She nodded, her face tense. Pompey stood nearby.

North muttered something under his breath and kept his eyes down until the queen at last entered the castle and the crowds began to disperse.

"I'm heading back to the inn," Owain said. "You folks coming?"

North shook his head, nodding at Pompey.

"I believe that's our minder for the evening," North said. The man's eyes widened in recognition, and he waved us forward.

"Good luck with that," Owain said, clapping North on the shoulder. "Come find me tomorrow, and we'll have a chat."

The steward reached us just as Owain disappeared into the sea of men and wizards.

"Pompey," North greeted him.

"It's been so long, Mr. North! Your mother has asked me to escort you to your chambers, but I'm sure you remember the way."

"Remember the way?" I repeated, looking up at him.

"I lived here before going to train with Magister Pascal, remember?"

I could have strangled him. "Yet another thing you conveniently forgot to mention?"

He tucked a stray curl behind my ear. "I know this castle inside and out."

"Are there any other secrets I should know about?" I asked. "Cousins? Secret rooms?"

He leaned in, grinning mischievously. "None of those," he said. "But there is a tapestry room—*and* a weaving room."

"Will you take me?" I was begging, but I didn't even care.

He laughed again. "I'm afraid if I take you, you'll never want to leave."

"You're right—"

"Sydelle?"

I turned around slowly. North's hand came up to rest protectively on my back.

"Sydelle? Is that you?" Even in the darkness I could make out the familiar shape of his face. My heart dropped into my stomach.

"Henry!" I said, walking toward him in a daze. He flung his arms around my neck, laughing. "Are you all right—have you heard anything from home?"

He hugged me so tightly he actually lifted me from the ground, then we held each other at arm's length. I tried to match my smile to his grin, but I felt like I could scarcely breathe.

"One question at a time!" he said, laughing.

"Is everyone well, at least?" I asked. "How are your brothers? What about my parents?"

"Everyone is right as rain," Henry said. "And speaking of rain—"

"Syd!" North barked. I turned around, startled by his tone. He and Pompey were still standing where I had left them, both looking cross. I turned back to Henry apologetically.

"I'll come find you later, all right?" I said.

"All right," he agreed, smiling. "I'm holding you to that."

I nodded, but my own smile slid slowly down my face upon seeing the wizard's eyes turned away from me, back to the ground.

*   *   *

Hecate made sure that North and I were in rooms on opposite ends of the castle. I wanted to protest being so far away from him, but after what had happened with Henry, North wasn't in any mood to speak to me. Pompey brought us to the second level of the castle, where North would be staying. The wizard didn't acknowledge either of us as he strode into his chamber and slammed the door shut behind him.

"Still has that bad attitude, I see," Pompey sighed. "Well, come on, then. We still have a ways to walk."

My room was located somewhere on the fourth level, in the west wing. Pompey chattered about this and that as we climbed staircase after staircase, but I kept to myself. My insides were still in such a jumble after seeing Henry that I tossed and turned in the ornate bed. If that hadn't kept me up, trying to fall asleep in an actual bed might have. I hadn't realized how accustomed I'd become to sleeping on the hard ground until I had a pillow under my head.

*   *   *

The next day, North seemed to disappear completely. He needed to find Owain, his mother needed to speak with him again—a hundred excuses for why I couldn't stay with him. He said good-bye at breakfast, leaving the insufferable Pompey to act as my minder and tour guide for the day. It was a blessing in a way—I wasn't sure I wanted to see him or Henry, not until I could sort out my thoughts.

"And *here*," Pompey said, throwing both arms above his head. "This ceiling was constructed in the last years of the Golden Age. Do you know how you can tell, Miss Mirabil?"

"It's made of gold?" I answered dryly, adjusting the strap of my bag. I had brought it with me in the hope that I could find a loom to finish North's cloak, but Pompey had other plans.

"Very good!" he said cheerfully. "Would you like to see the armory?"

"Actually," I said, a new thought striking me. "Would you mind showing me the tapestry room?"

Pompey gave me a strange look. "Why would you ever want to go there?"

"Humor me," I said sourly. He gave me another curious look; he'd been given orders to watch me, not appease me, but the chance to launch into another long, tedious history lesson was simply too great for him to pass up. He took my arm again and we ducked down a different hall, his uniform looking especially smart next to my simple brown dress.

The door was locked, and it took several minutes for

Pompey to flip through his enormous ring of keys to find the right one. Even then, the iron key was hard to twist, and the lock stubborn. It took both of us to pull the door open, and we were rewarded with an explosion of dust for our efforts.

"The tapestry room"—Pompey coughed—"hasn't been viewed frequently over the years."

I frowned, taking in the bleak scent of mold, never a good sign where fabrics were concerned. The room was virtually black—both from dirt and lack of light. Pompey fumbled his way through the darkness, pulling the heavy draperies away from the windows one by one.

Each burst of light hit the opposite wall to reveal a new scene, a new moment in history perfectly captured in thread and time. There were battles and coronations, wizards and kings. The very first tapestry depicted Astraea blessing the holy grounds of the capital. The red and gold thread used to create her long, flowing hair had been caked over with dust. My hand came up to touch my own hair.

"There we are!" he said. "Just needs a spot of cleaning."

I placed my fingertips lightly on the landscape of faded colors. The tapestries had suffered serious neglect over the years, and several faces had been eaten away by bugs and moisture. "You'll need to be careful," I warned. "They're quite old, and you wouldn't want to ruin them."

Pompey waved me off. "We'll just have new ones commissioned."

I whirled toward him. "But these are part of our history—they were created by the master weavers of the kingdom!"

"Yes, well." He pushed his finger through one of many holes. "They haven't held up very well, now, have they? And anyway . . ."

The midafternoon bell rang, drowning out the rest of his words. He drew out his gold watch.

"Oh, dear, time for tea!" He moved toward the door.

"Will you take me to the room that they do the weaving in?" I asked.

Pompey hesitated. He had far more pressing things to attend to, I was sure, than looking after a troublesome nobody.

"All right— hurry up, then."

I nodded, letting out a deep breath as he led me back into the darkened halls of the castle.

The weaving room wasn't truly a weaving room, after all—rather, it was merely a workroom, bustling with women washing, dyeing, and sewing. It was cramped and humid, and all ten of the women working there were red-faced and sweating. A woman with thick, dark hair and a severe expression met us at the door. Her apron was stained with Palmarta's dark purple, as was the skin of her hands.

"A new worker?"

"Just a visitor," Pompey clarified. "You'll behave yourself, won't you? I'll return later to show you back to your room."

The woman studied me, her hands on her hips. "Not many would choose to visit the washrooms on a grand tour of the castle."

"I asked to see the weaving rooms," I said, looking around for any sign of a loom.

The woman's face immediately softened. "We used to do a lot of weaving on the big looms, but the king began to import tapestries and cloth from other countries."

"That's terrible," I said.

"Are you a weaver, miss?"

"Sydelle," I said. "And yes, since I was a little girl."

"I'm Serena," she said, holding out her stained hands. "If you promise not to tell, I'll show you where we hid a few of the frame looms. It seemed like such a waste just to throw them out with the rubbish."

In the back of the chamber was a small closet, and inside, stacked against each other, were two frame looms—much larger, nicer versions of my old one.

"May I borrow one?" I asked. "I'll keep it down here, and I promise I won't tell anyone. I just have to finish something; I won't forgive myself if I don't."

Serena looked startled, but she helped me string the cloak onto the loom, showing me how to adjust its frame.

When we were finished, she stepped back and called a few of the women over to see it as well.

"This is excellent work. I'm surprised it held up so well for how many times you said you took it off the loom." Serena leaned in to examine the dragon's scales. "Are you making this for someone?"

"Yes," I said. "I should have finished it by now, though."

"You must care for this person a lot to make him something so beautiful." Serena looked at me knowingly.

"Well," I said, trying to stop the color from rushing into my cheeks. "He deserves it."

They left me to return to their own work. I worked on the cloak for an hour, adding Arcadia's hills to the scene I was depicting. Weaving put me in a peaceful mood, but it also gave me time to think about the events of the day before, to wonder what use the Sorceress Imperial would have for us. North had been so furious, violent even—and that worried me more than anything. The problem of Henry was nothing compared to what was going on around us. I would meet him later, but first I needed to find North.

Without waiting for Pompey's return, I said good night to the women, telling them I would be back the next morning. I cast one final look at the cloak before escaping into the cool, damp air of the castle. Every passageway and staircase looked exactly the same to me in the darkness of evening. Though it took me far longer than I had hoped, I did eventually make my way to the east wing of the castle, to North's room.

I started up the last worn staircase just as an argument spilled out into the corridor above me.

". . . have no sense!" Oliver, the Sorceress Imperial, and

North stood a little ways down the hall. I stayed where I was, listening.

"Stop right there, Wayland," Oliver warned. "I won't have you speak such treason."

"Let's go inside," Hecate said. "This isn't a conversation for the castle's many ears."

"As if that really—" The door to North's room creaked as it pulled open and shut, the voices disappearing. I traced their path down the hallway, straining my ears.

I stood close, my ear pressed against the wooden door, and listened.

". . . will you do when the city is destroyed?" North asked.

"If we keep Auster in the Serpentine Channel, it won't even come to that," Oliver said.

"Fine, but even if you hold them there, what will you do about Saldorra marching from the west?" North said. "Dividing the Wizard Guard is a terrible idea—you won't have anyone left here to defend the city, especially if Dorwan takes it upon himself to pay the queen a visit."

"If you believe that, then why won't you stay and fight?" Oliver demanded. "You criticize our methods of leadership, and yet you won't lift a hand to aid us?"

"I did help you. I brought you everything you needed to stop this war," North said, "but it obviously meant nothing coming from a dirty, unranked vagrant."

"Wayland," Hecate said, her voice hard. "Now is the time for you to come back, don't you see? Everything will be forgiven."

"No!" North said. "I didn't come back here for you, or for this life. How many times do I have to tell you that?"

"You're doing your father a great dishonor," she said severely.

"As far as I'm concerned, I'm the only one doing his memory justice," North shot back. "He would have done everything in his power to deal peacefully with this threat."

"Really, Wayland?" Oliver asked, sneering. "Auster is no more of a threat to the people of Palmarta than the girl you've brought here."

I tensed, my heart giving a strange lurch.

"She has nothing to do with this," North said.

"Don't think we didn't realize what she was the moment we both saw her," Oliver said. "Other wizards may not be powerful enough to sense it, but unfortunately for you, we are."

"Oh, how foolish of me," North said. "How could I *ever* forget how very powerful you are, Ollie?"

"You know what we've done with her kind in the past," Hecate said. "I thought at first that you were bringing her to me to use in the war. That kind of power would devastate Auster's armies."

"Sorry to ruin your plans," North said, "but I've been sorting out the threads of her magic since the first day I met her. It's not as simple as you would think. She radiates magic, yes, but all the different kinds are knotted together, so she can't necessarily control the effect she'll have on the world. I've closed off most of her ability to use it, willingly or not. She's no danger or use to you, not anymore."

My mind, or at least the portion that wasn't slowly spinning it all together, was telling me to stop listening. To turn and walk back down the stairwell, to leave before I learned the full truth.

"All you've done is repress her magic," Hecate said. "A single wizard can't strip that type of power, Wayland. She's not like us. She doesn't just channel magic; she creates it—*is it*. You must understand why the Guard has handled things the way they did in the past. The jinxes were detected and put to death before the age of seven, when their magic would have manifested.

"Does she even know?" Hecate continued. "Does she know what she is, or have you kept that from her, too?"

"She doesn't," North said. "And I'll skin the both of you alive if you tell her."

Oliver laughed. "Oh, this is too good! The dumb thing follows you around like a lovesick puppy, and she's never put it together?"

I cringed, shrinking away until Hecate's voice caught me and held me there.

"That's unfair, Oliver," she said. "How could she possibly know? Most wizards wouldn't recognize the magic, let alone a human. I'm assuming that's what the duel with Genet was about? And the quake that followed?"

"I had to fight," North's voice was strained. "She releases so much magic into the world that it draws other magic to her, and there hasn't been a wizard who's been able to resist it."

"I felt I had to touch her," Hecate said. "Even with the bracelet, I could still sense it, weakened as it was."

"Yes, and I noticed how well you resisted it, Mother."

"You touch her all the time," Oliver snapped. "It's disgusting how little restraint *you* have."

"Because I want to, not because I feel compelled to! There is a difference!"

"Wayland," Hecate said. "I'll use her, or I'll end her life—either way, she will not leave this city until I've made my decision."

North was practically pleading now. "Magister helped me create a lock. I've been strengthening it over the past few days, making sure that no one else can sense her power. It's contained completely. She's not any danger to Provincia!"

I could hear Hecate's sharp breath, even through the thick wood. "That is highly unsafe, Wayland! If the lock breaks, all of the repressed magic will spill out—who knows what disaster that would create!"

"She's created very few disasters," North said sharply. "A drought, a quake, a storm, and a landslide—that's *it*. And the only reason they came about was because she was upset!"

"So she stubs a toe and creates a whirlwind?" Oliver said scathingly. "Tell me how that isn't unnatural or dangerous?"

"That's not—!" North began fiercely.

"The truth is, my son, that you were irresponsible in taking this on," Hecate said severely. "You don't know what kind of destruction she's capable of—no one does! How many have died or lost their homes and possessions in the towns you've passed through? Do you even know if the magic you're using on her is causing her pain? Will repressing her magic kill her? Or, worse, kill you?"

I couldn't breathe. My vision had blurred, and my throat constricted. This couldn't be real—whoever that girl was, she wasn't me.

"I don't—" North tried again.

"Exactly, you don't. You're no less of a child than she is, full of pride. You never stopped to consider her once in all of this!"

"Of course he wouldn't have," Oliver said. "I know very little about jinxes, but I do know the legend. Their blood heals all kinds of things, doesn't it? Especially curses."

"Did you try it?" Hecate asked eagerly. "Did you see if her blood would help with your curse?"

There was a very long silence, and then, faintly, "Yes."

I flung myself away from the door, scorched by my own foolishness. Pascal and North talking in Arcadia—the bloody handkerchief he never let me wash. The tears that dripped down my cheeks burned; every part of my body felt as if it was on fire. I couldn't get away fast enough.

"The amount of blood I would need to cure the curse would kill her."

I stumbled down the steps, trying to control my thoughts long enough to find the way out of the castle—out of Provincia—as far away as I could get.

Why me? It all made sense, as if the final piece of the riddle had fallen into place. Every piece had been right in front of me, but I had trusted North too much to put them together. I had to find a way out, to get away from the wizards—away from what they would do to me and what I could do to them.

I continued downstairs, and when my steps finally slowed, I didn't know where I was. Surrounding me was a sea of white pillars, no doubt supporting the castle above. Everything was dark and still, save for the steady drip of water. Somewhere along the way I must have taken a wrong turn. I would have to retrace my steps to find my own way out. Unless there were side passages that led to the shipyard.

No sooner had I taken another step than there was a sharp tug on my arm. I looked down past my shoulder, expecting to find a gloved hand, but there was only air and nothing else. I moved forward again, but something kept me there with an invisible grip on my wrist. I tried wrenching my arm free. Every other part of my body could move, but it was as though an invisible rope had chained me to the nearest wall.

I took a step back and my bracelet made a light tinkling sound as my arm fell limply to my side. My bracelet, which seemed to glow unnaturally in the torchlight. My bracelet, which I cherished.

My bracelet, which had been given to me by North.

I sagged against the nearest pillar. I stared at the silver chain, the three perfect stones—so beautiful that they might not have been of this world—and touched it gently. There was no clasp to undo the chain around my wrist. I turned it around, searching. I had never noticed, because before that moment, I hadn't thought to take it off.

It was too small to pull off over my hand, and the chain was too strong to simply break. The more I pulled, the warmer it seemed to become. I finally recognized the presence of magic for what it was and began to cry. Really cry, from deep inside my chest, the sobs clawing their way out. And when that wasn't enough, when I felt like I would be crushed by the weight of it all, I looked at the dripping ceiling and let out a silent scream.

What else did this bracelet do? Why had he given it to me—why had I just accepted it, without another thought?

"How . . . stupid," I sobbed. I pressed my hands to my face. *How incredibly* stupid *you are, Sydelle.*

CHAPTER FOURTEEN

I waited for the dark to settle in before moving again. My knees hurt from hugging them tightly to my chest, but I had been on the cold, wet floor for so long that every other part of me was numb. Even the ache in my heart had lessened from a stabbing pain to a dull, heavy throb.

I stood unsteadily, looking around. The smoldering torches lit the water at my feet, showing me the path out. There was another stone archway at the opposite end of the chamber that looked as if it led into another room—perhaps even a passage to the outside. If I could escape the invisible chain holding me back, I would have a good chance of finding a way to leave the castle. It seemed a better idea than going through the same door by which I had come in. Less chance of running into someone.

I went forward tentatively, bracing myself for a sharp yank

back . . . but there was no resistance at all. I took a step, and then another, and another.

I was free from whatever had been holding me back before. I moved quickly, so much more lightly than a moment earlier, splashing through the dirty water toward the other archway. *I can do this,* I thought. *I'm going to be fine. I will be alone, but I will be fine.*

"Syd?"

The voice that echoed through the chamber was laced with incredulity and relief. My body lurched to a halt. With that single word, my heart suddenly constricted, the blissful nothingness gone. All I could feel was hurt, and then, suddenly, a hot flash of anger that raced down my spine and curled my toes.

"Did you get lost down here?" he asked, laughing. "I've been looking for you all day! Come on, we've missed dinner."

I couldn't turn around—I wouldn't. I was one of Mr. Monticelli's little glass animals, teetering at the very edge of a shelf, waiting to fall and smash into a thousand pieces. I took a deep, calming breath and continued walking.

"Where are you going?" North called.

I walked faster, feeling the first burn of tears. Unfortunately, North was walking faster, too. His long strides overtook mine in a moment, and he blocked my path with a look of annoyance. When his hands reached out to touch me, to stop me, I shattered, like one of the glass animals.

"Don't touch me!" I yelled. "Don't look at me, don't talk to me—just *leave me alone*!" I pushed him away with all my strength. North stumbled back a few paces, but recovered quickly and seized my shoulders before I could fight back.

"What's wrong?" he asked. "Did something happen? Did someone hurt you?"

I struggled to pull out of his grip, fighting the urge to scream. "I think you know *exactly* what you did."

"I left because of that other man!" North said. "I don't know why you had to hang all over him like that."

I shook my head in disbelief. "I don't believe you."

"If that's not it, then what?" North cried.

"Explain to me again," I said, "why it was that you chose me."

Even in the faint light I could see the color drain from North's face.

"I told you," he began weakly. "I needed an assistant."

"So it wasn't because you wanted to study me?" I asked, unable to stop the tears from filling my eyes.

"What are you—?"

"It wasn't because I was a *jinx*," I repeated, "and you wanted to use my blood?"

North's hands released me. He opened and closed his mouth wordlessly.

"You really had me, you know." I took a step back. "I wouldn't have believed it if I hadn't heard the words come out of your own mouth."

"What did you hear?" he demanded.

"I heard everything!" I cried. "You want my blood? You want a *fresh* sample? Isn't that what Pascal said? Then take it if you want it so badly!"

He stared at me, horrified, but unable to deny any of it.

As I turned to go, he grabbed my arm and spun me back around. I tried to pull free, but he held me in a crushing grip.

"Don't you dare walk away from me," he shouted. "Not after everything!"

"Everything? Everything was a lie!" I said. "You said you came to Cliffton to give us rain, but it was because you sensed me, wasn't it? All I ever wanted from you was the truth, and you couldn't even give me that!"

"I'm sorry," he said desperately. "I never meant to hurt you. I needed to try, to see if there was any hope left for me. I didn't want to bring you here, Syd. I didn't want to even try to break the curse anymore. After you ran away, all I wanted to do was take care of you, *I swear*."

I would have given him my blood, I would have given him anything, if he had ever *asked*. All I could do was shake my head.

His grip on my arm tightened as he hauled me closer. For a single, stupid instant I thought he might try to kiss me. Instead, he simply pinned me there, staring into my eyes.

"All of those people, North," I said. "All of those homes and families . . . How could you take me to those cities, knowing that I could destroy them?"

"If I had told you that you were the cause of those storms, would it have made it any better?" he asked. "Would it have lessened your hurt or guilt? How do you feel now, knowing that you inadvertently caused your entire village to suffer for years? I never wanted you to feel that kind of pain."

"But it's still my fault, if I hadn't—"

"If you hadn't been born?" North said. "Syd, there was nothing you could have done about this! It is *not your fault*, and it has never been. Your powers, like the power of all magic users, manifested themselves when you were around seven years old. I believe those new powers fed into and worsened the dry conditions that already existed, so instead of a quake or storm, a drought occurred. You didn't ask for it or even recognize it."

"You should have told me from the beginning!" I pressed my hands to my face, taking in a shuddering breath. People had *died* because of that drought. My parents, my grand-parents, my friends—all of my loved ones had suffered from constant hunger and fear that they'd be forced to leave their homes. And why? Because I had been born with this curse, because I was that random anomaly in nature. Just by exist-ing, I had caused them to suffer.

I felt like throwing up more than anything. Leaning for-ward, I braced myself against one of the pillars.

"How did I do it?" I demanded. "What did I do to cause all those horrible things to happen?"

"It's . . . complicated," he said. "You have a kind of web

of magic around you. You let off magic, rather than channel it for use. Before I was able to find a way to restrain
it, your presence disrupted the natural balance of magic in
the world, and when you were angry or upset, you let off
more magic than usual, and it would set off a storm or a
quake."

I shook my head. "Is that the real reason why all of the
jinxes have been killed in the past? Tell me, if it hadn't been
for your curse, if you hadn't needed a cure, would you have
killed me when you realized what I was?"

"Syd, no!" he said, taking my arm again. "How could you
think that?"

"I don't know what to think!" I said. "I trusted you! If
you had told me this before, I would have known to control
my emotions, but instead you kept it secret, so you could do
your little tests with my blood—"

I caught a movement out of the corner of my eye, a flash
of dark purple in the pillars behind us. North must have
seen it, too, because it broke his concentration long enough
for me to pull away.

"Is someone there?" North called angrily. His only reply
was his own voice, echoing back to him. For a moment we
stood there staring at each other, breathing heavily.

"And this bracelet?" I asked, feeling stronger now that I
was away from him. "What does it really do?"

North took a deep breath. "It suppresses your magic so
that other wizards aren't able to detect it."

"What else?" I demanded. His eyes fell to the ground, as if he couldn't bear to look at me.

"I put a spell on the bracelet to tie you to me. You won't be able to go more than a certain distance away from me."

"So I'm your slave after all, then? Only now you've added the chain."

"That's not true!" he said sharply. "I put it on you so you couldn't be carried away or hurt by another wizard!"

"Which makes me nothing more than your property," I said. "Property you don't want anyone else to use before you can."

"Is that really your opinion of me? Do you think I'm some kind of monster, that that's the only way I think about you?"

"No, but you think *I'm* a monster," I said. "To be toyed with and manipulated. How dare you treat me this way? You're no better than Dorwan!"

Even as the words left my mouth, I regretted them. North took a step back, his face hardening into fury.

"You're cruel, Sydelle," he said, his voice a whisper.

"I'm *right*," I said. I held out my arm, the bracelet a symbol of his betrayal. "Take it off."

"No," he said. "Never."

There was a part of me that realized he was right, that by taking it off I would be opening myself up to the possibility of hurting someone else when my magic got out of control, especially as upset as I was. Still, I felt as if the bracelet was on fire, and I couldn't get it off my arm fast enough. That was all I wanted, to be rid of any signs that he had been in my life.

I pulled my hand back to slap him, but he caught my wrist and pushed me back against the closest pillar.

"Let me go!" I cried, landing a hard blow to his gut.

"Not until you've calmed down!" he said desperately. "Sydelle, please listen!"

A third voice joined ours.

"Let that girl go immediately!" Pompey stepped out from the shadows. His lush purple robe billowed out behind him as he strode toward us. "I said, release her!"

"This is none of your business, Pompey," North snarled. "I didn't realize you made rounds down in the undercroft."

"And I didn't realize you were both a vagrant and a brute," Pompey said. "Release her now, North, or I'll have the queen throw you in the dungeons for all eternity. Do you think you'll ever see her then?"

North's grip faltered, and I wrenched myself free.

"Come with me," Pompey said softly. I walked stiffly over to him, taking his offered arm with an overwhelming sense of relief.

"Syd!" North choked out. "Don't!" I felt his fingertips brush my back as Pompey and I turned to go.

"Stay where you are!" Pompey barked. "I'll be back to deal with you later, but in the meantime you will not speak to or touch this girl again!" His narrow face looked down on me with concern.

"The queen sent me to find you," he said by way of explanation. "You don't have to worry—you're safe now."

I nodded, and Pompey led me out of the undercroft, ignoring North's furious yells.

"Sydelle! SYDELLE!"

✻   ✻   ✻

Pompey brought me not to my own room, but to the queen's
wing of the castle.

"Where are we going?" I asked. "Why—?"

"The queen has requested your presence this evening."

"The queen?" I echoed. "Please, not now—"

"She wishes to converse with you. She's expressed interest
in hearing your story."

At any other time, the prospect of speaking to the queen
of Palmarta would have filled me with excitement. Now, I felt
hollow. My cheeks were still hot and flushed from my tears,
and my throat was so raw I could barely breathe. How could
I face the devastatingly beautiful queen now?

"Miss Mirabil," Pompey said sharply. "I don't think I need
to tell you that it is very improper to turn down a personal
invitation from the queen."

"Please . . . ," I said weakly, but it was too late. Pompey
held my arm a little too tightly as he escorted me down the
hallway.

The four guards outside the queen's chamber parted as

we approached. Pompey knocked twice, and a high, feminine voice replied, "Enter!"

The first thing that caught my eyes in the airy space wasn't the bright tapestry, nor the intricately painted wall and ceiling panels, but a table of four ladies playing a game of cards, one of them the young queen, wearing her crown.

Pompey cleared his throat loudly. The other ladies ceased their conversation, turning to stare at us with great interest.

"Oh, you're here! How wonderful!" the queen cried, her voice high and girlish. She came toward us at once, her long yellow dress flowing out behind her. "You look positively dreadful—is everything all right?"

"Fine, now," I managed to squeeze out. I held out my hand, but she only stared at it. I pulled it back and tucked it in my skirt.

"Your Majesty, may I present Miss Sydelle Mirabil," Pompey said. I curtsied clumsily, keeping my eyes low to the ground.

This close to her, I could see just how truly flawless she was, her eyes a shade of blue so brilliant that it seemed almost unnatural. She was smooth lines and pale skin all over. She watched me, never once betraying what she was thinking. I curtsied again, unsure of what she expected of me.

"I've waited a very long time to meet you, Miss Sydelle," she said. "May I call you Sydelle?"

"Of course," I mumbled, looking down. I had never been given the chance to go away to a fancy finishing school. There was a schoolhouse in Cliffton, a one-room building that boys and girls shared. We had learned how to read and write and do arithmetic, but I certainly hadn't learned how to set a table correctly or speak another language. There were only two or three years' difference between the queen and me in age, but the confidence with which she held herself made her seem much older than me.

I felt like I was six years old again, cheeks stained with dust and scabs on my knees. The slightest movement made me feel boorish and clumsy.

"Well, Sydelle," she began pleasantly, "I'm so very glad to make your acquaintance. I've heard rumors that you had quite the adventure coming here."

"Your Majesty." Pompey bowed. "May I take my leave to inspect the Wizard Guard's progress?"

"Would you mind getting Oliver for me?" Queen Eglantine said. "I have a question I'd like to ask him."

"Of course, Your Majesty." Pompey bowed again and shut the door silently behind him.

We took a turn about the room, arriving back at the table of ladies.

"Leave," Queen Eglantine said brusquely. The ladies-in-waiting stood, curtsied, and practically flew from the room.

"Now, Sydelle," she said with a smile. "Please sit down. Would you like to play a game?"

I balked, wringing my hands until they were bright red.

"I'm very sorry," I said after a moment, "but I don't know how to play cards."

"Don't know how to play!" she repeated, looking astonished. "Where are you from?"

"Cliffton," I said. What had my mother said? Not to look your elders directly in the eye? I tried to straighten my spine and keep my eyes trained on the beautiful carpet, but I was so tired that it didn't seem worth it.

"Oh, that pretty little shipping town in the south!" she exclaimed.

"Actually, it's out west," I said, hesitating. Even before I saw the brief flash of annoyance on her face, I knew it wasn't proper to correct her. Her smile quickly recovered, at least.

"Right, of course." Queen Eglantine waved her hand dismissively. "There are so many cities and villages that it's easy to confuse them. Are you homesick? You look a touch sallow."

"A little," I said, bringing a hand to my cheek.

"I'm homesick all the time," she said. "I'm not from Provincia, you know, and I'd much rather move the capital to Estoria, or at least build another palace there."

I nodded.

"Did you get a chance to see Estoria while you were traveling? We have such lovely shopping markets and flower fields there."

I shook my head.

"You're not very talkative, Sydelle," she said a bit sourly. "You haven't told me anything about yourself yet!"

"Well . . . ," I began slowly. "I'm from Cliffton. . . ."

"Yes, we've already established that," she said. I bristled slightly.

"Do you know what's going on right now in Cliffton?" I asked. "In all of the western villages? They've been overrun by Auster's ally."

"Yes, I'm aware, but I didn't realize that your village was one of those affected," she said. "There's a plan in place to protect them now. I promise no harm will come to your family and friends."

"Thank you," I said.

"Now, what else? What other exciting things have you done? I feel very sorry for you that you've had to put up with that scoundrel for so long, but I'm sure *something* exciting happened!"

"Nothing terribly exciting," I lied. "Just a few duels."

"Duels!" Her eyes lit up. "I love duels!"

She reached across the table and eagerly took my hand again. "Tell me, were they for your hand? You're a precious little thing—it must have been so romantic!"

"Not really," I said, swallowing my first touches of anger. "It was actually quite terrifying."

"That wizard's not very powerful at all, is he?" the queen mused, resting her chin in her free hand. "I'm glad he's down where he can't bother us anymore. Pompey will throw him into the dungeons."

"How did you—?" I began. Pompey had brought me

directly to her chambers—how could she have learned what had happened already?

"No matter, Sydelle. It will all work out." The queen squeezed my hand, a slight smile on her face. "Now, I couldn't help but notice that pretty little charm bracelet you have on. Where did you get it?"

"It was a—" Now that I knew the truth, the word was hard to get out. "It was a gift."

"Oh, how delightful!" the queen clasped her hands together. "Someone had very good taste to give you that."

"I'm sure you have much nicer things," I said.

"May I try it on?" she asked. "I'm sure it'll fit. I have delicate little wrists."

My heart leapt to my throat, and my body felt heavy and frozen all at once. I shook my head.

"I can't take it off," I said lamely. "I'm very sorry. There's no clasp."

"No clasp?" she said. Her long hair fell over her shoulder and into her lap like a golden river. "However did you get it on, then?"

"It was put on using magic," I said.

At that moment, someone knocked on the door to her chambers.

"If it was put on using magic, it can be taken off by magic," the queen said. "Come in, Oliver!"

My mind raced with possibilities. With the bracelet off, I could find a way out of the castle; I wouldn't be tied to North any longer.

"Yes, Your Majesty?" Oliver asked. He crossed the room, eyeing me warily.

"Sydelle can't get her bracelet off," she said, flashing her big eyes at him. "You'll take it off so I can try it on, won't you?"

"Of course," he said, favoring her with a confident smile.

I held out my wrist to him, looking away so I wouldn't have to see the three blue stones and everything they had represented. It was just a piece of jewelry, nothing more.

Nothing more.

The moment he touched the chain, Oliver knew. Perhaps he sensed the magic woven into it, or maybe he could tell just by looking at my down-turned face. But he knew. I felt his fingers still against my skin.

"I'm sorry, I can't," he said, pulling his hand away. "There's no clasp."

The queen let out an annoyed sigh. "Of course there's no clasp. She just told me it was put on by magic. So take it off using magic."

"Yes," I said, through gritted teeth. "Take it off."

"I really don't think I should . . . ," he tried, catching my eye. For the first time, he was looking at me with something other than disdain. The mask he wore as the commander of the Guard was ripped away, and standing before me was nothing more than a horrified young man.

"Take it *off*, Oliver." The queen came up to his side, sliding her small pale hand down the length of his arm.

I felt him stiffen, his fingers poised to pull the chain apart. He closed his eyes and let out a harsh breath. There was an audible snap as the chain fell away onto the floor. I half expected a blast of emotions or a frightful storm to suddenly erupt and consume us all, but all I felt was a deathly calm as my connection with North was cut.

"Thank you, Oliver," Queen Eglantine said. Oliver had turned his face away, his eyes still closed as if he couldn't bear to witness what he had just done. "You are excused. Send Pompey in on your way out. He should be waiting outside."

Oliver's head snapped back toward us, caught between her tense smile and the bracelet on the floor.

"What are you—?"

"Good-bye, Commander Swift," the queen said.

He turned away from us, looking back at me urgently as he left the chamber. It wasn't until we heard the door to her sitting room open and close that the young queen broke the silence.

"Now," she said, stepping on the bracelet as if it wasn't there. "You'll have to confirm something for me. I've recently heard a very nasty little rumor."

My body lost feeling entirely.

"Pompey mentioned to me that he overheard a conversation between the Sorceress Imperial and her son, and do you know what he told me? He told me that you have the ability to destroy a kingdom."

"No!" I whispered in horror. "No, that's not true—I would never—no, Your Majesty!"

She folded her hands together. "I don't claim to understand magic very well, but I do know that kind of power is a
useful persuasion tool, not only for Auster's king, but also for
the Sorceress Imperial."

"What?" I whispered. "No, you don't understand. I can't
control it. I don't understand how it works."

"Don't be afraid, you silly girl," she said. "I don't mean to
kill you. The king of Auster contacted me privately just this
morning, asking me if I had a visitor with your features. He
said if I was willing to send you to him, he would cease his
pursuit of my crown and withdraw from the war entirely."

"You're trading me for peace?" I asked.

"Yes, in a way," Queen Eglantine said. "I'm also sending
the king the means to his own destruction. Once you're in
Auster, your powers will reduce it to rubble."

"No!" I cried. "I told you I can't control it!"

"Precisely," she said. "The king has no idea what he's
asked for."

I felt the weight of Pompey's hands as they came down
hard on my shoulders. My back collided with his chest, and I
knew I was trapped.

"You're in charge now," said the queen, looking at Pompey.

"Thank you, Your Majesty," he said. "I have taken care of
everything. The boat is waiting and will leave for Auster as
soon as she's on it."

"No!" I cried, struggling against his unyielding grip. The
queen crossed the room to one of the wall panels. I watched

in horror as she undid a hidden latch and pulled it open, revealing a perfect escape route. Pompey pushed me into the cramped passageway ahead of him. I didn't even realize I was screaming until the captain delivered a harsh backhanded slap and covered my mouth with his leather glove.

"Forgive me, Sydelle," I heard the queen call from behind us. "But I will do what I must."

*　　*　　*

The passage narrowed as we went farther down. I never gave up trying to fight Pompey, even as my limbs tired and he grew agitated enough to throw me against a wall.

The long, winding path came to an abrupt end at another, larger underground passage. Moments later, thin strips of moonlight guided us out of the complete blackness of the tunnel into cold, wet air.

In front of us was what had to be the South Gate. Beyond the imposing, black iron gate were the outlines of trading ships, trapped after the city was sealed off for war. They bobbed helplessly against the angry waters of the lake, which rose and spilled through the gate and into our small water-way. The only other path to take led deeper under the castle.

"Are you there?" Pompey called gruffly. I looked up at him in fear, his hand still over my lips.

From a dark fissure in the castle's stone wall came the shape of three large men. They approached us cautiously, silently. They wore simple clothing, nothing like the silk robes I had expected to see. Their skin was a touch darker than that of Palmarta's natives. They had twisted the strands of their long, black hair so that each braid resembled a snake.

I lashed out at Pompey in one last, desperate attempt to escape, but his grip across my chest increased until I thought he would crush me alive.

"This is the girl?" one asked.

"It is," Pompey confirmed. "Do you have the papers?"

The men laughed, the sound carrying through the passage.

"What papers?" the first one asked.

"The treaty the king promised to sign!" Pompey growled. "I need to see the proof before I give her to you!"

"On behalf of our great king, we thank you for your assistance. Regrettably, we have to rescind our gracious offer," the man said. "After all, this land now rightfully belongs to our king."

Pompey let out an enraged snarl, throwing me behind him. I screamed and stumbled back, looking up just in time to see him forced to his knees as he fought, growling and spitting like a rabid dog. I turned to run, but I wasn't fast enough. One of the men had me by the throat.

"You cannot be going back on your word! I know all about your ways!" Pompey yelled. "Your people see it as the highest dishonor to break an oath!"

"Then you are in for a sorry surprise," the leader said, pulling out a small dagger.

The man raised his arm in a wide, graceful sweep. I watched from the ground, too stunned to move.

I remember the sight and sound of the blood from Pompey's throat as it splattered against the cold stone at our feet, the horrible gurgle of his last breaths, and the way his eyes went wide at the impossibility of it all. I remember how the passage caught and echoed the terrible laughter of the men as they came closer.

But more than anything else, I remember the briefest flash of North's hurt face in my mind and the way I cried out for him as the darkness finally swallowed me, too.

CHAPTER FIFTEEN

I slept a very long time.

We crossed the channel to a strange continent. I saw none of it. All the while I slept, waking only for dry, stale bread and a bitter draft that tasted of rotten fruit. No sooner did the liquid touch my tongue than I returned to that place of dreams, of shimmering tall grass, soon to be covered by snow. To the sounds of children in the valley, the warmth of North as we sat close together. The feeling of his hand as it closed over mine.

*   *   *

A touch of warmth against my cheek. My eyes blinked open, to be met by the heart-shaped face of a little old woman.

"Time to eat, love," she said. She padded quietly across the room to retrieve a plate. I shook my head when she brought it back. I felt sick to my stomach.

I touched the fabric against my skin. Someone had dressed me in a sleeping gown of red silk. And there was more silk strung up around the room, from wall to wall, the different colors and shapes running together. My eyelids stayed open only long enough to see the little woman's kind face.

"Where . . . ?" I breathed out, unable to finish.

"You are finally home," she whispered into my ear. "We've been waiting so long for you to come."

*   *   *

The old woman woke me from my nightmares. She held my head in her lap, brushing and combing my hair away from my face. Mostly, she told me nonsensical things, hushed me when I tried to speak.

In the early light of one morning, I heard her voice across the room, whispering urgently.

"—must make that demon lift his magic. She hasn't eaten in days, and I fear—"

"He said that she would wake long enough to eat. Are you telling me you can't get her to, Beatrice?" The man's voice was deep and strong. I saw him through a thin veil of lashes; he was dressed in deep red robes, with a head of graying black hair. The silver crown was worn low on his head. He looked like a god of war.

"She won't stay awake long enough!" the woman said. "I'm afraid she'll die if you don't right this."

I tried pushing myself away from them, toward the wall. My arms felt as though they were full of sand. They flopped about helplessly, twisting in ways that would have hurt had I not been so numbed by sleep. *Poison,* I thought. *I've been poisoned....*

I made a distressed noise, squeezing my eyes shut. Beatrice was at my side, pressing her warm hands against my face.

"Please, Your Majesty!" she cried. "Please."

I saw his face as he knelt beside me, studying me closely. I blinked, fighting desperately to keep my eyes open.

"Salvala," he said, the name of the goddess falling from his lips like a prayer. "This humble and obedient king welcomes you to your kingdom."

*   *   *

I found North in the small garden. The flowers and green sinews of life that he had brought back with his magic lay scattered around him, burning.

"I did it," he said. His back was to me, but he always could find me. "I ruined it all."

"North," I cried, wrapping my arms around him from behind. "I'm sorry, I'm so, so sorry."

"Syd," he whispered. "You need to wake up."

"No," I said. "I won't leave you."

"Sydelle." His voice was louder, suddenly not his own. "I said *wake up*!"

I glanced up, feeling his form shift and change in my arms. He glanced back over his shoulder at me, a low laugh rising in his chest.

I was looking not at North, but at the mutilated face of Reuel Dorwan.

*　　*　　*

I sat up with a scream, kicking and thrashing at the sheets. My sleeping gown was wet with sweat. A nightmare. *Please, Astraea,* I thought, pressing my face into my hands. *Just let it be a nightmare.*

"It's lovely to see you again, too, Sydelle."

Dorwan sat across from the bed, in the chair usually occupied by Beatrice. If he hadn't been wearing that rotting pale coat, I might have taken him for a stranger. As the burns from his duel with North healed, the skin of his face had been pulled back, giving him a perpetual sneer.

Beatrice was nowhere in sight. I tried to pull myself off the bed to escape him, but I got no farther than the edge. I didn't have the strength.

"I don't advise that," he said. "You've been asleep for nearly a week. Your body needs to wake itself up.

"I had to keep you asleep," he continued. "We couldn't have you getting upset enough to cause another quake, could we?"

"What . . . are . . . ?" The words scratched my throat. The wizard handed me a glass of water from the nightstand, but I turned away from it.

"Come now, Sydelle," he said. "No poison this time. Wizard's honor."

I accepted the glass and downed its contents in one large gulp, though a part of me wished it were poison.

"That's better," he said.

I turned my head away again, looking around the small room. The fire crackled and hissed, but I could still feel the coldness radiating from Dorwan.

"Do you know where you are?" he asked.

"In hell?"

Dorwan let out a burst of laughter. "Close. You're in Auster. The king's summer palace on the coast."

"If I'm in Auster, what are *you* doing here?"

"I'm just a messenger," he said, "who brought wonderful news to the king." Dorwan inched closer to me, and I drew my knees up to my chest for protection. "Tell me, Sydelle, do you know anything about Auster's faith?"

I took a deep breath, humoring him. "They believe that Salvala's gift of the sword to man was better than Astraea's gift of magic."

"And they expect their goddess to return and reclaim the throne of the heavens," Dorwan finished.

"What does this have to do with me?" I asked.

"It has everything to do with you, and that's why finding

you was so delightful," he said. "When poison and duels didn't work, I had to figure out a different way to take you from Wayland. He wasn't ever going to let you go unless I put a sea—or a lake—between the two of you. Luckily for me, I caught the king's ear, and he was willing to listen to the word of a wizard."

"What did you tell these people?"

Dorwan's face pulled back into another uneven smirk. "That I had found his goddess, of course. Their legends said that one of their most hated enemies would bring her to them. There are a lot of strange similarities between the two of you: a beautiful girl with the ability to control the magic of the world, to harness the power of storms and other terrible calamities. Crimson hair and a vengeful temper, too, of course."

"You lied to them?" I said. "What will they do to you when they discover I'm not a goddess?"

"They won't ever know," Dorwan hissed. His eyes narrowed, and the splotchy pink of his scarred skin went white with anger. "Because if the king were to find out, he would kill us both—rather horribly, I'm afraid—and then move on to slaughter everyone in Palmarta."

"They'll just use me!" I said. "*I'll* be the one to kill everyone! Don't you have any kind of loyalty—to Palmarta, to the other wizards? They'll be the first to die in the war!"

"Settle yourself," he said dismissively. "I have far more self-preservation than that. My plan all along has been to use you against them. When the other wizards are dead, I'll have your blood for myself. I'll be the only wizard, too powerful for any human army to stop."

I moved away from him. "I may be a jinx, but at least I'm not a heartless snake!"

Instead of being incensed, Dorwan's mouth parted in surprise. It was only for a moment, but his one good eye widened with wonder.

"He told you, then? Finally told you?"

"I figured it out myself," I said.

Dorwan let out a laugh. "It really is a sad story, you know. I think he did mean to save you from all of this. He needed you most of all, but now he'll never see you again."

"Leave me alone!" I couldn't get my voice above a whisper.

"Don't cry, Sydelle," he said with a mocking smile. "You're finally home."

I squeezed my eyes shut, willing myself to wake up from this nightmare, too.

✳   ✳   ✳

I pretended to sleep through the rest of the day, opening my eyes only to reassure Beatrice that I was still alive. The moment she left the room, I swung my legs out from beneath the covers and stood on weak legs. The dark red silk of the sleeping gown they had dressed me in felt like scales against my skin. Red—I *hated* red.

My favorite color, North had said. The memory was enough to stop me for a moment.

I rummaged through the small wardrobe and chest at the foot of the bed; my dress was nowhere to be found and neither were my shoes. There was only a single brown cloak—the old woman's, which meant that she would be back soon. I would have only so much time to find a way out.

I had seen flashes of the guards outside my door when Dorwan finally left. I wouldn't make it a step past the threshold without being stopped. The only option was the small window that Beatrice had left ajar. I stuck my head outside, taking in the faint salty scent of the afternoon air. From this height, I could see the blue line of the Serpentine Channel, but also the hundreds of feet I could fall into the gardens below.

There was a small ledge below the window, not even a foot wide, but it looked stable enough to support me. It was enough.

I wrapped the woman's cloak around me, pulling the hood over my hair. The window was tight around my body. I sucked in my stomach to get through, twisting so I could hold on as my bare feet found the ledge.

"Just go." I took in one last deep breath. "*Go*, just go."

I pressed my body against the cold stone, keeping my eyes focused ahead and not on the distance between my feet and the ground. There was nothing for my hands to hold on to until I reached the next window ledge.

It didn't get any easier, and I couldn't see any way to climb down to the windows a dozen feet below. There was one last window, and then the wall of the castle came to an end.

The room was empty, as far as I could tell, and the window was closed. I hit it once, twice with my fist, but it wasn't until the third and fourth time that the latch unhooked itself and the window swung open into the room.

I didn't waste another second after I made it through. My arms and legs were still shaking with the strain of my climb, but I pushed myself away from the window and pulled up my hood. I waited by the door, listening for the sound of footsteps, then slipped out into the hallway.

I was surprised to find bright, lush carpet beneath my feet instead of the dank stones of Provincia's castle. The walls of the palace weren't stone, either—not even plaster. They had been plated with perfect uniform blocks of gold.

I found a staircase, probably one used by the servants, and held my breath as I ran down the steps. When my bare foot touched the bottom step, I forced myself to slow. The hallway was well lit and free of rodents and filth. Two women dressed in blue silk walked past me, jolting my arm.

"Terribly sorry, ma'am," one of the women whispered, bowing her head. "Pardon me."

I nodded in return, trying not to panic. I had wanted to avoid any contact with the Austerans, not only for my safety but for theirs as well. I wasn't sure what I was capable of anymore.

I followed the women down what had to be the servant's hall toward a wall of sunlight. Outside, the steps down the side of the palace were lined by lush green gardens, each tree and bush molded into a distinct shape. The women talked of little things like their families or the meal they had been asked to make. At the bottom of the steps, they turned and waved good-bye to each other.

"Excuse me," I called.

The dark-haired woman walked over to me. "Is there something I may help you with?"

"How . . . how can I get down to the channel?" I whispered. She didn't look like any devil—if anything, she looked like my mother.

"Oh," she said, surprised. "It's a bit of a walk. If you plan on going somewhere, you'll have to ask about a boat in the center of town. I'm headed that way, if you'd like some company."

"It's all right," I began weakly.

"It's no trouble at all," she said, folding my arm under her own. After a moment she lowered her voice and said, "Are you in some kind of peril, dear? What happened to your shoes?"

"I prefer to go without them," I said, my mouth dry. I reached up to pull the hood farther over my face.

"You and my son both," she said, and led me down the steps of the palace. "Don't worry, my dear. Whatever the trouble is, you'll be perfectly safe with me."

*   *   *

We entered the small village through the shaded marketplace. I kept my eyes on the knotted lengths of silk that covered the stands of flowers, vegetables, and fruit. The tiered, round roofs of the buildings were visible through small patches where no silk had been tied. Instead of the uneven stone surfaces of Palmarta's cities, stones that were covered with years of moss and dirt, the buildings were smooth, clean, and soft to the touch. Even the stone path beneath our feet was white-washed. If I hadn't been in the world of my enemies, if I hadn't passed a statue of Salvala the sword bearer, I might have thought it beautiful. Now all I felt was the creeping of unease across my skin. I reached for the necklace that wasn't there.

The woman, Elema, waved to several of the vendors and bent to stop an apple from rolling away from a cart. She threw it back, smiling at the man who caught it.

"I'm going to introduce you to my brother-in-law," she said. "He has a fishing boat and is one of the few who has obtained permission to sail in the channel during the war prepara-tions."

I shook my head. "You've already done enough for me."

"Nonsense," she said. "You know the Word as well as I do—life in the service of others. We're all here to help one another."

I knew those as Astraea's words, not the violent, blood-thirsty Salvala's.

"I don't have any money to pay for passage," I said as she brought us down another road, wide enough for us to slip past two horse-drawn carts. Elema greeted both drivers.

"That's perfectly fine," she said. "We don't have much use for money in these parts. If you can trade something or some kind of service, you should be just fine."

I felt my face relax into a smile. With all the sordid history of wars between our countries, I hadn't expected the peace of that village to soothe me into something that resembled calm.

"Here we are," Elema said when we reached a long line of doors in the white walls. She opened the closest door and pulled me inside.

The stew over the hearth smelled sweet, like apples, and I found myself taking a step toward it, even as I noticed the man standing beside it.

"Evening, Elema," he said. "Sallie's gone out for a bit. Can't believe she actually trusted me to watch dinner."

"I can't believe it, either, after the stew fiasco of last week," Elema said, embracing him. "I've brought a guest with me. I hope you don't mind."

"Course not," he said, and bowed in my direction. "My name is Ben Crom."

"I'm Sydelle," I said. Maybe I shouldn't have been that honest—Elema gave a little start when I said my name.

"That's a beautiful name," she said. "One we don't often hear around here. Are you from Palmarta?"

I looked back and forth between their faces.

"My father was from Fairwell. He had a sister with that name," Elema said. "I thought you looked awfully nervous! Is that why you still have your hood up?"

"I'm sorry," I said, taking a step back toward the door. "I'm sorry, I'll go—"

"None of that," Ben said. "No one in this town would harm you. Many have come from Palmarta, and many have left for it. Is that why you've come to see me?"

I nodded, keeping my eyes on my bare toes. "I was brought here against my will."

"And without your shoes, it seems," Ben said with a small laugh. "Elema, Sallie should have an extra pair for Sydelle to use."

The other woman smiled and disappeared up the small stairway.

"Come here," Ben said, motioning me closer to the hearth. "That's better—a bit warmer, eh? Am I to understand that you're trying to return to Palmarta?"

"If possible," I said. "I don't have much to offer—I can sew and weave, even mix elixirs . . . but they're wizard elixirs."

"Probably won't need those, then," he said, inclining his head toward Salvala's symbol on the wall. "I have to tell you that it might be a few days before I can take you anywhere. We have very limited opportunities to go out into the channel. The only reason I'm allowed is to bring food to the soldiers stationed on the boats out there."

"Are you allowed to go near Palmarta's coast at all?" I asked. Elema returned a moment later with a pair of green silk slippers.

"Unfortunately not, but I think you might be in luck," Ben said. "Ewald Amert is bringing grain down the channel to the soldiers in the southern part of Saldorra. Is that close enough to Palmarta?"

"That would be perfect," I said. "The only luck I've had in months."

"Listen, Sydelle," Ben said. His face lost his easy smile. "I think we both know how dangerous your country will be in a matter of weeks. Are you sure you wouldn't rather stay here, where you'd be safe?"

"Nowhere is really safe," I said. "It would be better if I went. I can find my way home from Saldorra."

But I couldn't go home—I couldn't go anywhere I would put people in danger. I didn't have the same insane thoughts the queen had about destroying Auster. I didn't want to hurt *anyone*, not if I could help it, but I didn't know where I could go so as not to be a menace to others. There wasn't any order or sense left for me, just the realization that everything was different. An unnameable feeling welled up from deep inside of me and stole the breath in my lungs.

"Ewald's going tonight or tomorrow, isn't he?" Elema asked after a moment. "I'll watch supper if you take her over to speak with him now."

"Of course," Ben said. "Let me get my cloak and we'll go."

I gave Elema a grateful smile, and she squeezed my arm reassuringly.

"I never thought—" I searched for the right words. "I don't know if there's any way that I can thank you for what you've done."

"You know how these things come around," Elema said. "All good favors are returned in the end."

"Ready, Sydelle?" Ben asked as he fastened his cloak around his neck. "The markets are busy this time of day, so stay by my side."

The markets were far more crowded than they had been earlier. I trailed behind Ben as we fought our way down the street. He drew me forward, passing out apologies to those we brushed by. As we approached the end of the street, the simple silk shirts and dresses of the Austerans gave way to the deep crimson of soldiers' uniforms. They marched down the street, knocking on doors and stopping every other person to question them.

Ben kept his face impassive and the line of his lips hard. If he suspected I was behind the sudden flow of soldiers into the town, he never suggested it.

"Are we—?" I began, but no sooner had the words left my lips than I was pulled back.

"A good attempt," said a familiar voice behind me. "But how could you be so cruel as to leave your people, my Great Lady?"

Dorwan's pale face was ghostly against the sea of blood-red uniforms. He stepped forward, throwing back my hood. The noise in the market died away.

Ben's face disappeared as the ring of crimson soldiers closed in around me, a shield against the sudden outcry of prayer and song. Hands reached out to touch my face, my hair, my arms.

No, I thought, squeezing my eyes, *no . . .*

"It's a beautiful thing, is it not?" Dorwan said, close to my ear. "To be worshipped and feared?"

CHAPTER SIXTEEN

I was returned to the same room as before. The old woman was there waiting for me, kneeling beside my empty bed. She formally introduced herself to me as Beatrice Hostenham, my humble and obedient servant, and I instantly regretted taking her cloak.

"I'm sorry for the way you've been handled, my Great Lady. I begged the king to awaken you, but he refused for so long—oh, please, please spare us."

I stared at her helplessly. "I would never harm you."

"When you left, we all feared it was because you were displeased," she said. "But I knew you would never abandon us, not ever."

I said nothing as she gently guided me behind the room's dressing screen. Her dark hair was marred by thick strands of gray, pulled back into a tidy bun. She was wearing a red dress, embroidered with golden snakes.

"There's to be a formal welcoming ceremony for you," she said, tugging my gown over my head. "Don't worry, my Great Lady; only our kind may enter the great hall. We did not mean to offend you with the presence of an Astraean, but the wizard was part of the legend of your retrieval."

"Yes," I said, seizing the chance. "Please keep him away from me."

"As you wish, so it will be," Beatrice said. She took the discarded clothes away, leaving me shivering and huddled behind the screen. A moment later she returned with a pile of folded silk robes. She unfolded a heavy gown. This one was the same shade of red as her own dress, crimson as blood, with the same golden snakes lining the hems. It was a beautiful piece of work, but I wanted nothing more than to rip it off my shoulders and throw it into the fire.

"I'll do your hair now, my Great Lady," she said, taking my arm.

"Please stop calling me that," I said, distressed. "Just call me Sydelle."

"As you wish, Great Lady Sydelle," Beatrice said, placing the chair in the middle of the room. "Please sit; I have much work to do."

Beatrice began by wetting my hair. I started to tell her what a terrible idea it was even to attempt to restrain it, but she actually began to hum over my protests. I lost track of the time I sat there, suffering silently, as the old woman pulled all the curls and kinks from my hair, leaving it perfectly smooth.

I brought my hand up to touch it, wondering what sort of miracle she had performed.

"You have beautiful hair," Beatrice said. "No one in Auster shares your color. The Book spoke of many signs, including your hair. 'Tresses the shade of my fiery spite,' it said."

I wanted to scream.

She twisted half of it up, pinning it in place with little golden clasps and flowers. The rest was left down, much longer than I remembered it being. Beatrice finished by sliding a golden diadem through my hair, allowing the long red veil attached to it to flow down the length of my back to the floor below.

There was a looking glass beside my bed, but I couldn't bring myself to look.

"It really is you," Beatrice said. "My Great Lady, thank you. You have given me the highest honor in allowing me to care for you."

"No," I said. "Please, don't thank me."

She bowed in front of me again and held out her arm. "The king has asked this humble and obedient servant to accompany you to the great hall."

I took a deep breath and closed my eyes. I was no goddess, but for my life, and for all the lives I had left behind in Palmarta, I could at least pretend to be. And maybe . . . maybe there was a way I could twist the impossible situation to my advantage. Dorwan thought himself exceptionally clever, but he had neglected to include my will in his plan.

"What's going to happen to me?" I whispered.

"You will be celebrated and loved," Beatrice said, not realizing I hadn't been speaking to her at all.

*   *   *

Beatrice brought me past the servants and commoners who lined the pathways to the great hall. I was led through pristine corridors, every stone evenly spaced, the marble floors shining with the light of the sun. Outside, the mountains surrounding the palace rose for miles on end, the blue of the Serpentine Channel blocked by their massive shapes. The final bridge on the palace grounds had been built seemingly between two mountains; it reached high into the air, toward the heavens. For a moment, I thought the bridge was carrying us over the clouds.

The hall itself was filled with light, striking and new compared to the dark halls of the palace at Provincia. The men and women were silent, kneeling as I passed them. I refused to be afraid, not when I knew the consequences of my uncontrolled emotions. If I could stay calm, I could get through this. The night before, I had dreamed of destroying the palace and every city in Auster in a fit of rage, but now, after seeing the faces of the kingdom, the idea left me horrified.

The doors to the great hall opened, illuminating the streamers of red and gold falling from the ceiling. An array

of foreign flags was interspersed between the banners, each
bearing the symbol of the snake.

Beneath them, hovering anxiously at the edges of a long
crimson carpet, were even more Austerans. They fell into
a hushed reverence when Beatrice and I stepped through
the door. Even the king and queen stood, making their way
toward me down the long aisle. Beatrice backed away, releasing my arm.

"No!" I whispered, reaching for her. She merely shook her
head, giving me a small smile.

"My Great Lady," the king said, kneeling in front of me
with his queen. "Your servants welcome you." He dwarfed
his wife, though in my hazy half-waking dream I had believed
him to be much larger. The queen was fair-skinned, but wore
her crown atop a cluster of night-black curls.

"Has Beatrice treated you well, my Great Lady?" the king
asked, rising. "We had hoped to spare your wrath in allowing
you to rest."

"She has been a great help," I said, forcing the quiver out
of my voice. As we approached the thrones, an elderly man in
golden robes stepped out from the crowd and walked behind
us. The scepter in his hands glinted with the light streaming
in through the enormous windows.

The king and queen left me standing as they reclaimed
their thrones. Five men stood behind them, and as I passed,
each slid a gold medallion over my head. I glanced down, reading the names and crests of the countries engraved deeply in

them—Auster, Saldorra, Ruttgard, Bellun, Libanbourg—all of the Salvalite nations in the world. The old man, obviously a priest of some kind, bowed deeply before unrolling a long scroll at my feet.

"The alliance has been assembled," the king said. "We have been brought together to further your cause, through sword and strife, blood and battle. All we ask for is your blessing."

"All of you?" I asked faintly, looking down at the scroll, a map of the continent. I had seen a near-exact copy of it in North's messy scrawl as he presented the information to his mother, only Palmarta did not exist on this map. The borders of Palmarta had disappeared, as if the small country had been swallowed whole. I took in every line with a sharp sense of dread, but an even sharper eye.

"Your blessings?" the king asked again.

"How can I give you my blessings," I began, steadying my voice, "when I do not approve of this war at all?"

The representatives of the other nations crowded in, their voices leaping forth in protest. The king held up a silencing hand, his face red as he turned to the priest.

"The scriptures said we would have to bring her into the world slowly," the old man said. "She knows not what she says."

I recognized my mistake immediately. Losing the king's trust and faith would also mean losing my life.

The king gave a curt nod. "Continue with the ceremony, then."

When the priest spoke, it was in a language I had never heard before, a tongue that sounded like the groaning of an old wagon. His words were deep and lyrical, thundering through the great hall. The spectators, as well as the king and queen, responded in turn. I strained my ears, trying to catch a familiar word.

The priest turned back toward me expectantly, touching his scepter to my forehead. The king lit a small stick of incense that burned with the smell of jasmine and sandalwood and held it out to me. I opened my hand to take it from him, but his other hand closed over mine. The priest began his strange speech again, waving his scepter above our heads twice. I would have dropped my hand from the king's sweaty grip had the priest not suddenly wrapped our joined hands together with a long, golden string. Suddenly the priest stopped speaking. All those in the hall turned their eyes toward me, the priest leaning forward as if to say it was my turn.

I nodded slowly, biting my tongue. That seemed to satisfy the two men, who broke out into smiles that turned my insides to stone. What exactly had I just agreed to?

I maintained my composure through the rest of the strange ceremony; they seemed to find it appropriate that the vessel of their goddess was reserved in both her words and outward affection. When the cord unwrapped itself from our hands like a snake, I snatched my hand away, withdrawing it into my cool, dry robes.

Men and women were allowed to approach us then,

stooping to place small gifts at our feet. At least, I assumed they were gifts until the king turned and spoke to me.

He waved his arm over the piles of fruit, weapons, and tools that surrounded us. "These are the requirements for your miracle, my Great Lady," the king said. "The Book mentioned the weapon you would construct for us from these parts. Everything is here."

I stared helplessly at the floor, feeling the pull of panic. There had to be a way I could play this.

"I claim no such power," I said. "You have misread the Book."

"My Great Lady," the priest said, his eyes narrowed slightly, "I assure you that we have interpreted the Book correctly. Please bless us with your power." I heard the crowd murmur.

"I can't . . . ," I mumbled.

"Silence!" the king bellowed to the nobles. He turned back to me, speaking in the same strange language as before, studying my face closely for any sign of recognition.

"She does not understand the holy tongue," the queen said shrewdly from her throne.

"Is that so?" The king seized me by the shoulders, giving me the slightest of shakes. He spoke again in the language I didn't understand, his words punctuated with flying spit.

My entire body began to shake, and I tried to pull away. "Let me go!" I cried, but the king was still shouting at me in that horrible speech.

"If I may interrupt," a voice called over the others. "I think you may need to give her a moment."

Dorwan stood at the very back of the chamber in his pale coat, and for the first and only time, I was actually relieved to see him. The king released me immediately, and I stumbled back.

"Get that lying demon out of here!" the king bellowed, sounding nothing like the gentle man I had met in private. "Throw him into the ocean for all I care! Let this be a lesson to everyone never to trust a wizard!"

A small troop of guards rushed toward Dorwan, but the wizard merely held out his hands to stop them.

"I tried to warn you that not all of her powers would have awakened yet," Dorwan said, coming closer to us. No one stepped in his way or tried to block his path, but many eyed him with a look of revulsion that had nothing to do with the scars on his face.

"You have brought me a false goddess." The king sneered.

"I have brought you the goddess of destruction herself," Dorwan said. "She is everything you need to crush Palmarta, just as your Book said."

"Lies, lies, all lies," said the king, pushing him away, down the steps. Dorwan reached into his pocket without thinking, to the talisman hidden there. If he revealed himself, there would be no chance for either of us.

I did what I had to do, what my heart, faith, and resolve told me. I left myself open to Astraea's will.

"I'll prove my power to you," I said, proud of how strong my voice sounded. "I'll prove myself."

Dorwan's eyes narrowed, searching for my motives. The king looked back and forth between the two of us. No one spoke. Even the priest remained silent.

Finally, the king said, "If she cannot level a mountain at the very least, I will have both your heads, but first I shall feed parts of your bodies to my dogs while you are still living."

I nodded, pressing a hand to my heart. Dorwan was no longer the architect of this game. "Choose a mountain, and we will leave at once."

*   *   *

Beatrice had time only to throw a fur cloak over my shoulders and give my arm a gentle squeeze before I was loaded into a carriage to begin our journey up the long road to the coastal mountains. I glanced back through the small back window, to the queen and noblewomen who had been left behind.

I shared the trip with Dorwan and two guards, whom the wizard had sent into slumber with a wave of his talisman; the driver sat on the outside of the enclosed carriage. I had hoped Dorwan would get into one of the other carriages with the king and the rest of the nobles, but he had stubbornly pushed himself into the carriage after me and shut the door firmly behind him. Now he watched me carefully.

"What spurred this plan?" he asked, his voice barely audible over the grinding of the carriage wheels. "What could you possibly be thinking?"

"I'm wondering how you'll feel when your plan unravels, and there's nothing you can do to stop it," I said.

"Oh, please continue," Dorwan said.

"All this time," I said, "I've been wondering why you didn't just twist us away from the king, but it's because you need him to destroy Provincia first, isn't it? So that you can sweep in later and take over, just when he thinks he's won the kingdom for himself."

"Very good," he said quietly. "Though I hope you're not laboring under the misguided impression that I no longer want to collect your blood. The amount I would need would call for your death, and that simply won't do until Provincia is nothing but rubble and memories."

I sucked in a deep, angry breath. "You don't have a curse."

"It has hundreds of uses beyond curses and poisons." Dorwan leaned forward in his seat, passing his talisman back and forth between his hands. "Your blood is pure magic. Mixing it with my own would give me power you can't even imagine. After you destroy Provincia, I'll be the only wizard left—and with your blood running through my veins, no nation will be powerful enough to defeat me."

"Spoken like the despicable hedge you are," I said. "No, you were too repulsive for them, weren't you? You disgusted even them."

His face curled into a snarl, and he backhanded me across the mouth so hard I tasted the very blood that tempted him.

I struggled to pull away from his gaze.

"You talk of curses as if they're some sort of rarity. They aren't. Everyone is cursed, from the farmer with the pain in his back to the girl who can destroy worlds," Dorwan said. "And do you know how you destroy a curse, Sydelle? You become one. You consume your fear and become it. You plague everyone and everything that dares to hurt you or stand in your way."

He pushed me back against the seat. Perhaps from the noise, the guards had jolted back into awareness, looking between Dorwan's flushed face and my bleeding lip.

"There's not a problem," Dorwan told them. He leaned back in his seat, pulling out a small golden pocket watch and flipping open its cover with a small smile.

* * *

We were only halfway up the mountain path when a soldier rode up on horseback and told us to beware of snow ahead. There was no way for the carriages to fight through the icy covering that awaited us at the mountain's summit, so the king improvised.

"That is the Sleven Mountain," he told me. We were standing on the road, near where the horses and carriages had been left. The king pointed to a mountain, just across from us in the small range.

"If you can reduce that mountain to rubble, you will have proven yourself to be Salvala's vessel."

I turned my face away from him and walked forward, standing at the edge of the road. In the distance, I could make out the faint line of blue that was the Serpentine Channel, but mainly I saw the heavily forested and rocky slope of the mountain below my feet.

The wind increased, kicking up a smattering of snow. I drew the fur cloak around me tightly.

I closed my eyes again, feeling Dorwan's presence beside me. "You heard the king, Sydelle."

I turned around to face the others, not bothering to hide my disgust.

"Get this filth away from me," I said.

"For what reason?" the king called.

"This man is a liar," I said to the king, and the reaction was instantaneous. "He may be a wizard, but he is certainly no prophet. He found me in Provincia, saw the color of my hair, and decided to use both of us to his advantage."

I relished the look of alarm that stole across Dorwan's face when fifteen firearms and even more swords were turned in his direction.

"A lie," Dorwan said, raising his arms slightly in surrender. "Your Majesty, I can prove her power."

"Take him!" the king barked, waving the soldiers forward.

"They'll kill us," Dorwan said as the soldiers came closer. "They'll kill us, you foolish little—"

He reached into his coat for the talisman waiting there, but even in my heavy robes I was faster. I shoved him as hard as I could; he stumbled back into the approaching soldiers, who pinned his arms behind him and forced him to the ground.

I was his curse now.

"*Sydelle!*" he snarled.

"Good-bye, Dorwan," I said. "Good riddance."

He saw my plan in my eyes: I would take down this mountain and everyone on it—the king, his men, but, most of all, Reuel Dorwan. And if I couldn't escape the destruction, so be it. At least the war would be over before it had the chance to begin.

"Take the girl, too!" the king shouted. I heard, rather than saw, a few of the soldiers rush toward me. I held out a hand to stop them.

"Don't touch me," I said calmly.

I closed my eyes again, taking a deep breath as I searched for the magic that had once held so much fear for me. Magic is a tool, Pascal had said. Wizards open themselves up to it.

I focused not on my fear or my sorrow but on the world slowly spinning beneath my feet, on the anger I felt inside of me. I thought of those who had wanted to use me, who had thought I was a pawn in their games, and let myself feel every lick of disappointment and fury. This time, I knew how to control my powers. All along I had been *feeling*, and those feelings had driven the storms and quakes. Now, as the torrent of emotions passed through my heart and out into the world, I felt the familiar warmth of magic rise up with me.

I seized the connection. A thousand threads of light in every color appeared in my sight, rising from the ground. The warmth began to work its way through every vein and sinew in my body. A light breeze of cold air caressed my cheek, but I hardly felt it. Instead, I focused on the sound of it, strengthening it, pulling on it as if it were tangible. My fur cloak blew up and away with the force of the new wind, fluttering down the slope of the mountain.

A startled cry went up behind me as several of the horses spooked. I did not relent. I felt the spark of magic the moment my fingers brushed the ground, and a great shudder ran through it at my touch. I dug my fingers into the soil and pulled on it as hard as I could. The force of the ensuing quake rattled every bone in my body.

I heard the thunderous roar of the snow at the top of the mountain as it came barreling down toward us. The king's soldiers scattered, trying to break the bucking horses free from the carriages.

"Your Majesty!" one of them shouted. "We must leave—"

The king did not acknowledge him. He held out his hand, palm up, with a reverential expression on his face. A light spray of snow fell down over us as the mass of it barreled through the line of trees above us, groaning and straining like a living beast.

In that moment my connection to the world snapped, and the only thing I was aware of was the voice in my head whispering urgently, *Run, Sydelle.*

I ripped the diadem and veil from my hair, leaving them for the snow to claim. The shuddering ground made it hard to climb over the jagged rocks and upturned trees. My long skirt gathered around my knees, the beautiful red fabric torn and dirtied as I cut through dead brush and rocks. All I could feel was the burning of my lungs and the beating of my heart. Nothing else touched me, not the cold against my bare skin nor the branches and rocks that cut my arms. Nothing.

I was running, but not fast enough.

The snow picked up momentum as it barreled toward me, forcing me in the direction of a cliff. I looked back and forth desperately for a way down that wasn't as steep, but the cliff seemed to line the entire face of the mountain. From my position at its very edge, I could see the blue water of the channel over the line of trees.

The drop was hundreds of feet below, but I lurched forward again, unwilling to surrender to the snow. I fell to my knees, crawling over the edge of the cliff. My feet slid against the rocks, trying to find purchase as my hands clung to a long tree root. I scraped my chin against the hard earth, my hands slowly slipping with the force of the quaking ground. I clenched my teeth, ignoring the mass of white barreling toward me, and forced myself to continue climbing down.

"Sydelle!"

My head turned toward the direction of my name. It wasn't possible.

"Syd!" Again, over the roar of the avalanche. *"Syd, jump!"*

I risked a glance down, looking back over my shoulder to the slope below, scattered with men and women in familiar black uniforms. Standing at the forefront were two dark-haired men, looking up. They were hundreds of feet below me, but there was no missing North's distinctive stance and unusual cloak.

"North!" I screamed in warning.

"Jump!" He yelled back. *"JUMP!"*

And because I was out of time, because I felt the ground begin to shift beneath me with the river of snow, I did. And I flew.

At the moment my feet left the rim, North threw up his cloak, and something caught my body and eased my fall. I fell slowly, slowly—without even a sound. The roar of the crushing snow gave way to perfect silence. There was a wall of wind carefully lowering me when I should have been plummeting. I almost laughed in exhilaration, but I forced my eyes to stay focused on North's determined face, coming closer by the second. His arms were reaching up toward me, straining. Several of the other wizards seemed to be helping him guide me down, but even more kept their eyes turned up to the tide of snow that hurtled over the rim.

Time sped back up, and so did my fall. I fell onto North, my arms wrapping around his shoulders. He used the force of the impact to drop us to the ground, bringing his red cloak up in one fluid, sweeping motion and pulling it over our heads. A moment later, the rest of the Wizard Guard unleashed a firestorm above our heads, incinerating the snow until only steam and air remained. I felt the cold water raining down around us. It soaked through North's thin cloak, but neither of us cared.

His arms came around me tightly, crushing me to him. "Are you hurt?" he asked, his face buried in my hair. "Syd, did they hurt you?"

I couldn't say a single word; I clung to his neck and tried to breathe.

CHAPTER SEVENTEEN

We stayed down until the plummeting water ceased and the ground stilled, and only then did North drop the protective red cloak. I winced at the shock of cold air, and my legs buckled beneath me.

"It's okay, you're okay," North said, scooping me up into his arms. I pressed my face against his shoulder as he wrapped the cloak around us for warmth. It covered us like a wet blanket but dried quickly with its own natural heat.

"Take her back to the ship," Oliver said, coming to stand next to us. "We're going to search for survivors."

"It was me," I whispered. "I did this."

North's arms tightened around me. "It's all right," he said quietly. "It wasn't your fault."

"Yes, it was," I said. "I did it on purpose."

Out of the corner of my eye, I saw Oliver and North

exchange a look. In the end, Oliver merely nodded, summoning a few of the other wizards around him. They drew out their talismans and, in the next breath, disappeared.

"Hold on," North told me, replacing the red cloak around us with his black one. I nodded and, for the first time, savored the feeling of our fall through space.

My body jarred with the heavy thud of North's boots against the ship's deck. Several of the sailors around us looked startled at our sudden appearance.

North ducked, squeezing us down the narrow staircase to the hull. The space was dark and cramped. North sat against the wall with a long sigh and pulled me onto his lap, once again wrapping the red cloak tightly around us.

"Where are we?" I asked again, suddenly exhausted.

"We're just off Auster's coast," he said. "It was too far for us to twist safely from Provincia. We had to sail most of the way."

"How did you find me?"

"The moment we came close to shore we all felt you, burning like a star on the mountainside. You drew us to you."

"Dorwan," I began, pulling away. "He was with me on the mountain—I don't know what happened to him—"

"What in the seven hells was he doing there?" I saw North's face glower in the darkness.

"He told the king I was their goddess," I said. "When I didn't understand their ritual, he asked that I be allowed to prove my power."

"And you did," North finished.

"On my own terms," I said. "I've never wished this on anyone, but I hope he's dead, and I hope he suffered."

I felt his hand come up to stroke my hair softly.

"I hope so, too," he said. "If he's alive, Oliver and the others will find him."

"How did you manage to get Oliver to come along?" I asked.

"I've been wondering that myself, actually," he said. "When the queen sent him away, Oliver came and got me immediately. I think he felt guilty for letting it happen, to be honest. He may not like me, but he's not a beast, and he knew you were innocent."

I pulled back from him, studying his face. "About before . . . I was angry," I whispered. "If it meant saving your life, you know I would give you whatever you needed."

"Don't say that, and don't apologize," he said gruffly. I felt him shift slightly beneath me. "I deserved it, every last word."

I pressed my lips against the line of his jaw softly, not pulling them away until I felt the tension there slowly abate.

"I'm sorry," I whispered again. It was his warm breath on my face that made the moment real; it was the light touch of his fingertips on my neck that nearly reduced me to tears. I tilted my face up expectantly.

The sound of two dozen boots raining down on the deck above us broke the spell. A moment later, Oliver appeared on the steps, his shape outlined by the setting sun.

"Wayland!" he called.

North cleared his throat but made no movement to stand, let alone move. I let my head rest against his shoulder once more.

Oliver stumbled around the crates and bedding, stopping short of us. Even in the darkness, I could see his eyes widen at the sight of us.

"We could only find guards and broken carriages," Oliver said. "Who else was there?"

"The king," I told him. "A few of the nobles and priests . . . and Reuel Dorwan."

"So he is involved?" Oliver asked North. "It wasn't some lie you spun to avoid the war?"

"Do you really believe I would do that?" North asked, and there was real hurt there.

Oliver looked away. "I checked the records. I wasn't able to find any trace of him, let alone track his movements."

"He's not a ranked wizard, so there was no trace spell placed on him, remember?" North said. "You were there when he confronted my mother about it, weren't you?"

"That was justified," Oliver said. "He was raised by hedge witches. His ranking is forbidden in our code of laws."

"It's more important you try to find him *now*," I said. "There's a chance he didn't make it off the mountain at all."

"And you're positive the king was there?" Oliver pressed. "This may change everything."

I nodded.

"Only if he's dead," North said. "If Dorwan was there, I doubt he would have let the king die. Not when it was advantageous for him to keep the king alive."

The thought was almost soothing to me, as if the lives of a few men being saved by Dorwan made me any less of a murderer. Of a monster.

I ducked my chin against my neck and closed my eyes. North seemed to sense my thoughts, because his hand came up to press my face against his shoulder once more.

"You did what you had to," he said. "You're alive and we're together again. That's all that matters to me."

"I wish . . . I wish there could have been another way," I mumbled. "None of those men were like Dorwan."

"The other way would have been death as well, only it would have been yours," Oliver said. "And that's no more honorable than what you did."

North and I were silent.

"And in any case, if the king is dead, the war will be over before it even began," Oliver said.

I felt North nod once before resting his cheek against the top of my head again.

Oliver hesitated a moment before leaving. "Are you going to . . . put it back on?" He looked at North, lifting his wrist slightly. I felt North shift beneath me, and I realized what he was asking.

"Yes," I said. "He'll put the bracelet back on."

Oliver relaxed. "I'll be on the upper deck, then."

"Commander Swift," I called as he began his ascent up the staircase. "Thank you for coming."

He shrugged halfheartedly. "I didn't come for you. I came for my friend."

I waited until Oliver was gone before looking up into North's face.

"You don't think he meant the queen, do you?" North said. "Because that would ruin a rather touching moment."

I elbowed him. "When things settle down, you should try talking to him again."

He leaned his head back against the wall.

"And I do want my bracelet back," I told him.

"I can hardly believe that," he said.

"You gave it to me." I could still picture it in a coiled heap on the floor of the queen's chamber. "Of course I want it back."

"With or without the magic?" he asked.

I bit my lower lip. "Either way you think best," I said after a moment. He reached into the pocket of his trousers, retrieving the thin chain.

"Just to hide your magic," he promised, fastening it over my wrist. "To contain it. I've added a clasp, so you'll be able to take it off if you need to."

He drew me closer to him once more, his fingers stroking my loose hair. The boat released a beastlike groan as the anchor lifted from the water. We felt the exact moment the wind caught our sails and set us in the direction of home.

I let my eyes drift shut, perfectly at ease. For a moment or two, I thought North might have fallen asleep.

Just then, he whispered in my ear.

"Syd," he said. "What did they do to your hair?"

*   *   *

After less than a day at sea, we reached Provincia. We landed in the courtyard of the palace, at the bottom of the stairs. The Sorceress Imperial was pacing the length of them, accompanied by a few members of the Wizard Guard. I remembered standing there several days earlier, seeing the queen for the first time. It seemed like a distant memory now.

Before she could say a word, I held up the bracelet for her to see, and she nodded in acknowledgment. I wore borrowed trousers and a shirt that North had scrounged up, but the Sorceress Imperial's extravagant robes no longer had any effect on my confidence.

"I need to speak with you," I said. "Immediately."

North looked at me in surprise, but Hecate's face did not betray her curiosity. After a moment she nodded again.

North took a step as if to go with me, but Oliver held out an arm and blocked his path. I cast a reassuring smile over my shoulder at him as we walked up the steps into the castle.

We made our way through the long halls and winding staircases in silence. The castle felt different to me now, subdued and dark. Everything in Auster had been so bright and clean, so well cared for, that in contrast Provincia seemed in danger of collapsing under the weight of dust and grime. How had the city—the kingdom—fallen into such neglect?

The interior of the Sorceress Imperial's quarters was sparse, decorated only with maps and shelves of musty old books. She sat down in a leather chair, never taking her eyes off me. I sank down onto a settee. A portrait of a dark-haired family— a husband, wife, and their mischievous-looking son— looked down on us from the fireplace.

"I have very little time to waste on you," Hecate said sharply. "If you're expecting some sort of apology, you should realize how blessed you truly are that I haven't had you killed."

"What would killing me solve?" I asked bitterly. "I'm surprised you won't just throw me out to the battle, hoping I destroy Auster without harming Palmarta."

"Keeping you alive poses more of a threat. I only allowed them to go after you so Auster wouldn't use you against *us*," she said.

I shook my head, my anger building as she continued.

"Having you here is an even larger risk. If any one of us were to obtain your blood, he would become the most powerful wizard alive. You do know what you are, of course, but you have no idea what your presence does to the balance of magic in the world. In the past, jinxes have always been put to death for this very reason."

"So why am I still alive?" I asked. "Why not kill me now and take the power yourself?"

Hecate held my gaze. "Why did you wish to speak to me?"

"I have information for you about Auster," I said.

"You and my son have already provided me with information."

"The situation has changed," I said. "The king may be dead."

"What madness is this?"

"They believed I was the vessel of their goddess, and asked for my blessing," I began. By the time I had finished relating the story, Hecate's face had gone stark white.

"Is there any proof of this?" she asked. "I won't base the policy of this country on the word of a silly girl."

"It's the truth; ask Oliver," I said. "This is your chance. If the king really is dead, there's no reason to go ahead with such a foolish war. Make amends with the queen and find a peaceful solution."

Hecate turned toward her desk, lifting a blank sheet of paper. When she looked up, I thought I saw real shame there.

"Get out," she said harshly. "I have letters to write."

✳   ✳   ✳

I made my way back to my former quarters alone, wondering if my things were still where I had left them. I had thought about trying to find North, but with men and wizards filling the palace to capacity, it was like searching for a drop of water in the sea. Some stopped to look at me as I passed, but no one bothered me. It was a nice change.

After a considerable amount of wandering, I found the dark corner of the palace the Sorceress Imperial had assigned me. *Unlocked,* I thought, *thank Astraea.*

Inside, my room was almost exactly as it had been. My clothes were spread out across my bed, washed and folded. I picked up the blue dress my father had bought for me years ago in Provincia, holding it up to the light streaming through the window.

"It's like you've never seen a dress before," a voice said from the door. I spun around, to see Henry leaning against the doorframe.

"That's my favorite," he said. "It matches the color of your eyes."

He took a step inside and shut the door behind him. My fingers tightened on the dress. I turned my back to him.

"I need to change and wash up," I said. "Can we please talk later?"

"I want to know what's going on. Why you're dressed like that. Why you up and disappeared a week ago." He put a hand on my shoulder, forcing me to turn around.

"I can't tell you," I said. Henry was staring at me with those brown eyes. I didn't want to lie to him, but there wasn't a chance in the world he would understand what was going on.

"Can't, or won't?" Henry asked. "The last time I checked, we were friends. We used to tell each other everything."

"We're not children anymore," I said, and threw the dress down on the bed. "You keep acting like nothing's changed, and you know it has."

Henry took a step back. "Nothing has changed, Sydelle, not for me. But I can see that's not the same for you." He nodded toward the bracelet on my wrist. "Do I even need to ask who gave you that?"

"I'm sorry," I said, choking on the words. "I don't want to hurt you, but I can't pretend anymore."

"Listen to yourself," Henry said in astonishment. "You're scaring me. Is this the wizard's doing? Did he do something to you?"

"No, of course not!" I said. "Please, you're making this worse—just go, Henry. *Please!*"

"Come home with me," Henry said. He reached out to take my hands, but I pulled them away. I saw the hurt in his eyes, and it felt like the walls were closing in on us.

"What's happened to you?" he asked.

"Nothing," I said. "Everything. I've changed. I don't know if I can go back to the way things were before and be happy."

"So you won't be happy with me, not ever?" I looked up as anger flooded his words. "You know we're supposed to be together; it's the way it's always been!"

But it was no longer the way it could be. How do you

tell someone that he is a part of your past, and not your future?

"Please go," I said. When he refused, when he tried to fold me into an embrace, I was the one to leave.

The door shut behind me, and it felt like a poor ending to a story that had been written long ago in the sands of a yellow mountain.

*   *   *

The weaving room was deserted by the time I found it, for which I was grateful. The thought of facing anyone, even a complete stranger, was unbearable. I wanted a place to be alone, to work in silence.

The other women had left the loom up. I rubbed my hands along the length of the cloak as I sat down, the threads smooth beneath my fingers. There was only a little still to be done, but I dove into the work with everything I had. I saw nothing else, felt only the warmth of magic and something else rushing through my veins.

CHAPTER EIGHTEEN

The next day passed as had the day before. The other women came and went, but I stayed behind long after they had gone, for what I hoped would be my final night of work. I poured every wish, every part of myself into each thread. I watched the yarn between my fingers take on a faint glow, even as my bracelet tinkled with the furious movements of my hands. I finished the row I was working on and sat back, a new thought coming over me.

I retrieved a sewing needle, and before I could begin to doubt myself, I stuck my finger. The droplet of blood, the same blood that had already caused so much strife, welled up against my pale skin. I pressed the finger to the upper left corner of the cloak. The effect was instantaneous—at the touch, the cloak lit up as if on fire, warming beneath my hands.

If my blood can do this, I wondered, *what else can it do?* Could it heal the curse of a dead witch, one passed from father to son? Could I give enough of it over time that it would cure him?

But, more important, would North ever take it?

Ingredients, plans, and tests flitted through my mind as I wove love—and more—into the remaining threads.

*   *   *

"Syd?"

I sucked in a deep breath, rubbing my face. The light in the room was a dull gray—an overcast morning. I had meant only to rest my eyes for a few moments.

North laughed as he helped me sit up. "Sleeping on the cold stone floor when you have a perfectly good bed upstairs. I was wondering where you had disappeared to."

"I'm in hiding," I said.

"From who?"

I sighed. "Henry. We had a fight, and it didn't end well."

"Does . . . ?" North paused, taking a deep breath. "Does he need to be dealt with?"

I had to laugh. "No, nothing like that. He's just angry that I didn't want to go back to Cliffton with him."

"Ah," North said. "Well, I can't blame you. You'd be depriving yourself of my charming company."

I rolled my eyes. "What a loss."

"In all honesty, though, I think you should find a way to make amends if you can," North said. "Real friends are hard to come by, and as annoying as Henry is, he'd throw himself in front of dragon's fire for you."

"And that's the definition of a real friend?"

"Oh, yes, just ask Owain." He laughed.

"I'll take that into consideration," I said. I reached up to brush a splotch of dust from his cheek.

"I keep forgetting," he said, pulling something from his pocket. "I've been carrying this with me for so long I just got used to having it."

In his hand was my necklace. He put it around my neck, still warm from where it had lain against his own skin.

"The king of Auster is dead," he said.

I looked up sharply. "What? You're sure?"

"Word came this morning to the Sorceress Imperial," he said. "You won't be hearing celebrations in the streets until she deems it the right moment to inform everyone else, though."

"That's good news, isn't it?" I asked. "Not for her schemes, of course, but for the rest of us?"

North blew out a long breath. "The queen of Auster and the remaining nobles want to negotiate for peace," he said. "On one condition."

I looked at the newly finished cloak, still hanging on the loom. I already knew what they wanted.

"They still think you're their goddess," he said. "What

happened on the mountain only proved it to them, even with the king's death."

"How do they know I'm still alive?" I asked.

"They don't," North said, running his hand through my hair. "We'll find another way."

I shook my head. "I'll go, if it means protecting you and everyone here."

He clucked his tongue. "As if I would ever let you do that. We'll find another way," he repeated. "Mother is letting me accompany the diplomatic party over to Auster for the nego- tiations."

He turned to look at the cloak. "You've been busy," he said. "What is this?"

"A gift," I said. "For you."

He pulled off a glove and pressed his fingers lightly against the dragon at the center.

"It's warm . . . ," he marveled, sensing the power woven into it. "But how can I take something like this into duels? I would never want to ruin it."

"All the more reason to be careful when you fight," I said. "Let me get scissors and a needle to hemstitch it."

I worked quickly, feeling his eyes on me the entire time.

"When are you leaving?"

"In an hour . . ."

"An *hour*?" I said, folding the cloak across my arm. "I thought it would be another few days, at the very least!"

"The Sorceress Imperial wants to move quickly," he said.

"I think a part of her still hopes these negotiations will break down."

The thought came to me suddenly. "But they don't have to. Do you still think they'll agree to peace if I'm not part of the treaty?"

"It'll depend on a number of things. The queen has prepared a list of terms and concessions that they might agree to, but I'm still concerned." North ran a hand through his hair. "They've lost their king, not their armies or their alliance to Saldorra. It won't help that we won't give them the one thing they truly want."

"What if you *can't* give it to them?" I asked. "What if I were dead?"

North looked horrified.

"Figuratively dead," I clarified. "They couldn't hold it against you if I had been killed in the avalanche as well."

"But where's the proof?"

I bent down to pick up one of the longer pieces of thread I had cut away. I smoothed my long hair back, tying it in place. Then the small scissors were in my hand, cutting through my hair before North had the chance to stop me.

"Don't—!" he said, but I was too fast for him.

"This was all Dorwan needed to convince them I was their goddess," I said, pressing the bundle of hair into his hand. "How do they usually bury their dead?"

"They don't," North said. "They use funeral pyres."

"Then tell them you did that when you found me on

the mountain," I said. "Tell them you did it to honor them."

"When did you get to be so clever and devious?" he asked. He brought a hand up to my much shorter locks.

"I suppose I've been spending too much time with wizards," I said.

"I have a favor to ask of you . . . ," North began hesitantly. "And you certainly don't have to. It's just a stupid old tradition for luck."

"What is it?" I asked.

"Will you come with me to the tents?" he asked. "A wizard is supposed to ask his lady to arm him. For luck, I mean. After that you'll go back up to the castle with the other women."

"Of course," I said, taking his hand firmly in mine. "I'll come wherever you need me."

✳   ✳   ✳

North and I twisted to the outer banks of the Lyfe. I held his hand tightly as we navigated the hundreds of colorful tents that housed the wizards and laborers.

"All right," he said. "Come on, we don't have that much time."

The supply tent North was assigned to was empty by the time we arrived. Trunks of armor and weaponry were stacked in the center, and though candles had been lit to compensate for the gray winter sky, the tent was still fairly dark and cold. North solved both problems with a simple flick of his old red cloak.

North and I said nothing as I slowly unknotted his cloaks, catching them before they could flutter to the ground. I handled each piece of the black leather armor with care, making sure it was in its proper place. North helped me with the arm and leg pieces without a word. I could see my own miserable expression reflected in the surface of the mirror across the tent. I fastened the last piece of armor with trembling fingers.

It was all over too quickly. I gathered his old cloaks, folding them in their proper order, and clipped the new cloak in their place. The vibrant colors I had chosen were dull in the poor light. His hand came up to take mine, but I wasn't finished.

I lifted the thin silver chain from around my neck and placed it over his head. The braided silver slipped beneath his armor, out of sight but still there.

"Keep this for me, all right?" I asked. Astraea would protect him when I couldn't.

I stood on my toes again, bracing myself against his strong form, and pressed my lips against the smooth skin of his cheek.

"For luck," I explained.

"Thank you," he said.

I waited until he had disappeared completely from the tent before moving. I sat down heavily on the bench, my face in my hands, as anger, love, and fear all fought to rise up inside of me.

The tent flap banged open. I brought my head up, and there was Wayland North.

I was on my feet in an instant, but he had crossed the distance between us in two long strides.

"What—?"

He pulled me to him, grasping my face between his hands. And then he was kissing me, kissing me so deeply, so fiercely that I could feel my toes curling in my shoes. The world spun away, and it was just the two of us.

Then it was over. North sighed deeply, and there was that heartbreaking half smile again, the one reserved for times of resignation and failing hope.

"I'm going to need," he said, "*a lot* of luck."

When I reached for him again, he was already gone.

*　　*　　*

The few women and children who had been left behind by the party of wizards made their way back up to the city's bridge in silence. Once or twice, someone tried to make conversation, but no one was in the mood to talk. I hung back at the very edge of the group, watching the afternoon light play on the blue-green water of the lake.

It was ridiculous to be so afraid when they weren't going off to fight a war. Even so, the party of wizards and diplomats was still in danger. We would *all* be in danger if the negotiations fell apart.

"Lass!"

Owain's enormous body pushed through the crowds on the bridge. He waved both arms in the air, not stopping until I was at his side.

"He's off, then?" Owain asked. He pulled me closer to him as we maneuvered through the lines of people, animals, and carts. There were several more guards at the gate than usual, but they didn't stop us. Owain seemed to have that effect on people.

"Wasn't the Sorceress Imperial closing the city?" I asked. We were wedged between a long line of street vendors and their customers as we made our way up to the castle.

"Queen wouldn't let her," Owain explained. "I'm starting to like that girl. She's got more nerve than I thought."

I hadn't realized how late it had gotten. By the time we reached the marble steps of the castle, night had fallen, and there wasn't a soul to be seen.

"Where are we going?" I asked.

"To your room, of course," Owain said. "I've got orders from the lad: *Do not let anyone in or out of her room until I come back.*"

I groaned. "He didn't."

"He sure as spit did, lass," he said. "Not even the queen will get through on my watch!"

But as we turned down the final hallway, it was clear that

the queen was a step ahead of him. Her violet dress blended with the darkness, and the dim light caught the strands of gold in her hair. Owain and I watched in silence as she lifted a fist and knocked twice on the door to my quarters.

"Is there something we can help you with, Your Majesty?" Owain called. There was no hint of friendliness in his voice. I had to push him to the side to see the queen's reaction.

She jumped, turning quickly to face us.

"Oh! Yes, I'm— It's— I need—" She wrung her hands until they were an angry red.

"Where are your attendants?" Owain asked, looking around. "Is everything all right?"

I watched the way her lips pressed together into a white line, the way one hand came up to smooth back her hair, and I knew something was wrong. The queen I had met before had been so self-assured.

"Did you need to speak to me?" I asked.

"Yes, in my chambers," she said tensely. "It is a matter of *grave* importance."

Queen Eglantine motioned us to follow her to her wing of the castle. If her words hadn't been enough to confirm my worst fears, the large purple beetle clinging to her skirt was all I needed to know who would be waiting for us in her chambers.

I grabbed Owain's arm, pulling him down so I could whisper in his ear. "Dorwan."

He pulled back, his brows drawing together. Dorwan was

using the beetle to track her, I knew, to make sure she couldn't run away or warn the other wizards.

The queen glanced back over her shoulder, her blue eyes wide. I wasn't sure that she had heard me until I saw her mouth the words *Help me, please*.

Queen Eglantine's wing of the castle was unnaturally quiet. The last time I had walked down this hallway, candles had been blazing, servants had been bustling back and forth, and a set of guards had protected the doorway. I saw the busts of past kings covered in the wax of the dripping candles, their vacant eyes following our path down the long hall. Everything was still and quiet, but I sensed Dorwan's cold aura reaching out to me, licking at my skin. I shivered.

"You need to get the Wizard Guard," I whispered to Owain. "Get as many wizards as you can."

Owain shook his head, a deep frown on his face. "Are you saying I can't protect you myself?"

"I'm saying I don't *want* you to," I said. "He's a dirty cheat—North barely made it out of their fight alive. Please, just get the Guard and hurry back."

He sighed. "I understand. But I'm coming back for you right away, you hear? Don't do anything to get yourself hurt; I'd never forgive myself." He turned quickly, fading into the shadows.

The queen waited by the door to her chambers, still pale and trembling. I came to stand by her side, looping my arm through hers.

"What was it that you needed to speak to me about?" I asked loudly. "What could you possibly have to say to me after everything that's happened?"

The queen cleared her throat. "I hope you don't expect me to apologize. I will always do what's in the best interest of my kingdom."

She pulled open the door, continuing, "You were a necessary part of gaining a peaceful resolution."

"There was nothing peaceful about it," I said, my eyes scanning the darkness. There wasn't a part of the room that hadn't been upturned. Her former Wizard Guard were piled one on top of the other near the window. I couldn't tell if they were unconscious or dead, but the torn draperies, burned carpet, and sprays of blood across the walls seemed to indicate the latter.

"Do you not like the way I've redecorated?" Dorwan's voice floated around us, but he was nowhere to be seen. Another one of his tricks.

"I'm sorry," the queen said, and I could see she meant it. "He came just before you got back, demanding that I fetch you. I had no choice; he would have killed the guards and myself."

So they were alive, then. It seemed a strange show of mercy from an otherwise ruthless wizard.

"Come out, you coward," I called, stepping in front of the queen. "I should have known your ugly face would show up the moment North and the others left."

"Some call it cowardice; others, intelligence," he said. "I hope you didn't think that little stunt you pulled on the mountain would be enough to kill a wizard as powerful as I."

"A roach can survive anything, apparently," I said.

Dorwan stepped out from the queen's bedroom, dressed in the black uniform of the Wizard Guard. In his fist was his dagger with its long, braided string of blue. He spun the cord around casually, the dagger slicing through the air in a wide arc.

"Why didn't you save the king of Auster?" I asked. "By letting him die, you've ruined your own plan."

"We'll see about that," he said, his scarred face turned toward the queen.

"I want you out of my kingdom," she said. "I am willing to consider your terms, as long as they do not involve harming my subjects." I didn't miss the way her hand reached back for the door. Dorwan did not miss it, either. He threw his talisman down with a harsh laugh, and a vein of ice sprang up, racing toward the door. The queen and I leapt apart, watching as a thick layer of ice overcame the door and froze it shut. Queen Eglantine looked at me in alarm.

"That'll keep our other friend occupied when he returns," Dorwan said, picking up the knife. "Now, Sydelle, on to more important things."

The queen lunged to her left, picking up one of the overturned chairs and throwing it at him with all her might. Dorwan ducked before it could hit him, but I used the distraction to grab at one of the ornamental swords on the wall. I wrenched and pulled at the hilt, but the ancient thing had been hammered into place.

Before I could take another step, a blast of water slammed into both the queen and me, knocking us back against the door. My forehead collided with the sharp edge of the doorknob, and it was enough to stun me for a moment.

I turned, searching until I found the queen a short distance away. She was on the ground, unmoving. Her dress was pooled around her, and for a moment I wasn't sure if she was alive at all until I saw her breathe.

I pulled myself up onto my knees, but Dorwan was just as quick to knock me back down.

"You still have such spirit," he said, laughing. "It breaks my heart."

"As if it hasn't already shriveled up," I said. I rolled onto my side, trying to ignore the sharp pain in my head. He knelt on me, forcing the air from my chest. I tried to push him off, but it was like trying to move a stone wall.

"You let them suppress your magic, didn't you?" Dorwan's eyes narrowed. "Why is it so difficult for you to understand that power is a blessing? Why do you let them make you feel ashamed of it?"

His fingers traced the length of my arm, a disturbingly gentle act, until they came to rest on my wrist. His eyes flashed in recognition and I felt, rather than saw, his fingers seize the thin metal.

"Take it off," I dared him. "I can control my magic with or without it."

Dorwan tightened his hand around my wrist until the pain was nearly excruciating. "Take it off and give you the chance to use your magic? Nice try."

The dagger slid deeply, unexpectedly, against the length of my arm, from elbow to wrist. I opened my mouth to release a scream of pain, but he pressed his hand firmly against my mouth.

"You asked me why I didn't save the king?" Dorwan said. "It occurred to me that if I had your power, it really wouldn't matter if they invaded or not. I'm tired of waiting for things to fall into place. I'll be more than capable of ruining this kingdom with your blood."

He pulled a flask from his side, twisting the top open methodically and placing it near the dagger. Dorwan was silent for a moment, bringing one of his bloodstained gloves up to my eyes. He licked the tip of its thumb. "Red, the color of life, of passion. You wear it so well."

Dorwan cut into my arm again, this time a little lower. The warmth trickled down the length of my arm, collecting in the gaping mouth of the flask.

"You won't win," I said through gritted teeth.

"I already have, Sydelle," Dorwan said softly. "Everyone above us will be overrun and torn—*augh*!" An unexpected crack sounded, cutting his words short.

The queen stood with one of the fireplace pokers in her

hands. The tip of it had broken off in her strike and landed near my face. Her shoulders heaved as she took in deep gulps of air.

"What a *vile, horrible man*!" she cried, still holding the black metal rod, as if waiting to strike him again. "Did I kill him?"

I crawled closer to Dorwan's prone form and, to my great disappointment, found him still breathing. I shook my head, and she sucked in a sharp breath.

Before either of us could do anything, the doors to the chamber burst open with a cloud of fire. I shielded my eyes from the intense light and heat.

"Lass!" Owain appeared out of the cloud of dark smoke, sword in hand. He coughed, waving a hand to clear away the smoke.

"We're here!" I called, and he rushed toward us.

A group of two dozen wizards flooded into the room. Owain knelt beside me. He pulled off his leather glove to hold against my wound, but it did little to staunch the flow of blood.

I'm in a room full of wizards, I thought, *and none of them have even looked my way.* North's bracelet really was a gift.

"What are you doing standing there like gaping idiots?" the queen shouted. "Someone take this man and throw him in the dungeons! If he's alive, make sure there are at least ten men on him at all times. Are you out of your minds with shock or stupidity? For goodness' sake, someone get the healers! If she or any of my guards bleed to death, it'll all be on your heads!"

It might have been exhaustion or the loss of blood, but I let out a laugh. Queen Eglantine turned toward Owain and me.

"And who says these wizards are invincible foes?" she asked.

"You made quick work of him," Owain noted in approval. "Cracked him on the head. Good girl."

I watched as Dorwan was carried from the room, bound and gagged even in his unconscious state, and for the first time in weeks, I felt safe.

A small group of healers appeared at the door a few moments later. Most of them attended to the wizards that Dorwan had attacked, but one, an elderly gentleman, went straight for the queen.

"*She's* the one bleeding, not me!" Queen Eglantine sighed. "Honestly!"

The healer went to work immediately, cleaning my cuts as best he could. "I'll have to stitch these," he said, glancing up at me through his spectacles. "It'll hurt something fierce."

I must have made a face because Owain suddenly slapped his hand on his knee and said, "Lass! Have I ever told you the story of Vesta's glorious birth? It started on a cloudy fall day, several years back. . . ."

It was enough to distract me from the needle, but I wasn't sure which was worse.

"—and it felt like coming home, lass, such a beautiful moment." He finished at the same time as the healer.

Meanwhile, Queen Eglantine was deep in conversation with two wizards. Finally, she glanced my way.

"Sydelle," she said, coming over to me. The two wizards trailed her like dogs. "I'm curious. Is this the same wizard who was involved with the king's death?"

"Both kings," I said. "He was the one who poisoned your husband, but he was also with me in Auster."

"A king slayer," Queen Eglantine said. "I don't think there's a punishment worthy of that crime."

The idea came so suddenly that I sat straight up. "I can think of something, though you might not relish losing your chance to punish him."

"I don't follow you," the queen said.

"Write to the Sorceress Imperial—no, write to her son," I said as the healer finished bandaging my arm. "Tell them that you have the man responsible for killing Auster's king, and they can punish him as they see fit. Trade him for peace between the kingdoms. That'll be retribution enough for Dorwan."

Queen Eglantine favored me with a brilliant smile. "I like the way you think."

When the message was written, she waved one of the wizards over.

"No," I said quickly. "Queen Eglantine, you have no better messenger than this man right here."

Owain leapt to his feet. "Lass—"

"It's true," I continued. "Let him take the letter to the port, at least. Have you heard of his horse, Vesta? There's no faster girl around."

Queen Eglantine smiled and seemed to understand me perfectly. "I've been in need of a new messenger. Are you someone I can trust, sir?"

"Your Majesty," Owain said, dropping into a clumsy bow. "There is no man and horse more faithful or willing to serve."

"Then I'll have you," she said. "I'd like you to take the letter to Auster yourself, to make sure it reaches Wayland North's hands directly—*not* the Sorceress Imperial's. If she protests this move, remind her whom she serves."

Owain's smile faltered. "But I made a promise to protect this one right here. Can't go back on that oath."

He rested a hand on top of my head, and the queen let out a laugh.

"I think she's proven to be more than capable of taking care of herself, don't you?"

CHAPTER NINETEEN

I rested, I ate, I rested again—for the next five days, I did little but sleep. There were times I woke in the middle of the night, surprised to find myself in a large, soft bed instead of on the hard ground. If I hadn't the scars to prove otherwise, it might have all been a dream.

I thought of Cliffton often, even as I walked through Provincia's crowded markets—not with that old, sharp sense of longing but with sadness and curiosity. Had the soldiers been called back? What did the valley look like now? Was it spotted with every shade of green imaginable? Had it rained since I had been gone?

I wrote a letter to my mother and father. I told them about Auster's king, about the possibility of peace, but I kept the rest of the story close to my heart. I signed with, *I'll see you soon*, and wondered if there was any truth in that. I had told

Henry that I didn't want to return with him, but going back to Cliffton didn't necessarily mean returning to the way things were, did it? Maybe I needed to go back, to truly close that chapter, before I could move forward.

Henry was doing exactly what I expected: packing. He and the rest of the delegates were staying in small chambers just off the castle's courtyard. The doors along the corridor were open, and men of all ages milled in and out of one another's rooms, laughing and chattering like they were having a grand party. They barely acknowledged me, even as I ducked my head into each room, looking for a familiar mop of brown hair.

Henry's room was the last door on the left, well past the rooms of the older men. I stood in the doorway, watching as he folded his trousers and shirts. They were new, I realized. He probably hadn't been able to escape from Cliffton with much.

"Are you just going to stand there?" he asked, not turning around. "You can come in. I won't bite."

"I seem to remember your biting me when we were seven," I said lightly.

Henry turned around, a faint smile on his lips. "You shouldn't have stolen my apple if you weren't prepared to face the consequences."

We stared at each other for a moment, until I looked away.

"I heard what happened with the queen," he said calmly. "Are you all right?"

"I'm fine," I said. "It wasn't anything to be concerned about."

He snorted. "I suppose this is the life you've chosen for yourself, then. One of danger and magic and handsome wizards . . ."

I looked down at my hands.

"It's all right," Henry continued. "I mean, I understand. Why would you want a dismal little desert when you can have the world?"

"You knew I always wanted to leave Cliffton," I said. "I talked about it for years."

"Yes, but I always thought I would go with you," he said. "And I don't think you'd still have me."

What could I say to that? It broke my heart, but it was the truth, and we both knew it.

"You mean the world to me," I said. I reached for his hand, but he pulled away.

"But I'm not your world, and I'll never be," Henry replied. "I wanted to . . . make a life with you. Raise a family. Grow old. I want you to know the truth because I love you, and that won't ever change."

Henry snapped the lid shut on his trunk and dragged it onto the floor.

"I love you, too, Henry," I said. "But I can't give you what you deserve."

He blew out a long sigh, running a hand through his hair.

I pressed a hand against my heart, and a part of me still felt like crying. "What will you do next?"

"Go back to Cliffton, help Father with the fields until I clear my head," Henry said. "I'm not much for politics, but if your father asked me to, I would take his place here. It's important work, you know? I got to cast Cliffton's vote to allow the queen to hold on to her title. I thought that would make you happy."

"It does," I said. "By the way everyone talked about her at home, I thought she'd be a pretty face and little more, but she's . . ."

"A bit of a lion heart," Henry finished. "I don't think the wizard leaders will be too happy with her when they find out she's taking back a generous portion of their power. From what I understand, the Sorceress Imperial will have to pass everything through her and give the queen final say."

I opened my mouth, but a distant roar of applause and cheers stole the words from my mouth. I turned toward the sound of it, wondering—

"We heard the news this morning," Henry said. "They were successful in getting Auster to sign the treaty, though I don't think we're in a better position than before. The brother of Auster's queen has assumed the throne, and from what I understand, he's a ruthless piece of work."

And we had sent Dorwan to receive whatever punishment the new king saw fit. What that meant for Dorwan, I wasn't sure, but I knew I wouldn't feel completely safe until word arrived that he was dead. There was still the chance that he could escape or somehow gain the ear of the new king. . . .

I didn't want to think about it, not when there was so much to celebrate.

"Are they really back?" I asked. Henry nodded. Trumpets sounded, announcing the queen's presence, and the cheers from the courtyard grew louder.

"I guess that's my cue to leave," Henry said. "Well, go on, hail the conquering heroes and all that. If you get bored of this life of adventure, stop by Cliffton and say hello to the simple folk."

"Of course," I said. I wrapped my arms around him, but it was nothing like our past embraces. "Will you tell my parents that I love and miss them very much?"

Henry nodded. "Come on," he said. "I'll walk you out."

*　　*　　*

I lost Henry's shape in the crowds as I pushed my way through the cheering masses, trying to squeeze my way up front.

The queen stood at the top of the marble staircase, wearing her ceremonial purple robes. She was surrounded by human ambassadors and advisors, while all of the wizards were on the ground below, holding back the crowds. Banners and flags had been strung up around the courtyard.

I glanced up at the queen, surprised to find her eyes fixed on me. She gave me a little nod of acknowledgment, but just as quickly her attention was drawn back to the courtyard, where the first horses appeared, as the crowd exploded in applause.

The Sorceress Imperial led the procession, followed closely by Oliver and several members of the Wizard Guard I didn't recognize, but not the one wizard I was looking for.

He and Owain were at the very end of the procession, chuckling about something as they guided their horses forward. Owain idly stroked Vesta's mane; his own hair, remarkably, looked as if it had been brushed and tied back. North was still in his leather armor, and the cloak I made for him was spread out over his shoulders. There was color in his face, and a smile that stretched from ear to ear when he observed the crowds. With the sun shining directly on him, North was happy and, for the first time, receiving the recognition he deserved.

I watched his eyes cast out over the crowds and took a careful step back. I didn't want anything to interrupt this moment for him.

They gathered with the others at the base of the stairs, dismounting from their horses. Several attendants rushed forward to lead the animals away.

North was still scanning the crowd as his mother walked up the steps to where the queen was waiting. Wordlessly, the Sorceress Imperial handed over a scroll, and the crowd hushed as Queen Eglantine read it.

"I would first like to thank each one of you for your service to our people," said the queen loudly. "It was at great risk that you traveled into our enemy's country, and that kind of bravery does not go unnoticed."

At her side, the Sorceress Imperial turned away from the crowd. North climbed a few steps and turned to face the crowd again. From that height, he spotted me right away. I gave a little wave, and the grin on his face was enough to send a flush of happiness through me. He jumped down from the steps and forced his way through the crowd. I ran forward, an enormous smile on my face.

"It gives me great pleasure," the queen was saying, "to accept Auster's terms for peace."

I threw my arms around North's neck, and the crowds flooded around us, sending up songs and shouts into the air. I laughed, pressing my cheek against North's warm skin, and felt one of his hands come up to tangle in my hair.

"Let's get out of here," he said, and when he bent down to kiss me, we had the time to make it last.

*　　*　　*

There was still a large crowd gathered in the courtyard later that afternoon, as I sat on the ledge above. North's notebook was open before me. I thumbed through it, taking notes of my own.

Fallbright leaves mixed with heartroot intensified the pain, I wrote inside the back cover of *Proper Instruction for Young Wizards. Fallbright leaves are rare but may have a better effect blended with a combination of georgeroot and cattail leaves.*

Now that he was back and things had settled down, there

was only one last problem pulling at my consciousness. The war might have been put to rest, and Dorwan shipped off to Auster, but we had yet to overcome North's curse.

"What are you doing?" North asked, coming up behind me. He wrapped an arm around my chest and drew me back toward him.

"A little research," I admitted. I snapped the books shut and turned around. I had a few ideas about the curse, but I didn't need to bring them up quite yet.

"Research!" he said. "Don't you know you have a companion of limitless intelligence and magic? What do you need books for, when you have me?"

"I'll keep that in mind for the future," I said. He leaned down to kiss me, but I pulled away at the last moment.

"Now, now," I said. "You'll have to treat me with a little more respect. They consider me a goddess in some countries, you know."

North laughed loudly, reaching for me again. "Yes, but I've always considered you a goddess, Sydelle Mirabil."

I smiled, letting him pull me close. Wizards, honestly.

"Can I see your hands?" I asked him. "Just for a moment?"

I could tell by the look in his eyes that he didn't want to do it. "Right now?" he asked, taking in the sight of the wizards and humans milling below.

"There's nothing to be ashamed of," I murmured. I lifted one of his gloved hands and kissed it. He seemed to relax.

"If you weren't so beautiful . . . ," he said, and slowly began to tug at his gloves.

I drew his hands closer to me, inspecting his skin for any signs that the curse had spread. North shifted his weight impatiently, but I kept my eyes fixed on where the black began and ended.

"It really hasn't spread since Arcadia," I said, turning his hands so his palms were faceup. "I feel so relieved."

"Yes, but I really haven't done any hard magic since then," North said. "The next time I have to cast a spell, I'm sure you'll see a difference."

"Wayland." We turned toward the dark-haired woman watching us from a short distance away. North yanked his gloves back on, turning away from his mother.

"I didn't realize it had already progressed so far," said Hecate, her face pale. She looked smaller to me somehow, though she was still dressed in the resplendent robes of her office. "Are you in pain?"

"I'm *fine*," North said. He tucked his hands into his pockets. "We'll be leaving soon. You don't have to worry about our causing more trouble."

She pressed her lips together, then said, "You could stay. We could speak to the healers about the curse, and you could help Oliver and me with the Guard."

"I don't belong here; you know that."

"Yes, but . . ." I felt North's body tense beside me as she continued. "You've proven yourself to be a smart, resourceful wizard. I like having you around, and I've missed you greatly these years. I know now it was the right choice to send you to be trained by Pascal, but that doesn't mean I don't regret the time we've lost."

"Don't go soft on me now," North said. "You'll need all of those hard edges to deal with the queen's new policies."

Hecate scowled. "I suppose I won't be reappointed when the rankings come next spring. If you'd like to participate in them—"

"You know that's not an option for me," North said.

"Not now," I said, "but maybe in the future?"

They both turned to me in surprise.

"I have some ideas," I said to North. "I'm not certain they'll work, but if you're willing to try, I am."

"Try, please," Hecate said. She brought a hand up to his shoulder, and for a moment I thought she would try to embrace him. Instead, North leaned down and kissed her on the cheek.

"Be good, Mother," he said. "If you need me, I'll come back. You know that."

"I hope to see you at the summer solstice. Both of you." As she turned back toward the doors of the castle, she lifted her hand in a small wave, and we did the same. When she finally disappeared from sight, North released the breath he had been holding. I watched his face for any sign of confusion or hurt, but I found nothing but perfect calm.

He turned to me. "What do you say we leave now?"

"You don't want to stay for the celebrations?" I asked, surprised.

"No," he said. "I just want some quiet."

North stepped away, reaching down for the bags I hadn't noticed before. He threw them both over his shoulder.

"I was thinking," he said, "that I would make you a loom. Would you be able to describe it to me? Exactly how you want it?"

"North," I began, but he didn't allow me to finish.

"It would mean a lot to me," he said. "It's something that I want to do for you. I'd only need a little guidance and to stop in one of the towns to pick up the tools I'd need. I think Fairwell would have something I could use, don't you?"

"North, I would love anything you made me," I began, wrapping my arms around his warm center. "But I was hoping that you could take me home to Cliffton. I realized after talking to Henry how much I miss it, and I need to see my family and friends. Could you take me there?"

"Of course," he said. "I'll take you anywhere you want to go." There was a strange touch of sadness to his words that I didn't understand, but before I could say anything else, he brought the cloak I made for him up around us and we were gone.

EPILOGUE

I t was nearly a month and a half before that same smile returned. Once North had twisted us out of the city, I carefully plotted our path west. We stayed on the Prima Road, the road we would have taken to Provincia if we had been able. After walking its straight path across the countryside for several weeks, I had to admit that the way we had taken before, however roundabout, had been far more interesting.

North and I stopped when we were tired, ate when we needed to, and worked when our gold ran low. It was a familiar routine, but one filled with far less fear and a lot more joy than our earlier trip. Everything had changed between us, and yet it felt as if nothing had. It was strange to me how I could go from hating everything about a person to loving even his worst faults.

As we neared the imposing barrier of the Sasinou

Mountains and felt the first wave of desert heat wash over us, something in North's demeanor changed.

"I think I can twist the rest of the way," he said, stopping suddenly. His eyes were on the mountains, not on me.

"Are you sure?" I asked. "It looks as if it'll be more than a mile."

"Do you really want to try to navigate those beastly trails again?" North said. "No, thank you!"

He brought up his cloak before I could protest. I clung to his shoulders, holding him close. When our feet hit the ground, the cloak remained up around us, as if he never wanted the moment to end. I would have been perfectly happy to stay there, cocooned in darkness and his solid warmth.

But there was that scent, just a hint of it, a mere memory. Though I had experienced it only once, I recognized the way the smell of rain combined with the yellow dust and created a scent unique and beautiful.

The cloak fell down around us.

We were standing on the smooth surface of a rock, overlooking a valley of patchwork green and brown. There were roads, the old houses of stone and mud, the small schoolhouse, and the markets all still showing signs of the Saldorran attack.

I knew this view very well. That was Cliffton below us, though it was no Cliffton that I had ever known. There were patches of green dotting the valley, fields of vegetables and maybe even fruit. Not only that, but I could see the irrigation canal they had begun to dig. The lingering traces of the most recent rain shower were around us, casting the valley in unfamiliar light. Heavy gray clouds hung low over our heads, and there was the delicious scent of wet dust and something else.

I walked over the ledge and looked out into the valley below.

"Do you not want me anymore?" North's words came out in a rushed breath, and I realized he had been holding them in the entire journey back. "Is that why you asked me to bring you back here?"

I turned around sharply. "No! Not that, never! You know how I feel about you."

"I don't do well without you," he said. "Who I was before—I never want to be that person again. But I told you when I took you away from here that when everything was over, it would be your choice. You would get to choose where you wanted to go and who you wanted to be."

There was a pleading look in his eyes. In that moment, he looked as if I had stripped him of his cloak and magic. I could knock him back into that darkness with a single blow.

But how could he think, after all this time, after everything we had done for each other, that I would ever want to leave him?

I looked from the fertile valley below, cocooned by the rocky brown-and-yellow mountains I knew so well, to the small splotch of wood and sand that was my home. All of it, every grain of dust, was a part of me, and that would never change—but Cliffton had never held my future.

This time, I chose him.

"I thought we could stay for a little while," I said. "To help them plant more crops and rebuild their homes. I think they could use the services of a wizard."

"Are you sure?" he asked. "If you want to stay, if you want me to go, I will. This is your home—I understand that."

"There's nothing to understand," I said. "My home is wherever you are. I just never had the chance to really say good-bye to the people and places I love. So if you'll stay with me here, just for a little while, we can go wherever we want to go and do whatever we want to do."

"That sounds nice," he said softly, as if too scared even to breathe. I watched his face as the fearful resignation finally gave way to the first touch of hope. North took my hand, and we began the long walk down to the village.

At that moment, it began to rain.

ACKNOWLEDGMENTS

One of my favorite things to do when I first pick a book up off the shelf is to read the acknowledgments page. Now that it's my turn, I find I have a lot of people to thank!

First and foremost, I'd like to thank my family. My sister, Stephanie, and my brother, Daniel, who make me so proud and so happy every day, and my parents, who have always made sure there was enough room for imagination in our lives. I also must lavish some gratitude on Uncle Cary and Aunt ☆, who read early versions of the story and believed that I could make something of my writing.

None of this would have been possible without the unfailingly wonderful Lindsay Davis, who championed this story from day one. Everyone at Egmont USA has been a constant source of joy and humor over the past months, and I'm so grateful that I've come to know and work with all of you. I have great admiration for my genius editor, Ruth Katcher, who was not only willing to hack down an army of adverbs but also to work around my crazy final semester of college.

And now, to my friends—I hope you don't need an acknowledgments page to know how much you mean to me. Mike, Garrett and the entire Bell family, Kevin, Julia—thank you! To Kevin Dua, as well as Maggie, Allison, and all of my lovely girls who wear the golden key—do you realize how wonderful you are?

Finally, to Carlin, who loved Syd and North from the beginning and did so much more than read and edit all of my early drafts. For all of your encouragement and our insane study sessions, midnight pancakes, oldies jam sessions, and amazing adventures—thank you! Happy (very) belated birthday!